A
NICER W
TO DIE

D1562001

Sam Mills was born in 1975 and studied English Language and Literature at Oxford University. Sam worked as a chess journalist and publicist before giving it all up to write full time.

Sam is now working on a second novel and contributes regularly to the literary magazine TOMAZI.

# A NICER WAY TO DIE

# Sam Mills

**ff**

*faber and faber*

First published in 2006
by Faber and Faber Limited
3 Queen Square London WC1N 3AU

Typeset by Faber and Faber Ltd
Printed in England by Mackays of Chatham plc, Chatham, Kent

All rights reserved
© Sam Mills, 2006

The right of Sam Mills
to be identified as author of this work has been
asserted in accordance with Section 77 of the Copyright,
Designs and Patents Act 1988

*This book is sold subject to the condition
that it shall not, by way of trade or otherwise, be lent,
resold, hired out or otherwise circulated without the publisher's
prior consent in any form of binding or cover other than that in
which it is published and without a similar condition including this
condition being imposed on the subsequent purchaser*

A CIP record for this book
is available from the British Library

ISBN 978-0-571-23079-2
ISBN 0-571-23079-2

2 4 6 8 10 9 7 5 3 1

*For K,*
*with all my love*

*And Cain talked with Abel his brother and it came*
*to pass, when they were in the field, that Cain rose up*
*against Abel his brother, and slew him*
*And the Lord said unto Cain, Where is Abel thy brother?*
*And he said, I know not Abel. Am I my brother's keeper?*

Genesis 4, 8–9

*'Tis dangerous when the baser nature comes*
*Between the pass and fell incensed points*
*Of mighty opposites.*

Hamlet (V, ii, 62–64)

**W**e weren't in the coach when it crashed. It was 3:15 p.m. when the driver swerved across the road and lost control of the wheel. Twenty-eight pupils and two teachers went tumbling over the cliff-face into the ravine. I keep picturing it over and over: the coach roly-polying down the hill in a tumble of sky and green, boys flying like astronauts in a space shuttle before gravity sets in and the coach went bombing on to the rocks in an explosion of metal. For a moment, an awful silence. Then the hiss of smoke and the shatter of glass and the whimpering of dying boys. Bodies severed, crushed, piled up, caught in metal teeth. Spiders and ants, crouching in the grass in terror, then scuttling out curiously, whispering over streaked faces. Flies buzzing, crawling into the caves of frozen mouths. A fox padding out delicately, picking up a severed limb in its mouth to take home to its cubs.

I wish I was there with them. It would have been a nicer way to die.

Henry was the reason I wasn't on the coach. The coach had been hired to pick us up at Paris and drive us to Le Mans. The driver was a Frenchman in his fifties, with curling, greasy hair, a moustache dangling over his lips like a piece of black spaghetti and a face like a slab of rare steak. Despite the 'Non Fumeur' signs peeling on every window, he was smoking a roll-up. As we – thirty fifteen-year-old boys in crisp black and white uniform, on day five of our French excursion – filed on to the coach, he ran his marble eyes over us, a tiny snarl tucked into the corner of his mouth, spotting the potential trouble-makers. It was obvious, I thought. The bad guys sat at the back, the try-hards sat in front of them, and as though in some arpeggio of descending rebellion, the squares sat at the front. Henry was on the back seat; I was on the seat nearest the driver.

I would have been happy to sit and stare out of the window, interviewing myself, but Ms Cave came and sat next to me, breezily saying, 'I'll keep you company.'

I knew she was trying to apologise for the humiliation she had enacted on me earlier before the coach had set off, not realising that by 'keeping me company' she was only enacting a fresh one.

'Thanks,' I muttered, forcing a smile.

Behind me Raf and Brian, who had been quietly debating how to spell 'cunnilingus', fell silent. I felt the warmth of their breaths tingle on the back of my neck as they pressed against my seat, listening in curiously: ammunition to gather and later sell to Henry when he was demanding their lunch-money.

'So, how are you this morning, James?' she asked.

Her voice reminded me of how the E string on my violin sounded when I'd tuned it too tightly. Her mousy blonde hair was looking even more messy than ever, static strands sticking against the seat.

'I'm fine,' I said.

'Nice day, isn't it?' she said nodding out of the window at the cerulean sky.

'Yeah.'

Ms Cave was always telling us to sit still, which was ironic because she was incapable of remaining still herself. She was a twitcher. Something would set her off and the shiver would go ricocheting through her body like a pinball, starting in the blink of her eyes, reverberating in the belly-dancer shiver of her breasts, and echoing in her hands, which splayed and fidgeted over her lap.

'I hope you're feeling all right. If you need some fresh air, do let me know.'

'I don't get travel-sick,' I said quickly, uncomfortably. I thought I'd concealed the churning in my stomach well. On the first day of the trip I had felt sweaty and limp and eventually puked in a plastic Hypermetro bag. For the whole of the journey, the bag had sat beneath the seat in front of me, knot twisted, plastic bulging, like some trussed up orange creature which had been killed and packaged for consumption. Henry and co. had kept sniggering at the back: 'God, what is that smell . . . Ooh, it's disgusting . . . maybe James has brought his egg sandwiches along . . .'

Behind me, Raf and Brian were bored.

'I think it's two "n"s.'

'No, it's three.'

'No, two.'

'And there's an "s" at the end. Cunniling –' he said in a whisper and then concluded loudly, '– *us*.'

At the back of the coach, Henry started up a sarcastic refrain of 'Ten Green Bottles . . .'

Ms Cave leaned in towards me and adopted a confidential tone which alarmed me: 'The coach is a bit dirty, isn't it?'

I hadn't noticed, but now she mentioned it, I supposed it was. Normally the coaches had been swept clean, but there were discarded sweet wrappers everywhere, curling like shards of orange peel, and empty Coke bottles rattled up and down the aisle as we swerved round corners. Ms Cave wrinkled her nose at the black ashtray in front of us, which a folded crisp packet was sticking out of like a handkerchief.

'And if one green bottle should accidentally faa-llll . . . there'll be eight green bottles sitting on the wall . . .'

I saw Ms Cave's eyes fall to the bandage wrapped tight around my thumb. I blushed and pushed it under the flap of my blazer.

' . . . there'll be seven green bottles sitting on the wall . . .'

'GARÇONS! BOYS!' the driver suddenly yelled. 'WILL YOU SHUT THE FUCK UP!'

Thirty boys fell into a stunned silence. The coach swerved round a corner and a Coke can rattled down the aisle like an exclamation mark.

'JUST SHUT UP!' he repeated.

I jumped; Ms Cave was so shocked, she didn't even twitch.

Mr Bellow was the other teacher on the coach. He was tall and thin like a piece of frayed rope. He went up to the front. Ms Cave hurried after him.

'I think there might be an "f" in cunnilingus too,' I heard Raf say behind me, but there was fear in his voice and Brian didn't laugh.

'We're awfully sorry,' Ms Cave said. 'I realise it may have been a little rowdy, but I'm sure you'll understand that the boys are restless, and –'

'I cannot concentrate!' the driver waved his hand, then caught hold of the wheel. 'I have a headache, their singing is driving me mad.'

'I'll go up and speak to them, and I'm sure we won't have any more trouble,' said Ms Cave, and Mr Bellow nodded gravely.

Mr Bellow sat down and crossed his arms, a frown halving his forehead. Ms Cave went fluttering up to the back. All the other boys turned and craned their necks to hear what she was saying . . .

'If you wish to sing, please join the choir back at school. In the meantime, I'd appreciate it if you could all make an effort to be quiet.'

The back row bristled. But Henry cut across them: 'Sorry, Ms Cave. We won't sing any more.'

That was Henry; that was why he never got expelled even though he should have been, ten times over. I had an obsession with doppelgängers because they featured in the *Horror* comics I was into. Henry was a doppelgänger. One minute he was a schoolboy, the next he was an adult. He could speak their language in their polite tone of voice, using their subtle riddles, their way of saying one thing and meaning another, with a slickness that filled us with awe.

'Thank you, Henry,' said Ms Cave, with a faint blush on her face.

'We'll leave you and Mr Bellow in peace,' he added, and there were a few titters.

'Right, Henry,' she said briskly, walking back down the aisle.

It should have ended there. But things got worse.

Ms Cave sat next to Mr Bellow. They spoke in worried, hushed whispers.

The coach drove on; the noisy chatter dimmed to nervous whispering. Behind me, they started discussing how to spell 'fellatio'. At one point someone on the back seat – it might been Henry – sung very quietly, 'One thousand green bottles . . .' evoking ragged laughter. The driver's head snapped round, his eyes demonic, and the laughter cut off abruptly. He turned back and put his foot down on the accelerator, muttering and swearing in French as other drivers tried to overtake him. Unease curdled in the pit of my stomach, bringing on a fresh bout of travel-sickness. I hated confrontation. I just wanted the whole journey to be over. In fact, I wanted the whole expedition to be over; I wanted to be back home, locked in my room, reading Dostoyevsky and listening to Coldplay on my headphones, the outside world a distant blur.

Suddenly, I became aware that the coach was slowing. Were we there yet? It didn't seem like it; we were in the middle of a country road, splitting down the centre of yellow wheat fields. The driver swerved on to a grassy verge, the coach pointing out at a dangerous angle to the road. He slid out from his seat and stormed to the back of the coach. Mr Bellow exchanged a terrified glance with Ms Cave, and they both hurried after him.

'You!' the driver pointed at Matthew.

Matthew was glugging from a lemonade bottle with the label torn off. He gulped loudly in surprise.

'You are drinking! No, don't try to deny – I can see you! In my wing mirror! You do not drink on my coach, do you understand!'

'It's only lemonade,' Henry interjected.

The coach driver didn't react the way adults normally did with Henry. He took hold of the 'lemonade' bottle, unscrewed it and took a glug, rolling it in his mouth like a marble. Then he grabbed hold of Henry's tie, yanked him up off the seat, put his face close to his and spat the drink back at him. It hovered on his cheek like a blast of semen, then slowly trickled down to his chin, dripping on his blazer. Henry looked utterly astonished.

'Please,' said Ms Cave, 'I think that's quite enough. I shall confiscate the bottle . . .'

'You can't go around spitting on boys,' Mr Bellow piped out.

The driver whipped around and Mr Bellow took a shaky step backwards.

'You break the rules – I break the rules!' he hissed. 'Your boys drink, I spit on them, okay? Do I make myself clear?' He turned and spun his glare 360 degrees round the coach. 'Does anyone else here have any alcohol?'

We all shook our heads sharply but you could see the same frantic fear passing across all our faces: what if he checks our bags?

Ms Cave's gaze slid uneasily in my direction, but I refused to catch her eye.

'Okay, fine, good,' he snapped, and went back to his seat and lit another roll-up.

Ms Cave stayed at the back, speaking quietly to Henry; I craned my neck to see. Through the heads, I saw a slither of his expression. I had seen that look before on his face, when I had stolen his Stanley knife, and I knew then that Henry would find some way to exact revenge on the driver. Indeed, as Ms Cave left him, he ignored his friends, crossed his arms and sank in on himself.

The coach rumbled on. Everyone was completely silent now, except for a few mutterings about the 'psycho' driver.

The driver, as though impassioned by the fight, drove even faster, funnels of smoke hissing out of the corner of his mouth. He was not impressed when, twenty minutes later, I slid from my side, forehead damp, throat hoarse, begging Ms Cave to let us stop for the toilet. My face burned red as I asked her. I hated to cause a fuss, but I knew that if we didn't stop now, I would throw up all over the seat and I had terrified visions of the driver grabbing my collar, smearing my face in the sick and yelling, 'Does anyone else feel like puking?'

'Do you really need to go?' she asked.

'I'm desperate,' I said.

'Okay, I'll ask the driver,' she said, looking petrified.

After five minutes of rather intense negotiation, the driver swore and said, 'Okay, okay, we stop.' He screeched into a small rural car-park and warned me: 'Five minutes! If you are not back within five minutes, I will leave without you!'

'This, er, place doesn't look very open,' Ms Cave faltered, noticing the locked up door with a *FERMEZ* sign dangling behind the glass. 'Perhaps we could stop at a proper café further on. I'm sure the boys would love to stretch their legs and buy some refreshments –'

'There is no café close by!' the driver bellowed. 'The toilet is over there! He goes here, or he does not go.'

'I'll go, I'll go,' I cried.

I clambered down from the coach and ran to the verge. It felt as though a fist was in my stomach, punching it upwards, and then it came: a spurt of sick, flecking orange and yellow over the grass. I wiped my chin and licked my dry lips. A fresh breeze caressed my face, mixed with country smells: manure and wheat. I stood up, feeling a little better. When I turned, I saw a row of faces staring out of the coach.

My bladder felt like a balloon. I checked my watch. I esti-mated that I could do it if I rushed: one minute to run over, one minute to urinate, one minute to run back on to the coach.

It seemed like the café owners had shut up for a long holiday now the summer was nearly over, for the place was looking darkly forlorn. The toilet was an unstable little white shack next to the café and when I tugged at the door it wouldn't open. I began to panic, tugging harder. The door pulled open with a rusty scream of pain; I'd finally killed the dying lock.

The toilets smelt horribly dank and were filled with flies. I drew in a deep breath and then ran in. I yanked down my zip, trying to piss as fast as I could, terrified of touching anything for fear I might catch some weird French disease.

Then I heard footsteps crunching outside on the gravel. *The coach driver*, I panicked, trying to stem my piss in mid-flow, *he's come to tell me off*. As I tried to push my penis back inside my trousers, the last of the piss streamed out over my shoe.

But it wasn't the coach driver.

It was Henry. He was out of breath, his face flushed and eyes glittering. He spotted my wet shoe at once and laughed.

'Nice aim, James. Ms Cave sent me to get you,' he said. 'Jesus, this place stinks. Still.' He was carrying a small bot-tle of mineral water, which he'd been hoarding at the back of the coach. He unscrewed the lid, poured out most of the water and then held it out to me, smiling gently.

Dread lined my stomach.

I knew then that we weren't going to be back in three minutes.

**W**hat did the noise sound like? It wasn't just a big explosion. It had layers to it. The more I think about it, the more I can separate them out, but it's not easy, like the time my father and I brought a bottleful of sand back from Brighton beach, sprawled it across a piece of paper and examined the grains. I was surprised that something that seemed so simple, like sand, had such a complexity of colours and textures.

But before the noise came, Henry and I were talking.

Henry said: 'It'll be so funny when we see his face.'

I clutched the mineral water bottle uncertainly.

'So you're going to . . . you want me to . . .'

'Uh huh. You pee in the bottle and we'll top it up with water. Then I'll sit at the back of the coach and sing again and wind him up. I'll pretend to drink it. Then he'll come storming down the aisle and yell "What zee fuck are you boys drinking?"' (Henry was good at accents.) 'And I'll give it to him and he can have a sample. You don't mind, do you, James? I mean, I figured there wouldn't be any diseases in your piss, not a little virgin boy like you.'

I felt the tips of my ears go red.

'We have to get back,' I said desperately, 'we don't have time to do this.'

'Oh, we have plenty of time,' said Henry, irritably waving away some flies. 'He'll wait. What, d'you think he's really going to go without us? He'll get sacked.'

'He'll be mad at us.'

'He can't hit us, you know. Think about it. You have to remember there are a lot of things adults aren't allowed to do; most of the time, they're just playing us. If he hits us, he'll go to prison. All he can do is pull the stupid ends of his stupid grey moustache and yell. And hey, yelling is just yelling.' Henry put on a child's voice. '"Sticks and stones make break my bones, but words will never hurt me."'

'But it's –'

'What?'

– not a very nice thing to do, I added silently.

'When I told Matthew I'd give you the bottle, he said you'd be too square. But I said to Matthew, hey, my brother's cool. James'll do it for a laugh.'

I knew he was laying down a dangerous trail of crumbs. Despite myself, I found myself wanting to eat them and fall into his trap. That was the thing about Henry. No matter how much you hated him, when he turned on the charm, it was hard to say 'no'. On the third day of our trip, he'd invited me to sit with his cronies at the back of the coach. They'd treated me with surprised respect. We'd laughed at Ms Cave together; I'd imitated her twitches and they'd broke into cheers and claps, amazed at my unexpected flash of cheekiness. I'd been one of them. All my problems seemed to disappear; I wondered why I had suffered so many hours hating them. And then the next day Henry wouldn't sit with me and I was the old James again.

'Okay, I'll do it,' I said, pulling my zip back down.

'Well, hurry up then,' Henry snapped. 'Or they'll go without us.'

I pressed the bottle against the tip of my penis and watched the yellow liquid slowly ooze into the plastic. Henry, meanwhile, went to a sink and peered at his face in the cracked mirror. He pulled down his eyes and rolled his eyeballs about like a parent pretending to be a monster.

Henry was always looking in the mirror. Sometimes he locked himself in the bathroom for hours. I used to assume he was just wanking. Then one day, a day that he thought everyone had gone out, I crept up and saw the door slightly ajar. I stood in the shadows and watched him making faces in the mirror and imitating voices: my voice, Ms Cave's, my mother's, his father's, even Sam's, as though we were all puppets he was playing in a theatre in his mind. It made me feel uneasy for a long time afterwards; then I remembered how Mrs Robson had told us in English that 'all the world's a stage' and I figured Henry was just rehearsing.

'Shit,' said Henry, suddenly cocking his head to one side. 'Can you hear that? I think he's going. Wait there!'

'But –'

'Just stay there and fill up the bottle – we need more water, it looks too yellow. Here. Catch.' He tossed the plastic blue lid at me but I missed and it landed by my feet.

'But don't go without –'

But Henry had already gone. I bent down and gingerly picked up the lid with the very tips of my fingers. Then I went to the sink, queasily wrenching at the ancient taps. There was a rumbling belch and a trickle of water emerged. I shoved the bottle under it. *Hurry up, hurry up*, I kept yelling at myself frantically. I twisted on the lid and turned to go, but something wet splashed across my trousers. The piss mixture. I hadn't put the lid on properly. I cursed like a madman. Without thinking straight, I spun on a tap, cupped a palm of ugly water and splashed it over the stain. Now my trousers were soaked.

I ran outside, through the café and into the car-park. Henry was standing on the gravel, smoking, shaking his head.

'Where's the coach?'

'They went without us.'

I looked about wildly. There were rough marks in the gravel from the swerve of the tyres, but I was convinced it was all an elaborate practical joke. Perhaps even Ms Cave had been in on Henry's conspiracy and they had arranged to drive the coach around the corner and wait there.

I started to run across the gravel. The water slithered down my trousers and dribbled on to my ankles.

'Where are you going?' Henry stopped me. 'They'll come back, you twat. If you run off, they'll come back and you won't be here. They'll send me out to look for you, and then maybe I won't be able to find you.'

I turned back and then –

There was the instant sound, like the bang of a bullet from a gun. Then a series of quieter echoes. Then a scraping noise, as though the coach, sliding down the ravine, was stretching out metal fingers and helplessly trying to hold on to the grass, the trees, the earth. Then the worst sound of all: a mess, a mesh of different noises, of screams and crashing and breaking and smashing and twisting and mangling. A distinct voice, crying out. Then a hissing, like water spouting from a cracked pipe, and a low moaning noise, as though the earth itself was weeping.

*

The voice that I heard that cried out belonged to Matthew. I don't know what he said. I keep thinking that maybe he said *I can't hear you* but I don't know why or what he meant.

The worst thing of all was that, even when I heard the noise and knew what had happened, I didn't think of them, or their slashed lives, or their families and how they would feel.

I just felt pure fear that I would be left alone with Henry.

**W**e were standing by the edge of the ravine, looking down. I felt I ought to cry. I kept trying to pull tears up but it was like grabbing air. I'd always assumed that tears were born in my eyes, but when I thought about it, I realised they came from a deep dark hole in my stomach, drawn up through my throat like water from a well. Then I thought how strange it was that I was thinking about crying, without being able to cry. All my friends are dead, I told myself. Matthew and Colin and Brian and Raf. Matthew who lent me three euros this morning so I could buy a cola, now dead.

But I felt just as I had felt three years ago when I found out that my father had died: empty, as though I was filled with smoke.

We were standing by the edge of the ravine, looking down. I thought of Ms Cave trapped beneath a jagged window, twitching even in her last moments of death. A hysterical desire to laugh bubbled up in my chest.

I remembered the first day of our trip, when we had been in Paris. The teachers had made us queue up in a black and white line, a patterned snake of twenty-eight. We were waiting for the tour bus. Ms Cave had walked up to me and said, 'You don't mind if I just check your rucksack, do you, James?' 'What, here in front of everyone?' I said. 'Yes, that will be all right, won't it, James?' I prayed: please just let her take a quick look inside, God, please, then nobody will notice. But she proceeded to take out every single thing and lay it on the red plastic seat of the bus shelter. Notebook, pen, a rolled-up dirty French mag. She picked up my pencil tin and she gave me a beseeching look as though to say: *Don't let there be anything in here, James.* By now, the line had become a curious circle of craned necks. Inside the tin: three pencils, a rubber, a sharpener, a fountain-pen. Laughter from the boys; a blush from Ms Cave. She left me to put it all back into my rucksack. She didn't even apologise. And someone from down the line called, 'Hey, maybe you should just check that sharpener, maybe he's storing materials for a bomb, Ms Cave, hey, Ms Cave.' She turned back as though seriously deliberating. She must have seen the look on my face because she turned away.

All because of the Knife Incident. Even though it had happened two months ago, even though I was innocent, even though Henry had set me up, the mud was still sticking to me, oozy and brown.

Then the bus came and we clambered on and as I sat alone on the top deck under the dusty sun I cursed Paris, I cursed Henry, I cursed Whittleby's Boys School, and most of all I cursed Ms Cave. I pictured myself defacing her face with the contents of my pencil-case; I wished her dead. And now she was dead and was it my fault; could I have cursed her, were thoughts that powerful or were they okay as long as you kept them safe in the dark caves of your mind?

*

We were standing on the edge of the ravine, looking down.

We couldn't see the coach because smoke was rising up in a mushroom cloud, which slowly dispersed over us. I could smell death in the smoke and I found myself retching again. I fell to my knees, bending over the verge, but all that came up was a glooping trail of saliva that stuck to the grass like a snail's trail. I felt Henry come up behind me and I sat very still. He put his hand on my shoulder, a comfort and a threat. Time seemed to slow down and hold in its breath.

He drew his hand away, and helped me to my feet.

We were standing on the edge of the ravine and now the smoke had thinned into tendrils that spiralled upwards. We could see the damage at the top: trees with broken arms, a flaky-painted danger sign bent over like an old man kicked in the goolies.

I didn't want to look down but I couldn't not look down. What I saw didn't seem real. It seemed like the sort of thing you'd see on TV, on the evening news, when an earthquake has struck an island, or a war has washed blood over a country. The news would come on while I was doing my homework at the kitchen table and my mum was cooking, and I'd try to focus on my physics but the images would flicker on to the retinas of my textbooks. It would remind me of the way my father used to sit watching it with sad eyes, and say, 'I just don't know what's coming to the world, why can't we just be at peace?' and later at night no matter how many times I rolled over or pressed my face in my pillow as though I could suffocate the images out, they were there, breeding and mutating in my mind: crying mothers and soldiers' faces twisted with hate and it made me want to be God and wipe it all out, blow out the candle of the world and start again with people born without darkness in their souls –

*Suddenly the rocks were sliding out from under my feet –*

I turned and grabbed Henry and he held me tight and we jumped backwards, shaking, as the earth crumbled away. It tumbled down over the rocks, spraying up brown clouds, and then settled.

And there was silence again.

When I turned to Henry, the look on his face scared me. He looked as though he might either break down crying or kill someone. Then, when he caught me watching him, his face smoothed out like a mask.

A black bird suddenly took flight from a tree as though in fright. There was a thrumming noise in the distance.

'It's a car!' I cried. 'It's a car!'

I started to run but Henry stood very still; he seemed unable to move.

'Come on!' I tugged his sleeve and he flinched with a violence that shocked me. I looked at him with nervous eyes and muttered, 'I think you're in shock.'

Suddenly he clicked back to the old Henry.

'No I'm not,' he said brashly, and started to run down the road.

I followed him.

The car was silver and there was a couple sitting in the front. They had turned off a small road on to our road and were now driving in the opposite direction. We ran after it, exhaust fumes laughing bitter in our faces.

'STOP! STOP!' we cried, waving our arms.

I saw the woman glance at us in the mirror and then quickly flick her eyes away. They weren't going to stop. I couldn't believe it: they weren't going to stop. I felt so desperate I wanted to grab the car so that my nails sliced furrows through the moon-coloured paint.

'STOP, YOU FUCKING FROGS!' Henry yelled. He picked up a rock and tossed it at the car.

'Henry – that's too –'

The rock bounced off the window and thankfully left it intact. I watched it thud back into the grass verge.

The car stopped.

As they got out of the car and I saw the anger on their expressions. I felt despair plummet through my stomach. They would not help us now.

I looked back and saw that the mushroom cloud of smoke from the crash was dispersing like a giant puffclock seed, trails of smoke floating across the sky, seeping into clouds, disappearing.

**A** man and a woman got out of the car. The woman was wearing a pink dress and a jacket with padded shoulders, her abundant hair pinned back from her face with a pair of tortoiseshell sunglasses. Her face was a strange shade of deep orange and a confusion of beauty and cracks. Her eyebrows were plucked into thin, pale caterpillars which rose and fell as she talked.

'*Qu'est-ce que vous les garçons –*'

Her husband cut in and started to shout at us.

I took a few steps back but Henry stood his ground.

'*Attends, je m'en occuperai,*' the woman said firmly and the man swallowed and stepped back, shaking his head. He glared at me. I looked back at him with pleading eyes.

The woman addressed Henry, as adults always did. They were always surprised when they found out that he was not the oldest.

'*Mais garçons, qu'est-ce que vous faites, jouant au milieu de la rue? Où sont vos parents? Avez-vous l'autorisation d'être là?*'

French was my weakest subject at school. I was particularly bad at French verbal and the words, firing from her drooping lips in staccato bullets, made no sense to me. My eyes flicked over to the man, who was standing by his car, arms folded, staring at me with snarling eyes. He wasn't even glancing at Henry; he seemed to have decided that I alone was responsible for all this trouble. Perhaps he thought I had been the one who threw the rock.

I tried to blot him out and pretend I wasn't intimidated. I fixed my shaking eyes on the woman. But there was something about her that made me feel uneasy. I thought of that film Henry had made me watch about aliens who had come down to do tests on humans. They knocked on houses, asking for glasses of water; they looked just like humans, but there were little, creepy things wrong with them that took a while to spot. A man who wore glasses to cover up his pupilless eyes; a lady with breasts halfway down her body.

The French lady didn't have low breasts; they were full, like Mrs Robson's. I felt comforted.

'We're English,' I stammered. 'We've lost –'

Henry cut in and said something in French.

Henry got 'A's for all his French essays.

The lady replied, and her voice was high and agitated.

Henry said something in reply and I heard the word *aide* and felt relieved. They would forgive the rock now; they would understand. Even Henry wouldn't play games in a situation like this. He would make sure she called our parents.

'*Il y a eu un accident.*'

'*De quoi parles-tu?*'

'*Un accident, imbécile. Tu parles même pas ta propre langue? Un accident? D'accord?*'

'*Tu inventes? Un petit garçon idiot qui le trouve amu-sant de danser dans la rue et d'inventer des histoires?*' Her voice became tighter and tighter, as though she was being strangled.

Henry gabbled a reply. I heard the word *merde*. My stomach turned. I knew what Henry was doing.

I realised then that he was in shock beyond shock; his reasoning had been thrashed with it and was crouched in the corner of his brain, whimpering.

'*Je suis perdu et tu ressembles à ma mère, espèce de merde.*'

Henry liked to play around with languages. Most of all, he liked learning insults. Not the obvious words, the four-letter-words, the *breasts* and *pisses* and *knobs*, the ones the guys who sat in the back of French classes howled over as they passed a French dictionary back and forth under the desks. Henry liked insults that were sly or subtle or silly. Like Latin classes, when he asked Mr Harris, *num saxum est calidora quam tu?* I recognised the word *merde* and remembered how we had laughed that it was close to *mère* meaning mother. As Henry insulted the woman, he kept his face wide-eyed, innocent, as though it was a slip of the tongue.

I should have been angry, because this wasn't the time for joking. But as Henry kept on saying *merde* and the French couple kept exchanging awkward glances, perhaps thinking, *Poor boy, he's lost, alone, can't speak French, he panicked, that's why he threw the rock*, and I found laughter bubbling in my stomach, and the more I tried to press it down, the more I felt my lips straining with the effort. A part of me felt startled by the sensation, for I had thought that Henry was the one who had lost it, yet this laughter was driving up against my mind like black water against a dam.

The moment I broke, Henry did too. '*Tu es merde!*' he said, and then his lips quivered and we dissolved into laughter, and we laughed and laughed, bouncing our hilarity back and forth like a ball.

'*Petits salauds!*' The man suddenly balled up a fist to strike us. The woman squealed and held him back.

I started to back up, but Henry broke into a dance, a little jig, crying, '*Merde, merde, merde!*' Then, as the man tore away from her and ran for us, Henry screamed, 'RUN!'

We ran. Down the road, feet pounding on the tarmac. Henry didn't turn back, but I made the mistake of glancing back several times. The man was charging at us like a raging bull. Pain ached in my calves, screamed in my lungs; the man was gaining on us . . .

'Here!' Henry panted, pointing.

'What?' I gasped raggedly.

Henry was pointing to the tall fence that surrounded a field of wheat. At first I thought he had the crazy idea of climbing it. Then I saw him yanking up the wire and slithering underneath. I followed him, and for one awful moment the wires bit into my back, tearing a strip off my shirt. I wriggled and I cried out; Henry ran over and yanked the wire away, and then we were running again. My nose was streaming and one of my shoelaces had come undone and kept waggling in front of me, but still I kept running. Through the fields of wheat that came up to my chin and Henry's shoulders, brushing and whispering against us as though quietly protesting against our invasion. I looked back and saw the French man was stuck. He had tried to climb under the fence, but he was too fat. He was waving his arms and legs about like flippers. His wife was also flapping her arms about and banging the fence ineffectually with her handbag.

Henry picked up a stick and, with astonishing accuracy, threw it and hit the man right on the head.

The man let out a scream of rage.

'Henry,' I cried, 'don't –'

'*Viens ici!*' Henry laughed.

We ran through the fields until we came to a ditch. The back of my throat rasped as though it had been sandpapered.

We couldn't see the man any more. Just an ocean of yellow bristlingness waving in the breeze. I looked anxiously for the mushroom cloud, but it had disappeared for good.

'Here.' Henry slithered down a ditch, papery with grass and dry leaves. 'We can hide here. If he comes, we'll have the advantage.'

I stopped to tie up my dirty shoelace with shaking hands before sliding down beside him.

We lay in the ditch. Trees waved behind us, showering lemony and pink blossom over our backs in giddy whirls. Henry got a handful of dirt and smeared it on our cheeks, so we were like soldiers. We peered out through the grass and wheat for the enemies, conscious of avoiding each other's stare, and then inevitably, deliciously, we looked at each other and burst into giggles again. I don't think I've ever laughed so hard, but it was a laughter that quickly became strange and lunatic, as though I was possessed by some spirit that made my ribs ache and tears stream from my eyes and pulse behind my forehead, until I felt I might vomit.

'I said, *shit, shit,*' Henry cried, and we exploded again. After a while I didn't need to laugh any more, but I carried on to please Henry, to perpetuate the warmth in my stomach. Despite the past, despite all that had happened, the

Knife Incident and the fight and the coach, I realised in surprise what the warmth meant. At that moment, I almost wished Henry really was my brother. Normally the coin of emotion I felt for him always came down on hate, but every so often I had an unexpected taste of it landing on the other side. Relief gushed through me; imagine, I thought, if Henry had been on the coach. If I had lost him and been left out here in the wilderness alone.

And then, quite suddenly, Henry stopped laughing.

'*Merde merde merde*,' I kept repeating, but the mood was gone and Henry's dark look crushed my laughter.

'We'd better stay here, hide, just in case he comes back looking for us,' Henry dropped his voice to a whisper. It wasn't really necessary to whisper, and it unnerved me.

Yet I found myself whispering back.

'Okay.'

I felt the warmth in my stomach cooling and I clung on to it, trying to stoke it up again.

'We should have got help,' I whispered. 'What about Matthew and the others?'

'They didn't want to help us anyway,' said Henry. 'That's why I started swearing at them. I told them about the coach and they said I was lying. Well, *baisez* them.'

'But – but – we need to go get help. We have to.'

'Yeah, well, they've driven away now, off in their flashy silvery vroom-vroom –'

'But you said he might come back! And, and, if they don't, we have to find someone else! You have to let me talk this time! I mean, you threw a rock at their car, what did you –'

'Look, just chill out, okay? You're giving me a headache with all your whingeing! Just shut up and let me work out what to do.'

25

A stinging pause. Henry shook his head. I swallowed.

'Look, we'll find someone else,' he said. 'Don't worry, James, my man, we'll find someone else.'

'Okay, okay,' I said, trying to sound cool.

'We'll just lie here and wait. A car will come by, or some dick farmer will come out to slice up his fields or whatever. It's safest just to stay put right now, okay?'

'Okay,' I said.

I felt uncertainty beat in my heart. I knew not to trust Henry, but what if on this occasion, he was right? Maybe if we walked down the road it would be one of those catch-22s where the more we walked the more cars and people slipped away from us until we walked into an eternity of loneliness. Normally, whenever Henry made one of his suggestions, my reaction was black or white. But now my head swam with grey confusion. The thought of making a decision seemed to spool a million what-ifs; I felt like a baby trying to make the decisions of a prime minister and all I wanted to do was bawl or sleep. And so, for now, I let Henry play the adult.

It seemed as though we had been lying in the ditch for hours.

Henry lit up his fourth cigarette. I watched an insect scuttling between grass stalks and tried to find humour in its clumsy excess of legs but all I could summon was a weak smile. I kept picturing the coach at the bottom of the ravine. The glass shattered in sparkles over the grass. An arm, hanging out from a shattered window, blood spider-webbing over its wrist and fingers. Who did that hand belong to? I tried to picture police arriving and going through the wreckage with their flashlights. The ambulance men would come. They'd carry off the bodies and call out names. They'd realise we were missing and come and look for us. But I couldn't seem to make the picture work; it was like a jigsaw with pieces missing. Instead, I saw the couple drive off and maybe the wreck would just lie there and the bodies would rot away and in fifty years' time people would suddenly stumble on it and think it was a crashed spaceship and put the bones of the boys in a museum.

'Maybe we should go back and see if anyone's alive,' I whispered to Henry.

He placed a hand on my back and pushed me back

down. He didn't look at me, just flicked his head with a nod, like his father did when I asked him a question and he was watching TV and didn't want to talk.

I felt a flash of anger, but I didn't get up. He left his hand limp on my back and I rolled over to shake it off and brushed my hands over the brown mud stains on my trousers. One of the hems was frayed, the cotton stained brown. I could just hear my mum's shrill voice saying, 'James, I just washed those trousers, don't you ever stop to *think*?' I wondered what she was doing right now. I looked at my watch and found that a crack had spidered across the glass circle, though the hands were still working. I knew that time was different in England and France but when I tried to work it out my mind kept sliding away and going back to the coach and the hand with the blood. Maybe it was two hours. I wondered if I had seen the hand twitch, or maybe it was just a trick of the light, or my memory changing the truth. Maybe it was eight hours. I remembered reading somewhere that if someone's head is chopped off by a guillotine they still remain conscious for up to a minute. Could your body still twitch after you are dead? Maybe it was night in England and my mum was asleep. I pictured her alone in bed, dreaming peacefully. Then I realised that was a fantasy; she would be in her big double bed with Henry's father. When I was home at night, I would go to bed at eleven o'clock and lie awake looking through a gap in the curtains at a slice of star-speckled sky. I would listen to my mum and Henry's father flush the toilet, spin the taps on and off, creak into bed, talk in voices too low to be understood. Then I would hear sucking noises and rustling noises and moaning noises and I would feel the blood throbbing in my cheeks and beating in my ears. When I saw

28

them at breakfast the next morning, looking tired and making toast and snapping at me, I always wondered if maybe I just dreamed the last part.

When Dad was alive, I never heard those sounds. They just went to bed. Then the house was silent for a while and gradually I heard Dad's snores. Mum moaned about his snoring but I liked it; I thought his snores sounded like the sound mountains would make if they could talk, and they sent me lulling off to sleep.

Two weeks before Dad died, he took me for a game of cricket. He was very thin and his face was yellow and his hair was like the summer grass that has cooked for too long in the sun. He moved very slowly, but I pretended not to notice and he pretended not to notice I was pretending. He hurled the ball at me, harder than he'd ever thrown it when he was well, and I thwacked it into the air and it soared in an arc before hitting and bounding across the grass. He walked very slowly to get it, and I ran very slowly between the wickets. He came up to me and said, 'If your mum wants to find someone else after I've gone, be happy for her. I just want her to be happy and looked after. Until someone else comes along, you have to look after her, okay, but after that you have to let someone else do it.' I looked down at the grass and said yes. He hugged me. My dad never normally hugged me. I wanted to hold him so tightly but he was so frail I felt as though I was a parent and he was a kid; I worried that if I squeezed him his ribs would crack inwards and spear through his heart. I wanted to tell him that I loved him, but I felt stupid and corny. Nobody in our house ever said 'I love you'. So I just said 'Yeah' again and then we packed up and walked home and two weeks later he was dead.

Mum only started to believe in heaven after Dad had gone to live there.

I watched ten more minutes tick round my watch. I could feel a change in the air; the smell of the day dying. I shivered with a fresh chill and whispered, 'Henry, we have to go and get help.'

Henry didn't say anything. I got up to go.

'Are you out of your mind?'

'What?'

'You want to go and confess, is that what you're saying? Well, James, you're very brave. I admire you.'

I sank back down into the ditch.

'What –'

'You know what will happen if they find us?'

'What?'

'They'll put you away. French prisons are much worse than British ones. You remember that film we saw about that con artist they locked away. They're very small and they don't let in any light so when they close the door you're in pitch-black. They just put food through a flap and you have to shit on the floor and sleep in your shit.'

I tried to tell myself that films were films, not real life but all the same, I felt my stomach turn to ice.

'Henry, I'm not going to prison, I haven't done anything wrong, okay?'

'You've done nothing wrong except cause a crash and kill off two of your teachers.'

'What?'

Henry didn't reply. He just stared straight ahead of him, keeping watch. A muscle quivered in his jaw.

I knew he was goading me. I told myself to keep calm. We had played this game before.

'If I'm going to prison, you're going to prison. We're in this together.'

'I'm not going to prison.'

Silence. The wind whispering in the grasses, a bird calling overhead. I waited, and he waited.

'Why not?'

'Because I didn't stop the coach, right?'

'I had to go to the toilet –' I heard my voice rise and I pushed it back under control. 'You don't go to prison for going to the toilet, Henry,' I said in a sarcastic voice.

'I know that,' said Henry amiably. 'But we were on a coach from Paris to Le Mans. There's a rule that on a coach trip, the driver is only allowed to stop once. It's a health and safety rule. We stopped once before on the way, and you made the coach stop again. If you hadn't done that and delayed it, he wouldn't have driven off so fast and crashed. Look – I know you're innocent and so do you, but the police don't care about that. If they catch you, you'll be interviewed in French and they'll trick you. You'll get stitched up.'

I paused for a minute. Sometimes Henry could lead me for hours through mazes of his stories, until we finally reach a centre of mockery and howls and '*James, I can't believe you fell for it.*' My mum used to ruffle my hair and tease me that it was because I had such a strong imagination. Now I tried to batter my fears back and think straight. Be logical.

'Henry, that's bullshit,' I said sharply. 'That's just crap.'

'Okay,' Henry backed down. 'Maybe it is, but the point is, you made him stop the coach, and that made him mad. If he hadn't been mad, he wouldn't have driven off. If you'd gone to the toilet in three minutes . . .'

'I . . . I . . .' There was logic in Henry's words; there was terrible truth. 'But I didn't mean – I mean – I didn't realise – I mean – you – *you* came into the toilets and slowed me down –'

'I was sent to get you. The driver was mad.'

'I'm not to blame – the driver's the one to blame, he was overreacting –'

'You and the driver are to blame.'

'But he's dead. He must be dead.'

'So you're the only one left to blame.'

'It's not my fault!'

'Not your fault? Wasn't that what you said to Mrs Robson after you pulled a knife on me –'

'That was your fault, not mine!' I grabbed his school tie and wrenched it hard. Surprise flickered in his eyes and it only made me wilder. 'You have to tell Mrs Robson the truth –'

'Shut up, shut up!'

I pulled harder and harder and suddenly Henry shoved me away into the ditch.

He stood up, brushing down his trousers, his face cold.

'If I were you, I'd run now, before the police get here.'

'You think . . . you really think I should run?' I stood up, swallowing. 'I could go through the field,' I stammered uncertainly.

'Wait!' Henry yanked me back. 'Don't leave me here,' he cried. 'I mean – we have to both stick together. For now, okay? Find help and all that. That's the most important thing.'

'But – but – you were just joking, then, when you said it was my fault – it's not my fault is it –'

'Stop wetting yourself. Look, we'll go down the ditch

and it'll come out on the other side of the fields, okay? Use your brains, *merde*-head.'

But it didn't come out on the other side of the fields. We found ourselves walking alongside a long line of railings. Henry stopped, curling his hand around one.

'We should climb over. There'll be a house.'

All I could see was a dense thicket of trees.

'It might just be a park. Maybe we should go back down the road, the place where that car passed by – another one might come!' I cried, looking back down the road. But when I tried to remember where the car had stopped, it seemed hazy, as though it belonged to a dream of another country I'd visited.

*Or maybe*, a small, scared voice inside me said, *you don't want to remember. To call and admit the crash was all your fault.*

It's not my fault. It's not my fault not my fault not my fault –

'If there's a house, which I reckon there will be,' said Henry, 'we can find a phone. Then you can ring and confess and all that. Look –' he pointed to the dark horizon, the rows of lonely wheat waving gently, '– there's no other houses for miles.'

I watched Henry begin to climb, one hand at a time, the way they made us shin up ropes in the gym. I had a burning feeling in my stomach that going into the woods was wrong; that once we were in them, there would be no turning back; the railings would enclose us like a huge cell. I thought about running back and trying to find the café by myself, but I was frightened of getting lost even further. I couldn't understand how we could have lost our direction, and the more I tried to pin the landscape down, the more it seemed alien, as though we'd been dropped on some desolate planet, and the trees weren't really trees, the earth was just dead skin and the sky a piece of cloth pinned up to trick us. I felt tears suddenly spurt up, hot behind my eyes, but I forced them back, gritting my teeth, fixing my jaw like a metal clamp.

I reached out for a railing and started to climb.

'You okay?' Henry paused, looking down.

'Sure,' I gasped, grabbing tightly.

But I didn't feel okay inside.

A kind of terror was swooping down on me. An hour ago, we'd been on a coach. Now this.

I felt as I had felt on the first day I had met Henry: as though suddenly my life wasn't in my control any more, as though some higher fate had taken over and thought it fun to throw cruelties at me and see if I would play along.

**I**sn't there a certain etiquette for when your parents decide to remarry? I knew other guys at school with divorced parents. They lived with their mums, saw their dads at weekends. Their mums' behaviour seemed to follow a set pattern. I thought I knew what to expect.

For the first year after the divorce or death, your mum cries at the kitchen table, cursing all men for being bastards. Then comes the revival period, lasting roughly three months, when a lot of new lipstick is bought and smudged, and strange guys start turning up for breakfast, stealing your favourite little box of Cocoa Pops from the variety selection, leaving you with something boring like the cornflakes. Then one of the strange guys stops being strange. He buys you a digital camera or a Gameboy, takes you to theme parks and forces ice-cream on you as though you're six, slowly slimes into your life until you can't wipe him away, he's your new dad and you have a new home and a new double-barrelled name that always fits the following formula:

[your name] + [your mum's surname] + [your stepdad's surname]

Your mum's surname, your normal name, always goes first, as a kind of concession. A token reminder of your blood history.

When my mum decided to find us a second dad, she didn't follow the rules. We had only been living alone for four months when everything changed.

The clock ticked. Cars hummed on the distant main road. The living room was so quiet I swear I could hear the custard creams piled up on the plate breathing, shedding nervous crumbs.

'They're late,' Sam suddenly interrupted, voicing the reality we were all trying to ignore.

'They'll be here,' said Mum. Her freshly permed hair formed a fuzzy halo around her head. She kept running her fingers through it and fluffing it out.

I felt as though I was having an out of body experience, hovering above and seeing us, our house, as a stranger might. Our street: a terraced row of red-brick houses with hunched shoulders. A front garden, once the most beautiful of the road, now a wildlife garden, butterflies skipping in the long grass. Our hallway, with its luxurious beige carpet, bought in a sale two years ago, its fraying edges concealed with a WELCOME mat. A line of coat-hooks, one now blank, the paint on the wall below it slightly yellowed from the smoke fumes that used to seep from an old blue anorak. Our sitting room, nervously clean, with a tray and a pot of PG Tips and a plate of custard creams. A bowl on the TV set, a goldfish swimming in circles of boredom. And us: me, thin and tall, with brown hair that wouldn't lie flat. Sam: twelve years old, giggly, with braces, and long fair hair in plaits. My mum, this woman with her breathless voice who, despite her bad perm and cackly laugh, had somehow managed to ensnare someone's father.

We heard the sound of a car pulling up in the road. Sam skipped to the curtains.

'They're here!' she cried.

I didn't move. I stared at the pyramid of biscuits. I didn't want to look out of the window, but it was impossible not to be curious. The car was red. A Ford. There was stuff piled on the roof-rack.

*Just for a week*, my mum had promised. *Their house got flooded and they've got nowhere else to stay and hotels are too expensive. Think of it as a holiday, only for once we're being the hosts. They're our new friends.*

Sam had been nervous, then excited at the thought of a new older friend around.

Mum had been disappointed when my nerves didn't turn into excitement.

What did she expect me to say? She was inviting two strangers to live in our house. And Mum wasn't a bad mum. She didn't neglect us or beat us or anything like that. It was all so surreal, like opening a book halfway through and trying to understand what the characters are doing. I'd spent so many hours lying awake, trying to make sense of it all, and now the doorbell rang and the pieces of jigsaw whirled, refusing to settle, creating the first pulse of a headache.

I went into the kitchen to get a paracetamol and when I came back, they were here.

And what did they look like to me?

Henry's father (later he asked us to call him Murrough but it never felt right) was very tall, with swirls of dark hair, hawkish eyes and round glasses resting on his Roman nose.

Henry was tall, too, with neatly combed dark hair and an arrogant air. I could tell his type at once.

When my mother introduced us, he shook our hands politely, and Sam repressed a giggle. His handshake was limp, so slight it was more like a passing current of cold air than a grip.

My mum's behaviour was very odd. She was quite formal with Henry's father, giving him a polite, frosty kiss on the cheek like some kind of Victorian, for God's sake. But Henry she pulled into a tight hug, pressing his head against her breast. She did that to me, sometimes, on kooky occasions, times when she was supposed to shout at me, like failing my Eleven-Plus when everyone said I was top of the class, and later, with the Knife Incident. I felt embarrassed and tried to catch Henry's eye, to send a message of silent apology, but his eyes were closed and he was holding her back just as tight.

In the living room, we sipped tea and made bits of conversation. Mum said to me, 'Why don't you go and show Henry to his room?'

'Can I go?' Sam asked.

I saw something pass over Henry's face, and it disturbed me, because I couldn't quite translate it. Mum saw the look too and she seemed able to speak his language, because she said quickly, 'No, Sam, stay here and let the boys be alone for a bit.'

'Oh – but I want to –'

'Sam. Enough.'

So we went upstairs.

'Your room's up here.' I pointed to the ladder.

Henry gave a sort of shrug. I kept deciding that I didn't like him, and then telling myself that it was too early to decide.

I climbed up into the attic. Henry glanced around. The attic room, the fourth bedroom in the house, had been pre-pared years ago for a third baby sister or brother that I was never to have. In between having me and Sam, Mum had lost a baby through a miscarriage; sometimes I saw it up here, sleeping in the bed, a greyish sort of foetus with pudgy arms and a sad thumb in its mouth.

Henry eyed up the room. He had the same expression on his face that Mum had had last year when we booked a hotel room and it had no curtains, and carpet and beds like old men's teeth.

I tried to think of something to say, something to spark a connection.

'What's your room like?'

'There's a really nice view from here,' I said, going to the window. 'It's the best in the house.'

Henry didn't reply. So I drew him back down the ladder and showed him my room, at the front, overlooking the road. It was smaller; I caught a gleam of triumph in his eyes. His sharp, flitting eyes stopped on a poster above my bed. It was of a seagull soaring above the ocean with a tremendous sense of vitality and underneath it said: *And the Lord God Made them All* . . . I'd always liked the poster, but the way Henry looked at it made me feel ashamed.

'I'm not into God or anything,' I said.

Henry smiled faintly.

'So you're coming to my school,' he said. There was an emphasis on *my*, as though he owned the place.

'Yeah.' I sat down on my bed. 'Yeah. I kind of decided to move anyway and Mum said your dad said your school was better, so . . .'

Silence. I watched Henry look around some more. I tried

to work out what had gone wrong, what I'd said to make him dislike me. It didn't matter that I didn't like him, but it bothered me that he might not like me.

'What's this?' Henry asked.

He'd spotted the treasure lying on the bed. I'd been looking at it before he came and meant to put it away safe in the box under my bed.

'Nice,' he said, fingering it. It was a small, stained-glass window of the Angel Gabriel. A silly smile of derision tickled his lips.

'My dad made it for me.'

'So your father made stained-glass windows?' The smile itched to become a laugh; I felt like tearing that smile off his face.

'It was his job,' I said hotly. 'It was a very specialised thing to do.'

'I'm sure.' Henry paused, staring out of the window. 'And he died, what, four months ago, if that?'

'Yes.'

'Your mum moved quick.'

I doubled up my fists, but he merely stepped backwards and laughed. I sat on my bed, shaking, listening to the creak of him walking across the landing and up to his ladder.

*Your mum moved quick*. Somehow I sensed he knew far more about this move than me. Why did she always have to wrap everything up in a tissue paper of lies?

I took the stained-glass window and threw it on the floor, smashing it into a hundred rainbow smithereens.

Later that evening, I picked them all up and spent hours taping and gluing them back together, but the angel's expression looked strange, like Frankenstein when he's put back together and sewn up all wrong.

At the end of the week I said to Mum, is their house ready for them to move back in yet? and she said, no, not qui– and then she looked up and saw the look on my face and laughed and said, Okay, James, it's not just the flooding, they want to stay a little bit longer, and I'm sorry maybe I should have let you all meet earlier, Henry's father suggested that, he thought I was mad just to ask them to stay, but look, I thought I'd just do it, just throw you all in at the deep end because if it wasn't going to work it wasn't –

but it is, isn't it, James, she said with an exhilarated face, you and Henry are getting along just great, I really think it's working.

**I**t wasn't easy climbing the railings. The metal was old and flaked with sharp pieces of rust that dusted our palms orange and embedded splinters in our skin. But we were helped by the forest, which was fighting a war with civilisation. The trees had pushed their arms through the gaps like a line of soldiers uniting to push the railings down. Some of the branches made good footholds, but halfway up I put my foot on a branch which bounced away and I found myself sliding, grabbing the railing and wrapping my arms and my legs around it. Henry glanced down and laughed; he had already climbed to the top.

I managed to climb up to the top without looking down. Then the fear hit me. It wasn't that I looked down, but simply the thought of looking down, of picturing that swerve of grass, was enough to make spirals unloop in my stomach. I kept thinking about a film I had seen where a spy pushed a man from a high window and he went crashing out in a waterfall of glass and hit a railing. It slit through him like a spear and he lay there groaning for some time. Then the film cut back to the spy and we never saw what happened to the man. I kept picturing the metal hot in the slime and slither of his guts; I wondered how long it took him to die.

Henry cried out. He had begun to slither down the railings but the collar of his shirt had got caught. He looked like a scarecrow struggling to be freed from his cross.

In order to grab the shirt, I had to lean over and two spikes of railing pressed threateningly against my chest.

'Hurry up, I can't hold on,' Henry called.

'I'm trying, I'm trying,' I gasped.

Henry was beginning to slip down the railings. His weight was making it harder and harder for me to pull the collar up.

'I – you need to –'

Henry lost his grip. He slid down the railings and there was a terrible ripping sound.

'Are you okay?' I stared down through the criss-cross of branches.

'I'm fine,' said a shaky voice from below. 'Come on. Hurry up.'

The remains of Henry's shirt billowed out from the spike like a flag.

I began to climb down, taking it slowly and carefully, telling myself to ignore Henry's impatient jibes of 'Hurry up!' or 'Okay, I've had enough, I'll go without you – you catch me up.'

'No – don't leave me here!' I cried.

No reply. I slid down the railings, crashing through branches, and found myself on the forest floor, winded and torn.

I grabbed a branch and pulled myself up. There was some sort of mouldy moss on it that left green slime on my palm and I winced, rubbing it on my trousers. The bottle with the piss-water mixture, stuffed into my jacket pocket, banged against my ribs.

Henry whistled and then came back into the clearing.

'Come on, then.'

I rubbed my palm again, and looked up at the spikes of railing, picturing an alternative past. I shuddered and turned away.

Into the forest we went. The sky was darkening like a bruise; the branches began to lose their detail and become silhouettes. As we plunged in, the patches of sky above the knit of trees became thinner and thinner. Henry and I walked as we did on the way to school – he on the pavement, me in the road, a few feet between us so that passersby could dissect us, yet never losing awareness of each other, as though we were bound by an invisible umbilical cord. Henry came across a large branch and he picked it up and thwacked nettles and bushes out of the way, like an army warrior leaving a path of devastation: bushes stripped and raped, foliage with broken necks and drooping wrists. He scuffed up dead leaves, cleaving open a smell of rotting vegetation and earth and badgers.

Maybe the coach crash is on TV right now, I thought. I pictured my mother sitting in front of the television, the scenes of devastation dancing across her retinas. I pictured her sobbing and Henry's father putting his arms around her. Or maybe she'll just smile at the TV, get up and ask him what he wants for dinner, a voice sneered inside me. After all, it only took her four months to find a new husband. Maybe if Henry and I really had died in the coach crash she would just have gone shopping on ebay looking for two brand-new sons to buy. Or maybe she'd be glad that it would just be her and my sister, Sam, and Henry's father, they'd make a nice trio; after all, we never fitted neatly around the kitchen table in our new home; the table fitted four and one of us always got a sliver of end table or an awkward corner, banging elbows every time we lifted a fork. Three might work better.

Occasionally, through gaps in the forest, I caught a glimpse of yellow stone, glimmering in the distance.

'Maybe we should go there.' I pointed towards it.

'Yeah.'

'There might be a phone . . .'

'Mum was talking about you the other night.' Henry had that tone of voice again. It sang *I know something you don't know.*

'Really?' I turned away, pretending to be busy looking for a branch.

'Uh huh. She was talking to Dad. They were watching TV, only they weren't really watching it.'

Finally, I found one: a long, clean branch with grooves and gnarls so deep they looked like the pattern on a snake's back. I picked it up. Henry waited until I was walking again.

'Your mum said that you were born a girl.'

I laughed, but it contorted into a hiss.

'It's not a joke,' said Henry, solemnly. 'I mean, it's kind of sad really. You know you had that accident when you were nearly three, when your mum put you on a slide in the playground and you sat at the top screaming and you wouldn't move and then that boy shoved you and you fell off?'

'How did you know that –'

'D'you think I'm making this up?'

There was a pause as we walked and beheaded nettles. I knew he was waiting for me to fall into his trap.

'Okay,' I said wearily. 'Tell me what they said.'

'She just said you were concussed and damaged your

45

fanny. It was the way you landed. I mean, you probably don't remember this, but there were sticks around the slide, and you landed . . . well, ouch. Anyway . . . It was all so tragic and you would never have got ah, periods, or had kids, so they did an operation to turn you into a boy and sewed a dick on you – I mean, it's amazing the advances in medical science these days, they can actually do that. And that's why your mum thinks nobody's ever liked you. I saw a programme about it. It really did happen – there was this boy and he got circumcised and the priest got overenthusiastic or whatever and chopped too much off, so they dressed him in girls' clothes and gave him dolls and all that but he never took to them, he was a bit like you – he felt strange in his own skin, he felt out of place. With you, it was the reverse. You started off a girl and now they're trying to pretend you're a boy, but it's not really working, is it? That's why you can't sleep at night.'

'Really, Henry?' I said in a bored voice.

'It's why your mum's always looked upon you as a freak.'

I knew his words were stupid, stupid lies, but it was as though he'd struck a match and tossed it into my stomach. Smoke was unfurling and I was trying to stamp the glowing embers out.

'Cancer is a psychosomatic illness, you know. People get sick because they're worried or scared or hiding a secret, or they know something's going on but they don't want to speak about it, so they bury it inside them and it eats away at their heart. I figure that's why your dad got cancer – worrying about his boy really being a girly –'

The fire roared; I turned suddenly and caught him by surprise, swinging my branch against his slack one. He stumbled backwards with a gasp. Then he collected himself quickly, tightened his grip on his stick and swung it at me. *Thwack, thwack, thwack*, we fought. He made a comment about me not having a knife on me and the red raged through me like a forest fire. I was starting to win. The anger bubbled in my muscles, shrilled and sang in my blows. I was driving him backwards, back into a huddle of bushes and I was winning, I was winning – and then, all of a sudden, he darted to the right, and then to the right again and I was hitting thin air and then I realised we had reversed and now I was going back into the bushes. It was just like those games of chess we played; Henry's father had bought us a set to help us bond in a more *educational* way than Gameboy screens shiny with knives and pools of blood; I'd be playing well until Henry suddenly made one move that destroyed me and my king would end up running sweating around the board. He never checkmated me, he'd just chase me, waiting for that moment when I'd put my finger on my king's cross and lower it, crucified, to the floor, so he could feel I'd surrendered before he'd yelled victory.

The bushes bit into my back. Henry's branch blurred before me. He dug it into my ribs and I let out a scream. He laughed and bounced closer.

'Get off me!' I yelled, lunging forward. He stepped aside and I fell headlong, into a bed of earth and leaves that arrowed pungently up my nostrils. I lay there, not wanting to get up, like a defeated boxer who knows he has lost. I closed my eyes and I heard Matthew's voice again, only this time the words were less distinct, like an echo fading poignantly. Suddenly I felt ashamed at the triviality of our fighting. We were losing time; we had to find a phone.

And then we heard the noise.

**A**s though a firework had exploded overhead. A group of birds cawed and burst into the sky in a flurry. Henry gazed up, and I used his precious moment of distraction to my advantage, shoving him away with a whack in the face and scrambling to my feet. Henry swirled his weapon, laughing coldly – and then there was another crack and a whizzing sound. I lifted my branch threateningly, but Henry put a finger to his lips and shook his head sharply.

'Listen,' he whispered.

I could hear the wind whimpering in the trees and the general rustling of forest nightlife. A bird warbled a poignant catch of song that thinned into the night like mist.

And then I heard what Henry's more acute hearing had already picked up: a rhythmic rustling. Whoever was walking towards us was taking care to make a minimal amount of noise.

'It's okay, we should tell him about the coach.'

'Are you kidding?' Henry whispered back. 'You heard that noise – it was a gun going off, idiot. He has a gun and we're trespassing –'

'*Mais que faites-vous dans ma forêt?*' the man called out in a harsh voice.

We jumped and stared at each other. My heart was thumping loudly in my chest.

'He might be friendly,' I whispered, so quietly that my lips barely moved.

'What?'

'He might be friendly.'

'Oh, right, James. You think a man with a gun wants to make friends with us?'

The footsteps were coming closer. I could see the bushes breaking apart in the distance as the figure advanced towards us.

'We're just looking for help,' I called out boldly. 'We're just –'

'JAMES, shut up!' Henry thumped me.

'*Vous êtes de retour, ah? Revenus pour emporter plus?! Revenus pour supporter plus?!*'

The man was shouting now, his voice hoarse with inexplicable anger. As though somehow he'd been expecting us. As though he was looking for enemies to hunt down.

It didn't look as though he was the right person to ask for help.

'What shall we do?' I whispered in panic.

Henry had already decided. He turned and started to run.

I followed him.

I was a faster runner than Henry; I had beaten him in the 400 metres. Running was the only sport I was good at. But I found myself slowing down, running with my head twisted back to check he was keeping up.

'Hurry up!' I hissed.

'I know, I know,' he gasped, sweat pouring down his face.

Trunks and bushes swerved past. Branches cracked underfoot. Leaves brushed our arms, insects landed in our hair. Birds, disturbed, yelled as though they were cheering us on.

We ran and ran and ran. I prayed to the rhythm of my footsteps. My lungs swelled until I thought they would burst. I gulped in air. It tore the back of my throat like sandpaper.

Then there was another gunshot. The bullet missed us but was close enough for me to see it splice into a tree trunk a few metres ahead. It tunnelled into its core and a piece of bark broke off, hanging loose for a few moments like a dead piece of skin, and then hit the ground.

Henry grabbed my arm.

'We have to hide!'

He found a dense bush and slithered beneath it, ducking his head and dragging himself to safety. I bent down and tried to follow, but a maze of thorns whiplashed my face.

'There isn't room for both of us!' Henry said.

I stood up. The pounding footsteps were coming closer. I turned – that tree – could I hide behind it? – no, too thin – that bush – not big enough – was there a ditch? – no – could I dig a – no – no time.

I ran a few more feet. Then I saw the branch, like an arm reaching out to me. I grabbed it. The bark bit into my palm. I clawed in a deep breath and grabbed another branch. The footsteps were very near now; I had to stop making a noise. I risked two more branches up and then stopped. I stood half-leaning against the branch, grabbing the trunk with one hand, a long bough with the other. My breath came in great heaves and I tried to still and soften them. A thorn throbbed in my cheek. There was a faint tension on the bough and I saw a small bird had landed. It looked like an English robin and its beady eyes circled over me curiously. I smiled at it. It sounds stupid but it made me feel better. I'd always felt a greater affinity with animals, more than people. The bird might be tiny, but it was like a good omen; I felt protected.

I heard the slow crunch of footsteps.

And then silence.

The throb of the thorn in my cheek had magnified into an itch. I ached to scratch it.

Two more footsteps.

Silence.

The bird bounced forwards a few centimetres on the branch.

I thought of the bullet splitting into the trunk. I pictured the tree howling as it died, a sound too high-pitched for human ears.

Silence.

A drop of sweat gathered on the rim of my forehead.

I prayed.

There was a clicking noise. A safety catch being released.

Silence.

I struggled to see if there was anyone below, but it was difficult to see through the network of branches. I pictured him standing right below me, gun pointed straight at me.

Silence.

He's right below me, I thought, I know he is. He's playing a waiting game. I mustn't make a noise. Not one millimetre of sound.

*There isn't room for both of us.*

There had been room, hadn't there? If I died, it would be his fault. He'd go to Hell.

The sweat drop fell. It rolled down my forehead down my cheek down my lips down my chin down my neck and into my shirt.

Silence.

And then: '*Je vous voir.*'

The bird at the end of the bough took flight in fright.

He wasn't right below me. He was a few feet away. He'd found Henry.

He pulled Henry up out of the bushes. Henry cried out a few replies in French, but the man wasn't easily charmed. I guess Henry told him about the crash, but the man didn't seem to care. *Henry*, I prayed to my stepbrother, *please don't tell him where I am.*

There was a scuffling noise and leaves flew up. I listened to their brief fight. Over the past few months, I'd fantasised about this exact moment: I'd had daydreams, red-misty with anger, whereby Henry pushed someone over the edge – a teacher, a sixth form boy, another bully – and as they pulped him, punched him into oblivion, I stood by and cheered. But the reality of it was unbearable. Every gasp that Henry hissed out made my stomach curl as though I'd suffered his punches myself, and I had to cling on tightly to stop myself from falling out of the tree. In my mind, I saw a braver James climb down with furious swagger, pick up a branch or a rock and thwack the man away, extending a brave hand to help Henry up. Inwardly, I screamed jeers at myself until my soul was hoarse. And yet still I sat in the branches, quivering.

I had just unpeeled one sweaty hand from the bark when it was too late.

Silence, punctuated by heavy breathing. The fight was over.

I could hear them coming closer and then they were right beneath me. Henry was lying on the floor and the man's fingers were curled under his shirt-collar as though he was a dog. In his other hand, he carried a gun, a long rifle like the kind you see posh people using when they go to shoot foxes and deer. He was a gamekeeper.

The gamekeeper was old. He was very tall and thin and knobbly, as though he'd been born with too many bones and not enough skin to cover them all, so it was tightly stretched over the joints. He was wearing an old cloth cap made out of checked tartan but I could see his profile and there was something shrewd and mean in the narrowness of his eyes and the hook of his nose. He was wearing a tweedy coat and brown trousers and black boots which looked a bit like the steel toecaps we were banned from wearing at school. He stood very still and held his nose to the wind, as though he was a hound picking up a scent. Because, I realised, he'd been right behind us. He'd seen that there were two of us. And now he was looking for me.

All he had to do was look up and he'd be staring right at me.

I mustn't make a sound, I told myself, I mustn't move a millimetre.

I boxed my breath inside my chest and prayed some more.

Still, he waited. He barely seemed to move his head, yet his eyes flitted from left to right and right to left as though he knew every colour and detail of the forest like a painting and could spot the tiniest brushstroke that had been changed.

Then he curled his fingers around Henry's collar and began to drag him forward, Henry yelping, and I knew that I was safe.

I became aware that I'd been holding all the muscles in my body like elastic bands stretched taut. I let them go, but instead of feeling relief, an aching spread through my body, the type I get if I run a long way and ignore the coach and don't warm up properly beforehand.

I heard another scuffling and Henry groan as he received a blow and I had to bite my lip not to cry out. I was no match for the gamekeeper. I had to sit still, wait until they'd gone and then run and run and get help.

The bullet seemed to come out of nowhere. I felt an arrow of air whizz past my cheek and then a dull thud as the bullet hit wood. I fell out of the tree.

I grabbed leaves and branches but they slid away like water. Wood hit my head and my back. I grabbed a branch and then – *crack!* – I fell and hit the floor and it was as though a large hand came up and whacked me on the back, winding me. I was terrified that I had broken my back. I remembered reading that if you moved just an inch when your back was broken you'd be paralysed. The gamekeeper walked up and stood above me, his hand still curled around Henry's collar and I saw the look in Henry's eyes and panic flooded through me. It was the first time I had ever seen Henry look afraid. He opened his mouth as though to speak and then clamped it shut.

'I think I might have broken something,' I whimpered.

But I knew that though my body ached nothing was broken, and he knew it too. He took his rifle and pressed it under my collar, dragging me up, only my shirt suddenly tore and I fell back again, banging my head. He barked something at me in French, which I figured meant: get up.

This time, he made us both stand up and walk ahead of him, alternating poking the rifle barrel in our backs. Every so often he would stick the barrel to the right of my spine, which I realised meant go to the right, and vice versa. We hovered in scared silence. I could feel Henry bubbling up with frustration, words aching to fly out from his lips.

'He thinks –' Henry burst out in a ragged voice. 'He thinks –'

'Silence!'

'He's mixed us –'

'SILENCE!'

He prodded the rifle hard into Henry's back and Henry shut up.

What, I kept thinking, what does he think? Oh God, what's happening, why are you doing this to us, we prayed for help. I kept thinking about those movies where two cops who hated each other but then turn out to be buddies get caught by a criminal and as they're being pushed forward by gun barrels they exchange glances and a signal and they know just what the signal means; one of them turns and kicks the villain in the face and the other karate chops his gun out of his hand and it's all hunky dory. But when I looked at Henry I didn't know how to signal or how to make it work and all he could do was look back at me, eyes wild with panic and unsaid words.

I composed arguments in my head, to explain to the gamekeeper about the crash, to say we came looking for help, but when I tried to remember the correct French I could only remember certain words and I couldn't work out how to stitch them together. Then I thought: if Henry can't make him understand, how can I make him understand? Mr Bellow had told us that the French had invented the guillotine. Maybe in France the laws were different and if you got caught trespassing you got your head chopped off. Or maybe that couple from the car had rung the gamekeeper and told him about the coach, how I had made it stop and probably broken the law. Only, no, that was just Henry's silly lie. Wasn't it? Or was it? Maybe that was what Henry had been trying to whisper to me. Maybe the gamekeeper had been waiting for us all along, like a Grim Reaper ready to take sinners to their judgement cells. I began to shake, and sweat dribbled down my back. And then I thought: surely they can't kill us if we're not yet sixteen? We were in that 'no man's land of adolescence', as Henry's father said whenever we did something wrong: no longer boys, not yet men. We were a danger to ourselves because we had energies but no responsibilities. Then I remembered reading that story about a girl from Nonsuch High, the girls' school across the road, who was nearly raped, only at the crucial point she said to her attacker, 'What would your mother say if she could see you now?' and he was so ashamed he ran off, and that's the thing with psychos, if you can just think of a word, a phrase, a key that turns the lock inside their chaos, the match that strikes a light in their darkness, you can escape. I tried and I tried so hard to think of a phrase, but my head seemed to become tireder and tireder, until the weight of trying to think made it feel so heavy I thought I might collapse, and the only thing which kept going through my head was that bit in the Lord's Prayer,

Forgive us our trespasses
As we forgive those who have trespassed against us

and I thought maybe it will work, maybe. And all the time it had been getting darker until we could hardly see where we were walking.

I wished I knew what Henry had been trying to whisper to me.

Then a light shone through the trees and we came out into a wide sweep of gravel: a driveway that led up to a house.

**I** say *house* **but it was more like** a mansion, a place you could imagine Marie Antoinette lived in when she was telling plebs to eat cake. It was huge, with a grand sweep of gravel that led up to a main entrance framed by a porch swathed in gargoyles and swirls of stone. In each corner was a fat turret that pierced the twilight clouds with a crown of castellations. There was a look of frowning sternness in the heaviness of its faded yellow stone and the multitude of windows that stared out like dead eyes.

If I thought about it, it didn't look like a haunted house, or one of those scary Dracula places you see in movies, but there was something about its shape and shadow that seemed horribly familiar to me, as though it had belonged to dreams so horrible my consciousness could not remember them clearly, just a colour of them. When we got to the entrance, something twisted in my gut and I felt so repelled I found it physically impossible to go in.

The gamekeeper pushed us up a series of stone steps. The front door looked thick and oaken. There was a gargoyle on the door; maybe he'd once been scary but the wind and the weather had worn him down so that he looked weary of holding the knocker in his mouth and just wanted to go to sleep for good. I felt Henry's eyes frowning on me. I looked at the gamekeeper. He was punching security numbers into a panel that resembled our burglar alarm at home. I looked down and saw that he was holding the gun loosely. Henry was saying: *Take the gun. Grab it.* Sweat formed slugs between my fingers. I looked at Henry: *Why don't you take it, go on, you grab it.* Henry glared back and then it was too late: the gamekeeper was barking: '*Alors, entrez! Vite!*'

Inside, it was like those castles you see in movie sets. The gamekeeper forced us up some stone steps with a scarlet carpet over them. Ahead of us was what would be termed a Grand Hall. You could imagine that it had once been used by aristocrats in the evenings, for marquises in frilly trousers to swing round maidens in big dresses. Now it looked as though the owner had tried to turn it into a museum, and then shut it down and let it sprawl into a junkyard.

The gamekeeper kept prodding us on sharply, forcing us left down a corridor, past some panelled doors, past walls with heavy oil paintings of old kings and queens, past holey velvety curtains that had become moth-zoos. Down another flight of steps without carpet on. I could smell a strange odour in the air. It reminded me of the smell I'd breathed in a few days ago when Ms Cave had taken us to visit a vineyard and we had watched French farmers crush grapes with their bare, hairy feet, red oozing between their toes.

Henry whispered something to me but he barely risked moving his lips and I didn't catch the words. Then the gamekeeper prodded us twice and made another grunting sound. I realised he wanted me to open the door. I faltered. Surely there was no telephone down here? I took the curved gold handle and twisted it to the left. The gamekeeper made an angry sighing noise. I twisted it to the right.

It was a cellar. Boxes of apples in various states of green and brown stacked up. Rows of bottles. The air thick with cobwebs, dust on the floor. This was all wrong. He was supposed to be telling us off and then helping us find a phone.

*Oh God, please let us make him understand, please help us –*

I broke off, remembering that I didn't believe in God any more.

The gamekeeper made a grunting noise, waving the gun at us. Henry and I glanced at each other in alarm. He made a more threatening grunting noise.

I waited for Henry to rebel, to overturn apples, to shout *merde*. But he just turned very white and backed up against the wall.

I followed him.

The wall was freezing, curling icy palms around my shoulder blades.

'Talk to him, tell him we're sorry,' I stammered.

'He thinks we're burglars,' Henry whispered.

'What – but the crash – but you told him about – how can he think –'

Finally, my fury for Henry erupted. And fury at myself, fury that lashed my heart and slashed my soul. If only I'd had the strength to say 'no' to Henry earlier, if only I'd listened to my inner voice when I first curled my hand around those cold railings, then we would have found a phone and be in a police car by now travelling past the crash site, seeing helicopters and ambulances and men in white slicing through twisted metal, dragging out dying bodies and breathing miracles of life into them.

'You're lying!' I turned on him. 'You're lying, you're a

*liar –*' I turned to the gamekeeper, drawing in a shaky breath and in my panic, the words I needed to say came to me, precise and clear: 'We're sorry. *On est vraiment très désolés, Monsieur, très désolés, très désolés!* Henry – he's lying – *désolés* – there was *un accident* and we just need *téléphone –*'

To my stunned surprise, the gamekeeper turned on me and yelled, '*DÉSOLÉS! DÉSOLÉS?*' He broke off into raw cackles of laughter.

'I told you,' Henry babbled. 'He thinks we're burglars, he said some boys came to his house a few nights back and they ran away and he just missed them and he thinks we came back for more –'

'But we're English, we're just –'

'He thinks we stole some guns, he thinks we're making the crash up to get away!'

The gamekeeper turned to go. What? He was going to leave us locked down here?

I gasped and tried to say, 'No –'

The apple falling. It wasn't my fault, you see? It's like that saying, that a butterfly flapping its wings can cause an earthquake that causes a tidal wave that causes a Martian to die on Mars. Fate took the apple in its hand and dropped it out of the box. It didn't even hit the gamekeeper. It tumbled down and perhaps grazed his back, or his shins. Then thudded to the floor like a cricket ball. I heard my father's voice in the back of my mind shouting: '*Catch!*'

The gamekeeper hurled the apple at Henry. Henry ducked and it hit the wall, exploded into pale green chunks. Juice bled down the brickwork.

The gamekeeper grabbed Henry by the collar and began to shout, pointing the gun down his neck. Henry yelled.

The gamekeeper slapped his ear. Henry started sobbing and yelling, 'James, help me, don't let him shoot me, James!'

When I saw the gamekeeper laying his hands on Henry, an emotion tore through me. It came before the fear and the rage. It shocked me, burned through me. As though he really was my brother. I saw myself back in the forest, sitting up in that tree, my ears bleeding with the sounds of Henry's gasps. I wasn't going to be a pussy this time. I ran at the gamekeeper's legs, ramming at him, trying to knock him over, my cheek bashing against the knobble of his knee. He stumbled, kicked. My leg howled with pain. I put my mouth to his trousers and bit hard. Right through the brown of his cloth. I felt the dough of his skin between my teeth. He screamed and swung the rifle round. It knocked over a crate of apples that tumbled to the floor in a cascade of *thump-thumps*. He tripped, fell. The gun flew away from him. I paused, waiting for Henry to grab it. But Henry was a statue with eyes like a bewildered baby. I grabbed the gun. I was surprised by how heavy it was. I heard Henry's cry and I turned. The gamekeeper had caught Henry in a grasp and was sticking his finger up Henry's nose; Henry's face was a stretching blur of pink pain.

I pointed the gun at the gamekeeper. He didn't respond. I curled my finger around the trigger. How much pressure did I need to fire? Then there was a sudden *bang!* and to my shock the bullet flew through a crate, speeding a tunnel through the apples. The gamekeeper let Henry go and he tore away, running and hiding behind me.

'James, go on, shoot him,' Henry begged hotly in my ear. 'He says he's going to lock us down here for weeks, to pay us back, we'll never find help if you don't shoot him – shoot him, shoot him, shoot him, for fuck's sake just do it!'

I turned and saw Henry's scared face. I saw the snot on the rim of his mouth and the red, pinchedness of his nose. 'Shoot,' he said, 'shoot.'

'I'm going to shoot,' I cried out. The gamekeeper laughed and spread open his palms, as though to say *So you want to play?* Then he was coming, taking slow steps towards me, his eyes intent on my face.

Sweat poured down my cheeks, soaked my collar. This was too quick. My hands were shaking so much I could see the barrel bobbing up and down. I needed time to think, dissect things; I needed Mrs Robson here to hold a debate of hands and voices and –

The gamekeeper grabbed hold of the barrel. I tried to tug it away but he held on tightly, a smile creeping up on his face. As the realisation dawned that he was much stronger than me, I let out a panicky cry and he laughed.

'*Je t'ai maintenant, espèce de petit merde.*'

I curled my finger around the trigger. Henry was yelling in my ear. I looked at the crates. I looked at the gamekeeper. I pulled the trigger.

I felt the gun kick back and bang against my chest, knocking out the air, and I stumbled back, banging against Henry, who yelled and fell back against the wall.

I hadn't expected to hit him. I'd thought it would fire between his legs and hit the wall. I'd only wanted to shock him.

The gamekeeper's eyes bulged until I thought they were going to fall out and hit the floor like marbles. And then a sound emerged from his throat, an inhuman cry, like the noise vampires make in movies when someone had just splintered a stake through their hearts. He began to hop about, clutching his leg. Blood gushed over his fingers. He kept shrieking like a bat. The gun burned in my hands and I dropped it.

Henry shouted: 'You idiot! Pick it up pick it up pick up the gun!'

I stood very still. It all happened very slowly, as though we were underwater. The gamekeeper staggered forward. He tried to bend down and let out a scream, clutching his leg. He reached out at arm's length, his fingers scrabbling around the gun, gained a hold, and pulled himself upright. He raised it and pointed it at me. My hands dangled down by my sides. My lungs swelled. I didn't move. I felt an odd pressure at the base of my spine. I realised my guilt was so great that I wanted him to shoot me, to share his pain.

He lifted the gun. A small tendril of smoke uncurled from the end.

His finger, bent around the trigger.

I closed my eyes and told myself to think of my mother, but it was not her face I saw.

I heard a crash and a loud bang.

I bent over, rolled on the floor. In my darkness I waited for the excruciating rush of pain. But – nothing. I pawed my body, my arms, my chest, my legs, searching for holes, for that warm gush of liquid. Nothing.

I opened my eyes and saw the gamekeeper was lying on the floor.

'What have you done!' Henry whispered.

'All your life,' my Dad had once said to me, 'people will tell you *you can't do this* or *you can't do that, life's not fair*, whatever. But remember, really: you can do anything you want. You can be whoever you want. You have your whole life ahead of you. And don't worry about the guys at school who are giving you a hard time over your grades. They're giving everyone a hard time. You know where they'll be? . . . In Tesco, stacking shelves. But you'll be a writer, ignore the teachers who say everyone wants to be a writer and you won't make it, you want to be a writer and you'll be a writer and you'll be the greatest writer in the country. I know school's kind of hard now, but just think of it as purgatory, before the heaven comes later.'

And I had seen my future heaven. I saw myself when I was really old, when I was thirty. I had a big house in the country with ivy crawling up the walls and a huge garden and dogs and cats and a wife and kids of my own. I'd have a study and I'd be sitting in there, the sunset on my page, words blurring into the gold, feeling peaceful with the thought of the long languid evening ahead. That was how my future was supposed to be.

The moment the gamekeeper toppled to the floor, I knew that from now on everything would be different and that I wasn't going to be a writer any more.

'**Y**ou've killed him. I told you to shoot him, not kill him!'

'I can't have killed him. All I did was shoot him in the leg.'

'Well, he fell –'

'I thought he was going to shoot me, I thought –'

'He fainted –'

'I thought he was going to shoot me –'

'He just stood there and then keeled over, just like that.' Henry clapped his hands together with a violent bang and I jumped. He smile-sneered and punched my shoulder.

I had taken a First Aid course at school a few months ago. I ran down the corridors of my memory, frantically flinging open doors, searching for instructions on bullets, on blood, on guns, but they were all full of useless junk. All I could remember was mouth-to-mouth resuscitation. Though they were completely irrelevant, the instructions persisted in jumping up into my brain. I knelt down by his body. *Tilt back the victim's head.* I looked at his head, the wisps of grey hair pulled over his walnut scalp. I saw a mark and my heart trembled but I leant closer and saw it was just a – a – what was the word, what was the word? A spotliver. That didn't sound quite right, but that was what it was. A spotliver. There was no blood. *Put one hand on the*

66

*victim's forehead and pinch their nostrils together.* No, that's no use, I told myself. I began to shake. *Seal your mouth over theirs and blow in two breaths.* How could I tell if he was alive? *And then blow in a breath every five seconds.*

'Take his pulse then,' Henry cried.

'No, you do it.'

'You killed him.'

'It was self defence.' I could hear myself shouting. 'You told me to!'

'I didn't, I just said pick up the gun. You should have used it to just threaten him. You should have pointed it at him and made him go upstairs and call the police.'

'It was an accident, it wasn't my fau –'

'Look, just check his fucking pulse!'

I crouched back down. Henry stood above me, his eyes deadly. My fingers were shaking like butterfly wings. I brushed their tips against the skin of his neck, but it felt like leaves in the autumn when they are so dry just one touch is lethal and they dissolve into pale green dust, and I drew back, afraid that I was jinxed, that if I touched him, the next minute he would be ashes. Henry kicked me gently in the back and I reached out again and pressed my fingers against his neck, drawing in my breath. I couldn't feel anything. Oh God, I prayed, I'm sorry I've stopped believing in you, I do believe in you now, I do, please let him have a pulse, please don't let him be dead, please don't make me a murderer, if he has a pulse, I promise I'll never doubt you again. I moved my fingers a millimetre: no pulse. Another millimetre: no pulse. Another no pulse no pulse and then I found it, suddenly, that flickering snake's tongue of life, and I felt tears of relief well up in my eyes. I held my fingers there, and I could hear Henry telling me that was enough but now I couldn't pull back, I had to keep feeling that safe throb, until his pulse and my pulse seemed to entwine and thump to the same rhythm.

Henry yanked me back and I fell back on the floor.

'He's alive,' I said. I found that I was laughing and I rolled from side to side like Sam and I used to on the hills behind our house when we were kids. 'He's alive,' I sang, and I remembered the song we used to sing in the playground, 'I'm the King of the Castle', and I made the words fit the tune and it sang in my head, *He's alive, he's alive, he's alive.*

'Yeah, okay, shut up. We have to take him upstairs.'

'Why?'

'Because it's cold down here. D'you want him to die? It's dangerous to be cold if you've been shot. We have to carry him up and then call someone.'

'I've been saying all along we have to call –'

'Well then! Take his legs.'

'You take his legs,' I said, staring at the bloody mess of flesh.

'No, I'm stronger than you, I'll take his head.'

As we carried him up the steps, I watched the blood pour down his leg. At his ankle, the river forked and some splashed on the steps and some trickled on my hand. I shuddered so violently I kept nearly dropping him. Halfway up the steps, I looked at Henry and saw sweat on his forehead, pain in his jaw.

My arms ached with his body weight and there was a pressure like an iron clamp squeezing my heart. A sudden panic had overcome me because I knew that we now really did have to call the police and I had to be the one to phone them.

I had to be the one to phone them because if Henry

phoned them, he would paint the story the wrong colour. He'd phone them, chatting away in French, smiling and winking at me and whispering it was all okay, when it wouldn't be. It would be the way it had been with the Knife Incident. I could still picture Henry, sitting in the head's office, knees apart, palms open and loose, smiling at the head as though they were two adults and I was an errant kid. Henry saying smoothly: 'I'm so sorry, Mr Jefferies, but I'm afraid I certainly don't know anything about a knife. I certainly didn't tell James to get one. I think he's got carried away and has been watching too many movies.' And when Mr Jefferies swept his spotlight of attention on to me, when I had to make the case for the defence, all I could do was stammer and sweat. I had to be the one to call.

I could feel the gamekeeper's left leg slipping away from me and I tightened my grip, but the trouser cloth slipped up and I found myself touching warm, hairy skin. When I looked back down the steps I saw that he had dripped a trail of blood, like a red snake that crawled back down the steps and into the cellar.

We came back into the Grand Hall. It was a large square filled with cabinets and surrounded by glass windows; a corridor ran around the side of the cabinets, leading off into other rooms.

We laid him down on the stone floor in front of a stained-glass window. A grim, colourful saint stared down at us with reproachful eyes. I said a silent apology to him. I hurried down the corridor and tried some light switches; to my relief, they worked. The chandelier hanging in the Grand Hall came to life with a thousand twinkles.

'Now what do we do?' I asked Henry, even though I knew what to do: *find a phone, find a phone.*

Henry stared at the gamekeeper for a while.

'Shall I –'

'Give me your bottle,' he said. 'You know – the bottle we filled up in the loos –'

'But I pissed in it and the water's dir –'

'Give it to me!' He spat the words out like bullets.

I pulled the bottle out of my jacket pocket. Henry grabbed the bottle, wrenching up the gamekeeper's trouser leg. He poured water over it in big gulps. The water, laced with red, sluiced over the skin, flattening the black hairs on his leg, flowing over the stone floor and lapping at the foot of the stained-glass window. As he did so, tears began to pour down his face and his body bucked with sobs.

I had never seen Henry cry before. Somehow, I found it even more shocking than the first time I had seen my mother cry, on that day when we had been sitting in the living room, dinner on our laps, the TV a happy glow on our faces, when my father casually announced over the top of a beer commercial, 'I have lung cancer and I'm going to die. I'm sorry.'

Henry sank to his knees, the bloody water wetting his trousers. I went to his side and put a nervous arm around him; he grabbed my lapels and clung to me, sobbing against my chest. I held him tight, my chin against the top of his head. I felt tears sting my eyes, but I had lost the urge to cry. Seeing Henry weaken was like a see-saw that made me strong.

'Look, I've got to find a phone,' I said. I tried to untangle myself but he clung on. 'You must let me go. I'll go and find a phone. It's okay. I'm going to find a phone. You stay here.'

Finally he let me go and nodded, whimpering: 'Find a phone, find a phone.'

'**L**ook. These are my father's pills.'

Henry held out the white plastic bottle. CLOZAPINE swirled in red letters round the side.

Sam and I exchanged uneasy glances. Today we were all meant to be going out for a day trip to the beach, before school started next week. Two weeks had passed and now Mum and Henry's father had stopped patronising us with platonic pretences and were sleeping in the same bed. In the evenings they watched TV, inviting us to join them. But I found myself retreating to Sam's bedroom. The pink glittery KEEP OUT sign on the door had once been for my benefit, but now she seemed glad to let my 'smelly' adolescent presence invade her world of teddy bears and perfume and boyband posters. We didn't talk much; we played games, like solitaire, occasionally teasing each other, or speculating what Henry might be doing up in his attic room. We always spoke in whispers, just in case *They* might hear.

Normally Mum supervised breakfast. I moved uneasily around the kitchen, trying to work out where a fresh packet of butter might be kept.

'My dad takes two pills every morning,' said Henry, rattling the bottle like maracas.

'What are they for?' I asked.

Henry ignored me. He pinned his eyes on Sam, who flushed scarlet.

'I dare you,' he said.

'What?'

'I've got some mints. Look.' He drew the bag from his pocket. 'They're the same shape and colour – but not quite. They're white and they don't have the letters on the side, but they're close enough. I dare you. Empty his pills and put these in.'

'No – we can't –' Sam stammered.

'Go on.' Henry's voice became cajoling, then a caress. 'Come on, Sam, you're not chicken, are you?'

Sam threw me a terrified glance.

'Don't, Sam,' I said.

Henry let out a tired sigh. I pictured my father's face again. I heard him telling me to keep my mum happy. I should try to get on with Henry. And it was just a joke, after all. Henry seemed to like his father, so maybe it was just a humour they shared, a ping-pong game of cruel, private jokes.

'I'll do it,' I said. 'It's okay, Sam, I'll do it.'

When they came down to breakfast twenty minutes later, we were eating cornflakes in silence. I was barely aware of Mum ruffling my hair affectionately – *Well done, boys, glad you've sorted yourselves out like adults.* Henry's father gave us a surly grunt for a good morning. He filled a glass of water. As he reached for his pills, unscrewing the top, Sam stopped chewing. I gave her a gentle kick under the table and she hastily pushed another spoonful into her mouth.

'It's poison,' Henry whispered across the table.

'What?'

'They're not mints, they're poison. You're about to kill my father.'

Sam went white. Mum hummed; the toaster popped.

'He's just joking,' I whispered to Sam. 'Ignore him.'

'Oh, you think I am?' Henry said. 'You want to take that risk?'

I stared into his eyes. If it had been any other boy in my class, there would have been a smile in their eyes at this point, no matter how hard they tried to keep the act up. Then a slap on the back and 'James, for a minute there, I had you!'

But Henry stared right back. His gaze was completely blank. Hypnotic.

*What if he was serious?* I knew he hated me being in the house, wanted to pretend I was the cuckoo and force me out of the nest. Who knew how far Henry might go? I had a lurking sense that he didn't seem to have the boundaries most people fenced up around themselves.

'Um, excuse me?' I asked Henry's father. 'Um, excuse me?'

He didn't take any notice. The pills were in his palm. He stared down at them. And then: 'Who did this! Where are my pills? Who did this? Henry?'

'What? What's going on?' Mum gasped.

'It wasn't me.' Henry was cool. 'I don't know what you mean, Dad.'

Henry's father's eyes fixed on me and ate through me like acid.

'I don't know anything about it,' I said. Why had Henry managed to keep his voice so level and why was mine so shaky?

Henry's father grabbed hold of my school collar and twisted it back so that I was gazing up at him.

'What have you done with my pills? I said, what have you done with my pills?'

'It wasn't his fault!' Sam cried. She had been swallowing her cornflakes and she spewed out a mouth of orange mush.

I looked at Mum with pleading eyes but she turned away, flustered.

'Sam – where are your manners –' she cried.

'It was Henry,' Sam wept, 'Henry did it, he made James do it, he dared him, he came up with the poison, he wants to kill his dad –'

'They're not poison, they're mints,' Henry said.

'I see,' said Henry's father, swallowing. 'I see.'

We all sat down for a polite breakfast. I fumed that Henry had got away with it without the slightest retribution. But later, when I came home from school, I saw that Henry seemed quietly brooding and had a bruise on his cheek. Over the next few days, the bruise blurred from purple to black to topaz to emerald. I began to find solace in it. I would look at it and remind myself that Henry would be too afraid to continue with his games. But I was quite wrong: for Henry, the games were only just beginning.

*Find a phone, find a phone.* I looked through the large glass windows into the Grand Hall. It was full of museum cabinets and clutter; there would not be a phone there. At the far end of the hall, directly opposite me, was a long marble staircase; halfway up it split into two, like a white dragon with two heads, and curved up, left and right, into an upstairs gallery. The gallery was shadowy, no lights on, and it made me feel uneasy; it led to a myriad of doors and a maze of corridors which I felt I would drown in.

*Find a phone, find a phone.* I ran down the corridor running around the rim of the Grand Hall until I came to a thick door, patterned with faded golden swirls and cherubs and a handle of twisted gold. I pulled it and the door creaked open.

I found myself in a dining room. Like the main hall, it was a blend of beauty and destruction. A large table sat in the centre. There was a dirty tablecloth rolled up into a ball and a row of candelabra, like small trees, old, grey lumps of wax clinging to their branches like birdshit. There were a few chairs lined up neatly behind the table, and a few broken ones in pieces on the floor, their golden bowels ripped open. One of the chairs had three good legs and a half-stump; it lurched to one side like the old man who got on our bus every day and forgot to bring his stick.

There were beautiful pictures on the walls. In the fading light, they looked as if they had been painted on, but when I touched them, I saw that they were made of cloth. They were oval portraits of soft faces and cherubs. I tried to think of what my father had taught me about art and different periods. I decided they looked a bit like the paintings of Leonardo da Vinci, the oil colours murky and mystical. *Find a phone, phone.* I had lost my sense of urgency; something was holding me back, slowing me down as though I was moving underwater. For a while, I persuaded myself that it was the house itself, casting its dark, sluggish spell over me. But I knew it was simply fear of what I was going to say on the phone.

What could I say? Every time we opened the newspapers at breakfast there was some new article about a Teenager With a Heart of Evil. A boy who'd shoplifted thirty times before the age of fourteen; a kid who'd drowned his friend in a swimming-pool; a boy who'd knifed or head-butted his enemy in the playground; all that. For all I knew, I might already be up there on French TV, some bad photo-booth photo of my face splashed over newspapers, for being the boy who'd made the coach driver lose his temper and crash a coach. The serial killer of twenty-eight boys. But surely I could explain about needing the toilet; surely the English would understand at least? My mother could explain that I had a weak bladder, just like doctors appeared in court and got murderers off by saying that they were mad. But the gamekeeper . . . what could I say? They might believe me; they might . . . they might check with the teachers to see my story rang true, to see if I had a sound character. The police might interview Mrs Robson. I felt my heart lurch. And then they would find out about the Knife Incident. Mrs Robson would protect me. Or would she? She might exaggerate, just to get rid of me. They would assume at once that I was a psycho, that after the Knife Incident and now the Gun Incident they had better lock me up before there was A Killing Spree Incident.

I began to shake. I wished I had left Henry to make the phone call after all. I was no good at smooth talking, at painting a situation in another shade.

I could tell them we had simply come into the building and found the gamekeeper lying on the floor, wounded. If I could just persuade Henry to lie with me. But it was Henry's word against mine. And he didn't have any black marks on his file; no Knife Incident; just a string of 'A's and proud parents. But I could lie, I could say I saw a man in a balaclava running from the house who was clearly a robber, carrying a briefcase with something gold sticking out of it. After all, that would fit, wouldn't it, with the gamekeeper's story about robbers. But then, what happened when the gamekeeper woke up? I might make the story worse; the gamekeeper might then declare that Oh yes, there was a robber, that boy was the robber, arrest him. Nobody would believe me over him, because he was the adult and I was the child, and nobody ever listened to children; it was as simple as that. Or maybe we should wait until the gamekeeper had woken up and try to make a pact with him . . . a pact, a *treaty*, just as we had learned in history about countries making up after the war. I could offer him money, send it every week, if he just promised to be honest but all I get was a measly three pounds fifty a week and anyway it seems the whole point of treaties is that people break them . . . I pressed my fingers against my pulsing temple; every way I turned seemed like a pit with a criss-cross of lies over it and the more I thought my stories through and tested them with my foot, the more I realised I would only fall into them.

*Find a phone, find a phone.*

I pushed open another door and found myself in another small corridor that linked back to the Grand Hall. There was a large partition screen with clumsy Japanese brushstrokes and I stood behind it, listening to the eerie sounds of Henry still sobbing. I turned, and wondered if I should go up the big marble staircase. I turned again and saw something in the wall that did not look real: it was a bookcase, but when I tried to pull out a volume of *Great Expectations* I realised it was just a fake spine. I pushed the bookcase, and found myself entering a hexagonal room.

It was a library. It had a curved white ceiling and the walls were packed with books upon books. In the far corner was a desk, and on the desk there were more books, and there was a phone.

It was an old-fashioned phone, one of those ones you only see in movies now, with a proper circular dial you had to push your finger into and spin round to get a number.

I sat down behind the desk. I stared at the phone and thought of Mrs Robson. I tried to unfurl her love out of mid-air, like a magician pulling a rabbit out of a hat. But the hat was empty. I closed my eyes and tried to find that sensation of curved softness, but all I could see was the pity in her eyes when she told me about lines that should not be crossed. She had said: '*Sometimes, James, we all have to do things in life that we don't want to do. It's part of growing up that we realise life isn't fair. We have to accept this and make sacrifices and be brave.*'

I realised then, my stomach caving in, tears hot in my eyes again, that this was what I had to do. I had to surrender. Because one of them, Matthew or Brian or Mr Bellow, just one of them might be lying in that wreckage still alive, praying for a miracle, and if I could save just one life, then I had to do it. For that person to live, I might have to go to prison and that wasn't fair, but that was life.

For a moment I felt brave. But as I picked up the phone, my hand was shaking and my heart was crying out like a baby that I didn't want an unfair life, I wanted things to be fair, and why couldn't they be fair, why, just for once, couldn't they be fair?

I stuck a finger in the dial and pulled the numbers round. My breath entered the receiver in hot clouds and echoed in my ear.

Then I realised that I had dialled 999. On the first day of our French trip Ms Cave had made one of her nervous speeches and told us the French code for emergencies was 112.

'Hello? *Bonjour?* Hello?' No sound. I clicked the receiver. 'Hello?' I clicked again, dialled the numbers, impatient with its swinging whirrs. No sound, nothing. I clutched the dirty white line, grabbing along its length like a blind man. It ended in a socket. I pulled it out and pushed it back in again and picked up the receiver.

The line was dead.

All the images I'd been holding back of the dying bodies, like wounds sewn up with ragged stitches and old plasters, burst open and blood sprayed through my mind, and I cried for them, for Ms Cave, for Mr Bellow, for Matthew and Raf and Tom and Tristan and for the gamekeeper and whoever else I might have saved with that call.

I cried until my eyes were dry and sore as though filled with sand and then I rested my cheek on the desk and lay with my arms curled around my head.

Outside, the sky slowly seeped from blue into black.

**H**enry's games were quiet for the last week of the summer. They began again when I started my new school. This was last October.

I couldn't go back to my old school because of the trouble I'd had there. Henry's father had suggested that for the final year of my GCSEs, I should go to Henry's school – 'There won't be any of that sort of behaviour there,' he assured us. 'James will be much happier. No bullying goes on at Whittleby's.'

'And he'll have Henry for a friend,' I heard my mum saying to him one evening. 'It will be much easier for him to go in if he has a friend to begin with.'

On my First Day morning, I spent most of breakfast trying to force my cornflakes down and drown the butterflies in my stomach. It made their wings soggy and heavy, but they kept on flying. I kept flicking my eyes at Sam. She was taking mousy nibbles from her toast crust, then went back to scribbling in her journal, the notebook covered with dayglo stars and glitter, cupping her hand around it so we couldn't see a word. But I knew what was in it anyway. I frequently read her journal when she was out at a friend's sleepover. It had become a habit since Dad died. So I knew that Sam was a virgin, that she'd only just got her period and was the second to last in her class, but now at least she felt like a woman, that she fancied an older boy called X only she was scared he might make her do it and that she hated Henry's father because he seemed weird and hoped he might take too many pills and disappear and that she wished Dad could come back.

Sam went to Nonsuch High School for Girls. It was only ten minutes walk further from my old school, Billingham Comprehensive. Sam didn't know that I followed her every morning, at a safe distance. Just to see her enter the school gates and make sure God or Fate had let her survive another day. Then I would run the ten minutes back to my school to be in time for register. My father had taught me to be a good runner.

As I sat at the table, watching her, I felt nervous. I kept thinking: *What if it's jinxed? What if the one morning I don't follow her, it happens? She steps out into the road and . . . ? Or some pervert picks on her, walks up to her, pretends he's a fashion photographer and then takes her away to be . . . ?* It could happen. Adults say all the time 'Don't worry, it won't happen' just like they said my father would be better after his chemo, there was no need to worry. When he died, I realised the reality of life: that every day is a dice roll: that any day, any time, anything can happen.

'So, you two boys can walk to school together,' Mum said, standing on the doorstep and waving us goodbye. I saw her look my new uniform up and down, pride in her eyes. She'd always wanted me to go to Whittleby's Boys. Henry's father had once donated a large sum to their school library; apparently he'd put in a good word for me.

I looked down the road. Sam was already walking off,

her ponytail bouncing. Goodbye, Sam, I said silently. Take care.

'Bye, Mum,' Henry said, putting emphasis on the *mum*, just for my benefit.

'Bye, Mum,' I muttered.

Henry and I walked in silence to the end of the road. There was a tiny, smug smile on his face. As though he knew how long I'd lain awake for last night, as though he knew every detail of what had happened to me at Billingham Comp, about me being the square, about Brian Jenkins. As though he knew that this time I wanted to recreate myself and become a cool guy. It was all down to first impressions, the place you carved in the hierarchy. I spent the night playing out scenes, whispering my lines, working out what I had to do. Punch a square, call a teacher a slag. Assert my territory.

But when it came down to it, I was scared I was going to get stage fright.

At the end of the road, I made a run for it. When I looked back, I saw that Henry was just strolling casually, that smirk still on his face. I felt as though he'd somehow won.

As I approached my new school, I passed torrents of boys wearing the black and white uniform. I could tell it was going to be a whole lot different from my old school because there was no sign scrawled with generation upon generation of graffiti. This one had a cream sign above the wrought-iron gates with elegant calligraphy that said:

WHITTLEBY'S GRAMMAR SCHOOL FOR BOYS
Est. 1889

I'd already visited the school and noted there was a phone box just across the road. I went in and dialled up her number; I knew it by heart now. The answerphone clicked on. I swallowed, checked my watch. It was 8:30. After Dad had died, she normally liked to go straight to work, but these days she lingered in the kitchen with Henry's father. I drummed my fingers against the smeary glass. It made everything look underwater, the boys drifting past like sharks. I started to hum 'Bittersweet Symphony', to hold back the images of Mum walking out into the road, Mum with blood pouring from her face, Mum with scars on her chest. I checked my watch. It was 8:45 now. Register began in five minutes and I was about to be late on my first day and I hated being late for anything. I slotted in another 30p and then, thank God oh God, I heard her voice say, 'Hi, this is Berkeley's Insurance, Pamela Frost speaking, how may I help?' This morning, instead of slamming down the phone, I lingered, cherishing the moment of relief, sweat cooling on my back. Then to my shock, she said, 'Who is this? You do this every morning – d'you get some kind of kick out of it –' I slammed down the phone, shaking. I shut my eyes, hearing Dad's voice in my head: *Look after her. Look after your mother and your sister.*

When I opened my eyes, my stomach lurched. *He* was waiting outside for me.

I opened the door and Henry immediately stepped in, so that we were crushed into the phone box. He drummed his fingers jubilantly on top of the phone, like a pianist getting ready to play. Then he turned to me, smiling.

'I need you to make a call for me,' he said, picking up the receiver. As he passed it to me, I felt the thin sheen of his sweat seep into my palm. It was a relief to know he sweated too, to know he was human.

'What call?' Maybe he was going to suggest a prank, calling up Henry's father at work.

'Call 999.'

'What?'

'Call 999.'

'Why? Why can't you call them?'

'It's an emergency, James. Jesus – will you just call them?'

'Okay, okay.' I stabbed in the numbers.

(I'd only ever rung 999 once and that was when my father died. My sister and mum were out at the time. My father was refusing chemo and he was lying in bed, in his ragged cocoon of a body. It was a hot day and I had been standing by the window. I walked over to his hand and touched it and it was dry as leaves. That's when I realised I needed to call 999).

'Police, ambulance or fire?'

'Police,' Henry whispered.

'Police,' I said.

A series of clicks.

'Hello?'

Henry was so close I could feel his whooshs of breath exploding on my ear.

'Tell them there'll be a bomb scare. This afternoon, at our school,' he whispered.

I stared at him. His face so close I could see the detail, the flecks of his irises.

'No.' My lips formed the word emphatically but it came out like a cowardly squeak.

'Tell them. There's going to be a bomb going off at school this afternoon at three.'

'No.'

'James, it's an emergency, d'you want people to die?'

'Hello, can I help you? Are you able to speak?'

'D'you want to die?' Henry whispered.

'How d'you know?'

'I overheard some guys on the bus, these really dodgy guys.'

'But-but –'

'Okay,' Henry whispered. 'Here's how it is. It's a custom at Whittleby's. Every new boy has to do a dare, prove he's not a square. If he doesn't have the guts, we all know he's a wuss and we all hate him.'

'Hello? Are you able to speak?' the operator persisted.

'There's a bomb –' I began.

'Where? Who are you?'

'Go on.' Henry nodded, his eyes bright.

'There's a bomb and it's made of eggs and flour and crap and –' I slammed down the phone, breathing hard.

'What the fuck did you do that for?' Henry cried, breath in hot blasts on my face. 'My God. You are such a dick.'

'I'm going.'

'Sure. Go, wuss-boy. Go, girl. Have a good first day at school.'

*Did you have a good day at school?* my mother asked later that day, when I got home.

*Great, Mum.* (I hated every minute.)

*Did you have a nice lunch? Was the two pounds enough for the canteen?*

*Nearly.* (I ran out of school in my lunch hour. I hid in the park and stared into the pond and watched the fish, they made me feel serene. I was too sick to eat.)

*What did you learn?*

*Oh, just geography, that sort of thing.* (I've learnt that

things don't change. Life repeats. Why do I always attract the bullies? What if I'm old and there are more Henrys out there, what if life is always full of Henrys?)

*I'm sure it will get easier as you go along. You've got Henry there, after all.*

Her voice so desperate for everything to be all right.

I thought: maybe there's time. She's only known Henry's father a few months. They haven't spoken about marriage yet. I saw that as the end; then there would be no escape. Maybe there would be time for her to change her mind. She misses my father. She's on the rebound, she's rushed into something crazy. There'll come a day when she realises that, surely?

She'll wake up and realise, and then everything will go back to normal.

**I** could hear a thrumming noise. Like bitter wasps.

I was standing in a corridor, on the other side of the Grand Hall. I knew, intuitively now, that I wasn't going to find a phone but I found myself still going through the motions. Because if I stopped going through the motions I would have to think about what to do next, and I couldn't think of any answers.

The corridor sloped away from the Grand Hall. The floor was stone with pieces of frayed red carpet thrown over it. I edged down a series of steps and found myself in a hallway with another choice of steps, one leading down to a stone place that looked like a kitchen, the other to another corridor filled with doors.

The thrumming noise was coming from the kitchen. I felt afraid, but I was also aware of how hungry I was. The last thing I had eaten was a few segments of satsuma at breakfast in the hotel in Paris this morning. Then Matthew had started a food fight and breakfast had finished early.

I edged down to the kitchen. A rotting stench pierced open my nostrils like tweezers and swam about blackly in my head.

The kitchen was a mass of blue and black shapes. I felt

about on the wall for a box-shape and found a switch. A fluorescent light zinged on and slowly leaked into the room.

Flies. The kitchen was full of them. There were unwashed saucepans lying about and overfilling bins and bits of vegetable and lumps of meat left on the surface. The flies looked as though they were celebrating some religious insect festival that had been going on for weeks. They swam over the food in black clouds, buzzing in ecstasy. I saw one or two reeling on the surface, feet peddling the air, glutted and drunk with food and rot.

I thought of flies crawling over Matthew's face and turned away, bile sharp in my throat.

Still, if there was food there, there must have been people. Perhaps, I thought with a flash of hope, the owners of the house had left in a hurry. Some sort of emergency or something had dragged them away. Maybe they would come back soon.

Maybe.

I spotted a First Aid kit by the sink and grabbed it. I was about to leave when I spotted a tiny window, about the size of a book. It was half-open and there was a small pool on the table, caused by the blown-in rain. The vegetation around the window was thick and determined and a black-berry bush had clawed its arm around the edge and was feeling its way down the wall. My stomach growled. I went back into the kitchen, swatting away flies wildly. I stretched out the bottom of my shirt into a cotton basket and plucked at the berries, piling them up, then ran back out into the corridor, breathing in the sweet air. Crouching down, I crammed them into my mouth in a purple mush. They tasted so lush, so good. I closed my eyes and smiled. I'd always liked the taste of blackberries, maybe because I liked the taste of the memories they conjured up more than the fruit itself. A memory of being five or six years old and going blackberry picking with my dad. Sam never wanted to come because she hated 'all the prickles'. So it was just me and him. He'd carry me on his back as he strolled across the fields, telling me stories, or the names of birds, or, if the sky was darkening on the way home, myths of how the stars came to be, and I'd cling to his back, my dad's back, wishing he would never put me down. I had played this memory over and over during his funeral so as not to cry; I stared at the coffin and concentrated on all the little details – the feel of his hair against my cheek, the little bald patch on the crown of his head, the strong, muscular feel of his back, like a totem pole I wound my legs around – because he'd told me that the only way he could transcend death was for me to keep him alive in my mind, like a sacred fire that would never be allowed to go out.

I thought about Matthew's dad, who was an architect. I wondered if he had been told about the crash yet, and if when I got out I would have to tell him about hearing Matthew's words, perhaps his dying words: *I can't hear you . . .*

The blackberries were finished and I realised how thirsty I was. I thought about going back into the kitchen to look for water, but I was worried that Henry would go mad at me if I didn't hurry over right now and tell him about the blackberries. I could just hear his voice: 'Why didn't you call me when you found them, why did you leave me here getting hungry, don't you ever think about anyone else?'

Then I hated myself for the way everything led back to Henry, every action shaped by him as though he was a king and I was his servant. I thought about tearing off the bottom of my shirt so he couldn't see the stain, and I was carrying this argument on in my head when I noticed the trapdoor.

Along the corridor, there was a length of frayed brown carpet that suddenly stopped. Then there was a square of wood with an old handle.

I knew I had to hurry back to Henry, but told myself it would just take a minute.

I put down the First Aid kit and had a go at pulling the trapdoor. I'd expected it to be like something out of those treasure-island-adventure books where the handle is rusty and you have to run and get a spade and hit it and dig under it. But I found that I could pull it, if I curled my hand tight. I felt the yank in my spine and then the trapdoor slammed back on the carpet with a thud. *Ker-boom, ke-boom, boom, boom, om, mmm*, the corridor sang back eerily. I stared down into the rectangle of darkness. It smelt of worms and old things. A metal ladder, eaten with rust, led down. I wondered if there might be some wires down there which could make the phone work. The shaft looked narrow and I remembered the last time I'd forced myself into a small space, when Henry's father had insisted we get into the lift in Debenhams and Mum hadn't been there to warn him about my problem, or Mum had warned him and he had forgotten. And now, crouched on my haunches, I swayed and nearly fell headlong, only just grabbing the top rung of the ladder in time. There was a wrenching noise. I felt myself pitching forwards: I heard a thin scream wail from my throat. In a second I saw myself falling: a dark flight, fingers clawing uselessly, the crash-smash of my body, and then I found myself lying on my back, staring up at the ceiling of the corridor, listening to the heavy ins and outs of my breathing.

When I sat up, I saw that the ladder had begun to come away from the wall.

I pulled up the trapdoor and slammed it back shut. I decided then that I wouldn't tell Henry about it. I told myself it was because I shouldn't distract him from the urgency of dealing with the gamekeeper. But deep in my heart I knew it was because I was pleased to have discovered a secret he didn't know about.

**H**enry and I took the First Aid kit to the gamekeeper. I was alarmed to see how heavily he was still bleeding; a pool was growing beneath his leg, slowly spreading its way down the corridor. We opened up the white plastic box, flinging aside plasters and scissors and ointments, arguing angrily over whether we should apply antiseptic to his wound and whether his leg might go green and fall off without it or if it might sting and make it worse. There was a coil of bandage and I gave one end to Henry, lifting up the leg and feeling the blood seep gently through my fingers whilst Henry attempted to roll the bandage around it. His hands were shaking so much it took him nearly a minute just to do one wind. I bit back the exasperation bubbling up in my throat, staring at him, willing him to hurry. Henry looked up at me, his pupils tiny dots in a sea of vacant blueness, like the addicts we saw in the anti-drugs videos at school. The bandage twirled and fell. Henry got up and walked away distractedly, shoving his hands in his pockets, whistling bits of Oasis.

'This is my last cigarette,' he said, without turning round. 'The last one in the packet.'

I twisted the bandage round his leg myself. Guilt made

me draw out the process as long as I could. I was just fastening it with a safety pin when the gamekeeper groaned. I jumped and fell back. His leg kept twitching but he was still unconscious. His eyes fluttered like dying flies, the way our dog's used to when he was having bad dreams. Occasionally he muttered something and bubbles of spittle seeped out of the corner of his mouth. I didn't have a handkerchief, so I bunched up the corner of my shirt and wiped his mouth. When I touched his forehead, it felt hot. I searched inside his jacket and found a brown leathery wallet with frayed edges. There were euros inside and some crumpled notes and a photo: a girl, aged six or seven, with an adult smile, and hair in a brown bob. I turned it over and scrawled on the back in green ink was the name: *Marie*.

I put my finger on the gamekeeper's neck, checking his pulse again. I closed my eyes. The rhythm was lulling, like a rocking train that sends you off to sleep. I kept seeing alternative pasts: the gun firing, kicking back, and the bullet whizzing through apples, grazing the gamekeeper's leg but not tearing into the skin.

I put the photo of Marie by the gamekeeper's face so that if he woke up, she would make him feel better. Then I passed from the corridor into the hall to get Henry.

'Henry, we have to go. There's no phone here and we have to go. Now.'

'Uh huh.' Henry didn't look up. He was trying to slide his fingers beneath one of the glass cases and lift it up.

'Where do you think . . . ?' I trailed off.

His behaviour puzzled me; he seemed distracted, as though I was nagging him over irrelevancies, drawing him away from the importance of studying the strange cases and metal objects.

I glanced around at the clutter. There were museum cases bathed in dust and cobwebs and a coffin, and boxes full of books, and a large black metal cage and –

And a guillotine.

Henry was standing behind it, eyeing it up as though trying to figure out how it might work, without having to take it all to pieces.

'Like I said . . . like I said . . . the phone wouldn't work.'

'Oh well. This is cool, hey?' he said.

The guillotine looked small and strange, as though it had been specially built to kill a child. Or maybe it was just a toy.

I came up and ran my finger under the blade. I shuddered as a ribbon of blood appeared on my forefinger.

'Ow, it's sharp!'

'You don't say,' Henry drawled. He spread out his arms. 'Look – all this stuff – the owner is some sick guy. He's even got a hanging cage.'

'That's for animals,' I said. 'In France they keep their dogs in cages, you know. I've seen them out in back gardens, I saw them on the coach on the way –'

'No it's not.' Henry pointed. There was a little plaque under the cage. Someone had scrawled on a white sheet of card in black, slanting ink and inserted it into a plastic wallet, which was now yellowy and coated with dust. I leaned in, trying to decipher it, but it was in French and the hand-writing was too small.

'What does it say?'

'Interesting,' said Henry in a flat voice which I knew meant he was excited. 'They strung people up and just let them hang in the cage and starve so the crows could eat them.'

'We have to go,' I said quickly. 'We have to get back.'

'In a minute,' said Henry, getting into the cage.

'But he might die –' I broke off, hearing the desperation in my voice. Showing desperation was like giving Henry lighter fuel and matches.

'He won't die,' said Henry. 'Jesus, he tried to kill us, you know. We could be lying dead now. Anyway, you only hit his leg. Look, just give us five more minutes, okay? Come on, we're never going to have a chance like this again.'

His words arrowed into my heart. Part of me didn't want to leave this house. I hadn't wanted to go on the school trip and once I was on the trip I hadn't wanted to go home. On the boat over, I had stood by the rail and watched the sea-gulls in the grey sky and thought sullenly that maybe I wouldn't go back home, maybe I'd stay in France for good, and then they'd be sorry. I'd nearly done it. An alleyway in France; Ms Cave's back was turned; everyone was ahead; I knew I could use my talent for running. I could run so fast they'd never find me; hide in a shop; sleep on a bench; begin a new life. But I had stood still and the moment had passed.

'Okay, five minutes,' I said, looking at my watch pointedly.

While Henry played with the cage, I wandered about. I didn't want to look into the cabinets. As Henry blew out his last stream of smoke, I watched it ascend heavenwards. The ceiling, made of glass triangles, seemed miles away and the light tried to shine down but by the time it reached us it had lost its power and became a weak yellow gloom.

I was aware of Henry's occasional gaze, pressing like a knuckle between my shoulder blades, mocking me. It was just like being back at home when Mum and Henry's father went out for the evenings to fancy restaurants or bridge evenings and Sam was locked up in her room, afraid of bumping into Henry. I'd be downstairs, trying to watch a nature film, when Henry would interrupt and insist on putting on some horror film. They were all over-eighteens, but he got them bootleg from some illegal immigrant trading them cheap. And so I had to sit and watch them through, image by image, and I couldn't even look away, because to look away would have let Henry know he'd won, that he was stronger than me. It wasn't that I abhorred the films; that was the problem. Henry seemed to sense that a twisted part of me took relish in the blood and gore and guts. But while the films would slip off Henry like water, they lingered in my mind at night, feeding off my imagination, mutating like genetically engineered creatures, mixing the scales and claws of the films with the fur and claws of the images I saw on the news until my mind was black with monsters and in that turmoil I ached to tear out my imagination by its roots and be clean like that poem we studied in class about boys who are innocent before the prison-house clamps them and their hearts lose their greenness and become shrivelled and grey.

So I made myself stare into a display cabinet. It was full of medieval French torture instruments, little pools of rusted black metal sitting in a sea of dust. Each had a little card next to it with an explanation that I couldn't translate. Somehow not knowing what they were for was worse than knowing. The lies of your imagination are always more terrifying than truth.

Henry's father had once taken us for a day trip to the London Dungeon. I had survived by looking at each thing and breaking it down so that it was no longer a whole, just a collection of metal and plastic pieces. But I was too tired to pull off this trick now. After the crash and the gamekeeper, I felt as though the layers of protective skin we wear around our brains had been rubbed away, leaving a raw, throbbing matter, bruised instantly by the slightest pain or ugliness. One of the instruments looked a little like a scorpion. There was something inertly active about it, as though it was holding its breath. I got paranoid that the moment I looked away it would leap, come flying out of the cage and sink its metal teeth into me, and so I stared and stared and stared at its rusty, glinting eye, until it became like one of those stare-out games where the chicken is the first to look down –

'Look at this,' Henry called me over.

He showed me his find. It was a small iron gadget with a hollow in it and a swirling corkscrew implement. 'Look.' Henry lifted it and showed me a slot, then he assessed my hands. 'I think they're the right size.'

I put my hands in my pockets. 'Henry, we have to go. Really.'

'Just put your thumb in here.'

'No!'

'I won't do anything with the screw. I just want to see how it fits.'

'Why don't you put your own thumb in?' I asked desperately.

'If you put your thumb in, then we can leave,' Henry said. 'Okay?'

I hesitated.

'Oh, so you really care about Matthew do you? I mean, he's just lying there injured, but no, you won't go and help him because your inky little thumb is too precious.'

'Okay, okay.' I knew that Henry's logic was skewed and cruel, but I played along. The Grand Hall felt cold; the walls, though large, seemed to be swooping down on me; I just wanted to get out. So I inserted my thumb. It only just fitted; I had to wriggle it hard. There was dirt in the hollow that caught up in my nail.

Henry began to twist the screw and I cried out.

'It's okay. I'm just doing it so it touches your thumb.'

I stood there, loathing the closeness of his presence. I thought of the gamekeeper and wondered how far his blood had flowed. I felt the tip of the screw meet my flesh – not piercing, not painful, but threatening.

'You really think we can go back?' Henry asked in a dead voice. 'They're all dead. I mean, you want to go back and see their bodies being put into plastic bags?'

I struggled to pull my thumb out, but it was too tight. I looked straight into the blue of his eyes.

'Look, they might not all be dead, okay? We have a responsibility to go and see.'

Henry was silent for a moment and then the force of his tirade shocked me.

'What kind of idiot are you? You think this is some sort of fairy-tale? I know, you think you can undo what you did to the gamekeeper, but you have to face it, James, they're all dead. I know you're thinking we can go out there and be heroes and drag them up the cliff and oh, be in the local papers for being boys who saved our friends –' He gulped, his voice laced with tears, 'But it's just a dream! Wake up! You saw how far the coach fell, it wasn't just a few feet, it must have been, I don't know, fucking fifty feet, maybe more, and nobody, not one single person will have survived. Haven't you read articles about plane crashes, planes falling two hundred feet and nobody surviving? And you want to go back and see all the bodies and know we're the only ones left, that for some reason we're still alive. We were late! We didn't go back to the coach in time and it crashed and it's our fault and we're just – well and truly – fucked – so –'

'Henry, you're hysterical – even if – even if they are dead – we have to go – we have to – we have to go now – and –' I struggled as he suddenly twisted the screw and I yowled and kicked him. He fell away and I staggered backwards, the torture instrument hanging from my bright red thumb.

'If you don't want to come, I'll go on my own!' I cried. 'You can stay here and you can look after the gamekeeper, I'll get help on my own, okay?'

Henry stared at me through slits of eyes. And then he ran. I swung round, bewildered.

'Henry?' Silence. 'Henry? Okay, fine. I'll go without you.' I looked down and untwisted the thumb screw from my hand, massaging the red indents, sucking my sore thumb.

And then: sudden footsteps. Henry was back. He was carrying the gamekeeper's rifle, and pointing it right at me.

'We're not going back. We can't go back. I won't let you.'

I erupted, then. My fear of Henry was lost in my frustration, my rage.

'WE HAVE TO GO! THE GAMEKEEPER'S LOSING BLOOD AND IT WILL BE MURDER IF WE DON'T GO! ARE YOU SOME KIND OF PSYCHO, YOU MIGHT HAVE KILLED YOUR MOTHER BUT –'

I hadn't meant to say that.

'What?' Henry's voice was like a whip.

I hadn't meant to say that.

Mum had told me after the Knife Incident. A way of trying to explain why Henry might be difficult at times, *though he means well*, she'd assured me. I'd saved the information, polishing it in my mind like a knife to draw and stab Henry with later. But this wasn't meant to be a moment of triumph; I saw the panic on his face and I felt ugly.

'I didn't mean that, okay?'

'I didn't kill her. I didn't kill her.'

'I know you didn't, Henry, it's fine, okay, we'll just go and –'

'Who told you that I killed her –'

'Nobody. I just made it up.'

'WHO TOLD YOU THAT I KILLED HER?'

'My mum, okay? She was just –'

'You're lying. You're lying. You, you're just so full of bullshit, but of course, nobody knows, because you, James, you're the perfect boy, with the perfect mother, and the perfect sister, and the perfect grades at school, and a *gift*, as Mrs Robson puts it, a poetic, *mature* writing style –'

'Jesus, Henry, I just heard –'

'YOU'RE A LIAR, YOU'RE A LIAR, YOU'RE A LIAR!'

He pulled the trigger.

I keep on playing the scene back. I see the bullet, like the slow-motion ones in movies, erupting from the gun, dancing through the air, skimming past the museum cabinets, heading towards me, me crumpling on the ground, the bullet passing by, hitting something, perhaps the wall, with a bang and a burst of stone. And then I rise, I rise above the scene like a ghost, and I see the gamekeeper lying in the hallway, whimpering, and Henry in the Grand Hall, shaking and cocking the trigger again, and me running, stumbling up the marble staircase, my shoelace coming undone, flapping around my ankles, nearly sending me back down the stairs as I turn the corner and then I'm upstairs in the gallery.

**It's going to be fine.** You shouldn't have said that about his mum, but it's going to be fine. Henry's just upset and he's over-reacted, even he knows this is no time for games, it's going to be fine. I sat on the top step of the marble staircase. The light from the Grand Hall glittered on my muddy shoes; the top half of my body was veiled in harlequin shadow. I stood up, squinting through the slits in the marble banisters. Henry was still holding the gun, staring into the cabinets. It's going to be fine, just go and see if there's a phone in the rooms upstairs, there might be a connection up here, you can call and then hide until the police come. Go and find a light. I took a few steps down the gallery, wincing at every squeak of my shoes. Henry's steps rang out below. I froze. Oh God, what if he's coming after me, oh God, please don't let him come after me. If only the gamekeeper would cry out, oh God, make him cry out and shock Henry into stopping and thinking. Silence. Where's he gone? I looked down into the twilight darkness of the gallery. I could see doors, faint light gleaming on the knobs. There had to be a phone somewhere. I pressed myself flat against the wall so that Henry couldn't see me from below and slid along it with crablike steps, like some spy in an action movie –

And then it happened. The whizz of a bullet and then the smashing tinkle of glass. Light bulb shards falling, falling, hitting the cabinets in the Grand Hall. Squiggles of chaos dancing in the wires; fuses burning and breaking, and then: darkness. Everywhere, pitch black. I stopped. I opened my mouth to call out, swallowed. I heard Henry's footsteps again. I wanted to slide to the floor and curl into a ball, but I forced myself on. Any hope of night-vision had been destroyed; the flare of the dying bulb was dancing on each retina. I pressed my palms flat against the stone walls, searching, searching for a light. The stone stopped and became wood. I felt the ridges of panels, and then, finally, the orb of a doorknob. As I twisted it, I heard another gunshot from below and I jumped violently. Maybe I should shout down an apology. A loathing for the house poured over me; I felt as though it was a series of babushka dolls and the deeper I plunged into it, the smaller and tighter the rooms and walls became. I turned the knob; a click, and then a small hiss of stale air. I should wait a few minutes for his temper to simmer down, then apologise. I pushed open the door. The darkness deepened. I paused, swaying slightly. A moment of *déjà vu*: of standing still, my breath in my throat, that night I had been feverish with flu and crept, sweating, to the doorway of my parents' bedroom, and seen them in the dark together. My father was holding her in his arms, but she was limp, and as he tried to kiss her, she ducked her head. He twisted her chin and kissed her firmly on the mouth and I saw, from the faint glow of the streetlamp, amber tears on his cheeks. He groaned and said her name and pulled her in tight; her eyes were blank with revulsion and as I watched them I shared her revulsion, wanted to help her push him away. Back in my room, I lay in bed, shivering and sweating, tossing and turning, pulling the covers up and down and deciding that it was her fault, that if I was going to pick a side, it would be his.

I stepped into the darkness, arms outstretched. No noise from below, but what if Henry had taken off his shoes and was creeping up behind me? I felt like Theseus in the labyrinth, plunging deeper into chaos. My palms met with paper; I imagined roses patterned across them. Why had I said that to Henry, why had I been so insensitive, so stupid? This wasn't the time to provoke him. I circled my palms and felt a patch where the paper had been torn away and the wall was cold. There had to be a light here somewhere. *I can't hear you.* Why had Matthew called that out as he died, had it been a message for me? A box, a switch! I clicked it. The darkness remained. I flicked it again, several times. Nothing. Henry must have caused a short-circuit. The whole house was blown, and there was probably a box somewhere, maybe down below in the dark tunnel, but . . .

You're not a baby. You're not afraid of the dark. Come on, move on, try to feel for a phone.

I walked forwards and my knees knocked something hard. I fell into the black, hit something both hard and soft, my face muffled in cloth. I felt about: cotton, silk, puffy things. Pillows. A bed. I breathed in; it smelt musty, of moths and rotting silk. But the thought of the bed was comforting. I lay down, curled in a foetal ball. I strained my eyes in the darkness, trying to see if the lump in the bed beside me was real or my imagination. What if there was a dead body in the bed? An old man who had died in his sleep and was now a skeleton with a ghost of skin stretched over it? Don't be silly, a dead body would stink. Just reach out and touch it and you'll see it's just a pillow. But I curled my arms tight, my breath warming my knees. Just half an hour, I told myself. That should be long enough for him to recover. I'll count down the minutes, minute by minute. Sixty backwards, thirty times.

I stood at the top of the stairs.

*I'm sorry. I'm sorry. I'm sorry.*

I kept on calling out the words. My voice sounded shaky; my echoes seemed to mock me with pathetic mimicry. I sat down on the top of the marble staircase. And then, at last, he began to reply, his words flying out of the darkness like spirits.

'James, James, won't you come out to playyyy . . .'

'Come on, James, what's the matter with you?
Cat got your tongue?'

Don't answer him, don't answer him,
don't let him draw you in.

'There's a lot of interesting things here to look at, you know. Like you saw earlier, or maybe you didn't. There's all these contraptions, and these quotes in French.'

(The flare of his lighter.) 'By the guillotine, it says "The condition of a man is a condition of war of everyone against everyone." Do you know where that comes from? No, I didn't think you did. It's from *Leviathan*. Listen to this:

"All men have a natural right to all things."

"For as long as every man holdeth this right, of doing anything he liketh; so long are all men in the condition of war."

'Interesting, huh? And I like this guillotine, I must say, I do.' I pictured him stroking his hands up and down its wooden edges, running his finger oh-so-close to the edge of the blade, enjoying the thrill of minute air between skin and steel. 'Do you know why the guillotine was invented, James? Well, you should do. We learnt it in French, remember? About that doctor, called Joseph-Ignace Guillton, who, incidentally, didn't even invent the machine, he begged the National Assembly to use the guillotine as a more humane form of capital punishment. I think that's kind of funny, don't you? They thought a nice, swift blow was better than all that hanging and being burnt at the stake and being hung, drawn and quartered. But still. Only the French could have invented the guillotine.'

He spoke grandly, as though the last remark was a clever, witty remark of his own, but I knew he was just echoing a remark of his father's.

After a silence had passed, I heard the sound of drinking. The plastic of a bottle hitting his chin, the sensual glug of water in his throat. My thirst was now a dry ache, so strong that I wondered if it would be worth fighting him.

'If I –' I broke off, my voice weak and cracked.

**'Did you say something?'**

**'I said, did you say
SOMETHING?'**

      *thing, thing, thing,* the hall echoed.
          *ing, ing, ing,* the rooms took up the refrain.
            *g, g, g,* the darkness whispered.

    **'If I come down, will you give me some water?'**

          LAUGHTER, echoing in ripples again.

I stood up. I grabbed the balcony and walked forwards, flailing the air with my other hand, the darkness around me like a great black moth. My footsteps clicked on the marble.

**'If you want water, you'll have to fight me for it. But I do have an unfair advantage. I mean, I have the gun.'**

    I stopped.

   **'Why do you want water anyway?'**

                'I haven't had anything to drink,
                not since we woke up this morning.
                      I'm thirsty.'

'But you shot the gamekeeper and you killed our entire class. Don't you think you're being selfish, wanting to ease your thirst, after all you've done?'

'That's not fair! If I hadn't shot him, he might have killed you!'

'I didn't ask you to shoot him. I mean, if the police came, and they questioned me, I don't know what I'd say, because I didn't ask you to shoot him, you took the gun and made that choice.'

How I hated him then.

'So I don't think you should come down here.' In the manner of our local priest at the height of his sermon. 'I think you should stay up there and think about what you've done.'

'You don't mean this. You're in shock. I saved your life and you're in shock. We're both in shock. I – learned about it in First Aid. Sometimes it can last for forty-eight hours and you can feel numb and blank. And then it hits you.'

'This isn't a shock.' Another glug.

'I have some food.'

Why did I say that? Why did I lie?

'If I give you some food, then maybe you can give me some water.'

'What food is this, exactly?'

'A sandwich.'

'Oh, a sandwich. Right. One of James's sickly egg sandwiches, right? There is egg in it, I guess right, right?'

'No, no, there's cheese.'

'I've already got some food, I don't need some egg sandwich.'

'Well, can I have some water anyway?'

'If you come down here, I will be forced to retaliate.'

I stood still, the marble chilling my palm.

'We can't stay here for ever,' I whimpered.

'Yes, we can.'

'You're crazy. What do you mean by that? You're crazy –'

'I like it here. Nobody will be looking for us, anyway, because by the time they deal with the crash, they'll just assume we died in that, and that our bodies have been eaten or lost or whatever. So we're cool. I'd like to stay for a few days, chill out, practise my French without lousy teachers breathing down my neck, without my dad hitting me every time I don't come home with a bloody A.'

'But we can't. If we don't leave this place now, and we come out in a few days, the police might have gone away and we might never get back.

Without food, we'll starve . . . we'll . . .'

'Correction. I have food. I've got water. You don't – well, except your egg sandwich, which may have more nutritional benefit than I might have imagined, I agree. But in the end, you'll starve, yes, because if you come down here and try to take my food, I'll shoot you. I have to, because there isn't enough for both of us. One of us has to starve, one of us has to die, and if you were in my position, you'd do the same –'

'I wouldn't, I wouldn't, I would let you come down. And if I die up here, when they come and find you, they'll see the gamekeeper's body and my body and they'll think you're the murderer and you'll go to prison and, like you said, French prisons are worse.'

'I was just saying that to wind you up.'

'Well, prison will still ruin your life. You won't get your GCSEs and you won't go to university and your life will be over.'

'But when are these so-called people going to appear? I mean, why is this place empty except for a gamekeeper? Think about it.'

Henry's catchphrase: Think about it. Well, I didn't want to think about it.

'I mean, why is there no phone?'

'It's a museum. I mean, that's why they've got display cabinets and stickers and that guillotine.'

III

'Correction – this was a museum. It's not any more. Maybe it was once, but it's not now. Why was it closed up, why did we have to climb over the railings? If it was a museum, there would be a proper entrance and there would be tickets. I don't see anyone coming here. I guess it's to do with the ghost.'

'There's a bit about it on the placards. It says that long ago, a couple lived in this house, and during the French Revolution they were executed. Maybe this is the very guillotine that killed them. So now they roam around the mansion, carrying their bloody heads under their arms, seeking revenge.'

'So I think the only person left is the gamekeeper, and the ghosts, and now the ghosts are going to get lonely. I reckon the people who own this place won't even bother calling the gamekeeper, they've probably gone away for the summer. I mean, it is July, so they'll be back, maybe September. Or maybe not. We'll see then.'

'WE CAN'T STAY HERE UNTIL SEPTEMBER. WE CAN'T!'

'Why not? Why d'you want to go back? It's not as though you've got a girlfriend waiting for you to help you lose your virginity.'

'Mind you, starvation is a slow way to die.'

'I doubt if anyone will care whether or not you go back home anyway. Sam won't –'

## 'DON'T BRING SAM INTO THIS!'
*this*
*this*
*this* echoed . . .

'Hit a nerve there, have I? Well, I'm going to sit here and eat. I'm sorry that there isn't any for you, but I think it might be good if you're hungry, it'll help you to stay awake.'

'I'm going to sleep.'

That's it; nice and cool. He'll be all right tomorrow. He's just in one of his moods, one of his worst moods. No point in talking to him; he just wants to stick the needles in deeper. It'll be different in the morning, in the light of day.

'I don't think you should go to sleep, James. I think that could be dangerous.'

'Why?'

'Because you don't know what could happen to you. It's dark. If you're asleep, your defences are down. Anyone can creep up on you. Anything could happen.'

'What d'you mean by that? What d'you mean?'

'Just what I said. Anything could happen. I mean, I'm the psycho, right? I'm the guy who supposedly killed his mother? So: anything could happen.'

I thought of a stained-glass window my father had once shown me, ten feet high. It had depicted a man

113

with a beard who looked holy and he had his hands clasped across his chest, only you could see through them, right into his heart. And in the centre was an angel, and a demon, side by side, holding hands.

'What you said about war earlier, I don't think it's true.'

'Oh?'

'People can be bad and they can shoot each other and drop bombs on each other and be at war with each other, but they can also do good things. They can help other people and, and, they can be like Saint Francis, my dad did a stained-glass window of him and he gave all his money to the poor and healed lepers by kissing them, and he loved everyone, and if you sit and think, Henry, I think you can . . . I think you can, you can . . . you can . . .'

'God, you have some nerve. What are you, some saint? You think you're Jesus Christ? You think I'm like Satan, and we're in the desert, and I'm tempting you? Is that what you think?'

'Well, you are evil, Henry, you're being evil right now and you have to let me come down.'

'There isn't any such thing as good and evil anyway. Nobody cares about that any more, just like nobody cares about the Bible and we don't have to read it in assemblies any more. It's just a case of who's stronger. It's a survival of the fittest.'

'Well, then, we may as well go around killing
each other, then, right? We may as well all just
die and give up on living on the planet.'

'No. I'm not saying that. I'm just saying that it's
me versus you. If you want to get out of here,
you have to come down here and get this gun
off me and kill me. And you're too much of a
saint to do that – so then you can just die.
You can die James the Martyr, right? Hey,
maybe someone will make a stained-glass
window of you.'

'You think you're so cool, Henry, but you're not,
some day this is going to happen to you, and
you're not going to like it, and maybe you'll die
then, it'll come back and you'll regret this, you'll
wish you hadn't done this. You're evil and you're
a murderer and you're going to go to Hell.'

'No such thing, James. No such thing.'

Quiet now. Wait for morning. Nothing else to
do but wait until morning. The gamekeeper
might be dead but there is nothing I can do.
Nothing I can do.

'Well, James, have fun up there tonight.
Make sure the bedbugs don't bite.'

'Well, goodnight, James.'

'Aren't you going to say goodnight, James?'

'Suit yourself.'

**S**tay awake, stay awake. I have to stay awake. Just sit by the top of the steps and think and stay awake. Listen with pricked ears, like an animal, be on your guard.

I remember just a few days before my father died, no don't think about that, think about Sam, no don't think about her, don't think about what Henry's done to her. Think about the myth behind the moon, how ancient people thought that a hare lived on it but how is it that my mum can say Henry's such a *nice* boy if she knew, if she knew. I remember just a few days before my father died, I was in the hallway and I saw him. I saw him standing in front of the mirror in his bedroom, naked, and he looked like a small bird who's been gradually pecked to death, a few hairs sprouting from his bald head like dying feathers, shoulders hunched, skin marble-yellowed, even his cock so small and shrunken it was almost absent and I couldn't believe it was him, that this was my dad. He sensed me in the hallway and called out my name and I ran downstairs out of the house and out to the park where I sat on the swings till it got cold and dark stay awake that's it keep thinking stay awake. And I hated my body, it felt like a prison and I realised that we are not living, we are all dying, every minute, our bodies decaying and sinking and slowing and breaking down, every one of us, and I felt so afraid that one day, sooner or later, I would be like him, it made me wish I could find a potion to make myself young for ever. But I remember Dad saying even though his illness made him old he felt young inside, he was still him and that is because our bodies are cages for the birds of our souls, and he said if I can keep him alive in my mind that means a little bit of his soul is in my mind and even if the body rots then the soul, the sweet winged soul lasts for ever

lasts forever

## Stay awake.

But then again people are always saying I look younger than my age. Matthew and Brian once sent me into an offy to buy them some beer but even with a fake ID the old man wouldn't believe I was eighteen – he laughed and said 'Get out, kid.' My sister, Sam, is the same, she is thirteen and she looks about twelve, with her long blonde hair all tied up in plaits and little pink ribbons, though recently she has started coming down to dinner wearing lipstick and Henry's father stared across at her and said, 'Has someone punched you in the mouth? Because that's what your lipstick looks like' . . . Oh God, what if there are ghosts? Don't think about that, just stay awake and the merry-go-round I saw them darting swimming

and it was going round

and round and he was chasing her laughing

# Stay awake.

I wonder if Matthew and Brian are in heaven now. If I close my eyes just to picture them . . . not to sleep because I have to stay awake . . . I can see them. They say your heaven is how you would like it to be but I think everyone thinks of a garden, a lush green garden. There are leaves falling softly from the trees and the sounds of children laughing hiding under the leaves and I'm lying on the grass and the sun is splashing warmth across my head and Henry isn't there, because Henry's down in Hell where he belongs he's being slashed and flayed by minotaurs with red eyes but I'm in heaven and I am lying in the grass and my father is talking softly to my mother, I know they're close but I don't need to speak I want them to keep talking to hear her telling him I'm sorry I made a mistake you were the one I always loved I never meant to push you away and it's so easy just to

sleep but I must

## stay awake

but he has to sleep too, doesn't he? Maybe if I could just go and search I could find a phone, if I could find some matches, maybe I could just go and check.

I can feel something. It's brushing against my foot but I'm not scared ghosts don't exist I know they can't exist otherwise I would have seen my father long ago. Though sometimes I wonder if by thinking so hard about him my thought might one day take form. I might recreate him some vapour some mist some essence of him and I have to stay awake

and maybe if I conjure up my father's ghost he will haunt Henry, will wait until he's asleep at night maybe if when I get out of here I will summon him and send him after Henry drive him mad in mazes of nightmares and he'll beg his father to go and but I shouldn't think these thoughts maybe thinking these thoughts will make me go to Hell and I can't help it

I can't help these bad thoughts my eyes hurt they want to fold over and maybe I should just give up oh God just give up and let go and lie down and let him kill me?

But then maybe I will be at peace like the time we studied *The Waste Land* in class and Mrs Robson had explained those final lines at the end

*Shantih shantih shantih*

which means *that peace which passeth all understanding*, and as she'd told us this she'd stared out of the window at the sun and the biblical rays streaming out of the clouds with a kind of longing in her eyes and I'd ache to reach out and touch her and say, nobody else in this class is really listening to you, they're all just sitting reading porn mags in their laps and waiting for the bell to go, but I'm listening to you, I am listening and I understand you, like none of them do.

But I do want to live I do I do I just wish things could go back to the old ways I wish Sam didn't shut me out of her room and treat me like the enemy too. I wish I didn't spend schooldays dreading going home and home dreading going to school I wish I could find some place some secret heavenly place to be at peace

## and what about the gamekeeper

oh God what about the gamekeeper?

this feels like being at home with Henry having to watch those videos I feel as though my head is full of scorpions this is like being in a nightmare. One of those worst nightmares, the babushka doll ones where you open your eyes and you find yourself in your bed in your room and you think you're safe and then the walls dissolve into blackness and the thing lunges at you again and you realise you've only fallen from one nightmare into another, a deeper, smaller core of the doll, and you kept screaming to *wake up, wake up*, on some level you can feel sweaty covers hot against your legs but your mind is possessed, trapped in a web of its fears and imaginings, and the question is, how many layers are there to the doll, when will you find the centre and if you do will you wake or be too far into the maze of darkness to ever wake up again so just so long as I stay awake I'll be fine stay awake stay awake

and maybe the gamekeeper is dying right now breathing in his last breaths slipping from his cage and maybe I can keep him awake maybe I can maybe I can maybe if I just pray for him, remember that article that Dad gave me about how scientists have found that prayer works and he asked me to pray for him every night. Only it didn't work for I didn't pray hard enough or long enough or the right way for God to listen and if only I had not been so selfish, if only the night before he had died I hadn't gone to sleep and forgotten to pray, if only I had stayed up all night I might have said a hundred prayers five hundred prayers and maybe on the five-hundredth prayer my prayers might have taken flight and found heaven and heaven might have said yes we'll keep him alive but I have to pray again I have to try again though I am in darkness I have to find the whiteness in my mind though I am in despair I have to find hope I have to keep the gamekeeper alive by saying God please let him live please let him live for Henry has a gun but the only ammunition I have are my arrows of prayer my bullets of love and so I will not go to sleep I will stay awake otherwise he will die he will die and once more it will be my stay awake my stay awake my fault stay awake

# B.

I stared closely at the letter, at the swirling curves of the B and then the blot where Mrs Robson's red biro had smeared against the grain of the paper. B. The first time in my English class that I hadn't got a straight A. This week I had been so confident; we had been asked to write a short story, so I'd written about Henry. A story about an old man who appears to be very kind, who adopts a young boy to keep him company in his cottage. Then he torments the boy, loving him one day, the next threatening to chop him up and eat him in a stew.

At the bottom, next to the B, Mrs Robson had written: *I realise this grade may be a disappointment to you, James, so see me after class if that helps.* All through the lesson, as we read our way through *Hamlet*, I felt my pen grow sweaty in my hands. At the end, I pretended to be engrossed in reading Act 5 while everyone filed out.

Mrs Robson smiled at me and leaned against the desk next to mine. She tossed back her head and her auburn mane rose in a static cloud and then subsided over her shoulders. She was wearing *that* skirt again. The one everyone in class talked about and took home with them in their imaginations. It was beige and there was a thin slit, like a lascivious grin, up the front. I kept my eyes on her face and not the slit. It took a lot of concentration to do this; my eyes burned in the back of their sockets and my fingers curled so tight around my pencil the knuckles protruded like sticks of chalk.

'Look, James, I did enjoy your story. I must admit, I thought the premise of an old man tormenting a child was a little . . . disturbing.'

'Well, I like Stephen King,' I said.

I don't know why I said that. It was a lie. Sam liked Stephen King. *Carrie* and *Pet Sematary* and *Misery*, all those dramatically titled horrors. But there was something about Mrs Robson that made me want to spin lies around myself like golden cobwebs.

'I see,' she laughed gently. She tossed back her hair and frowned, that little gathering of lines in the knot of skin above her nose, and said, 'My only problem with this story, James, is that I felt the old man, Harry – I think his name was? – didn't work as a character. I know that I told you to create interesting characters. But one minute Harry is kind to the boy and gives him apples. The next he hits him with his walking-stick, when the boy has done nothing wrong. He doesn't make any sense. Do you see?'

'Yes, Miss,' I said, nodding. 'Mrs Robson.'

She smiled and I thought she almost looked relieved, which unnerved me.

Then she looked down at the desk, playing with her pen, and said, 'Perhaps there's something you want to tell me, James.'

I felt panic in my throat. I thought: tell you that I think you're beautiful? Tell you that I write poems about you?

Tell you that you float into my dreams at night and day-time? And then I looked up at her and saw the pity in her eyes and I realised this wasn't what she meant. She wanted to know who the old man really was.

I wanted to tell her. But then I remembered the last time my mother said to me, 'James, I want you to tell me every-thing.' When she'd really meant, 'James, I want you to tell me what I want to hear.' Because when I'd tried to tell her the truth about Henry, she'd said softly, 'James, don't you think you can at least *try* to be friends with him? You never even look like you're trying, you always act as if you don't want it to work. I mean, for goodness sake, James, can't I have a bit of happiness for once? I feel I deserve it, God, after all these years.'

Bit of happiness? I scoffed inside. She had years of happi-ness with my father; now she was enjoying endless happi-ness with Henry's father. What about me and Sam? I wanted to cry. What about our happiness? I mean, can't you see it? Can't you see Henry's father isn't interested in us in the slightest, that he's given up on us? I pass him in the hallway and he looks at me through his glasses with his weird pebble eyes as though I'm an insect on his shoe. At dinner he can only just summon up enough interest in us to ask if we had a good day at school and then if we do talk he tells us we're giving him a headache and he can't focus. And what do you do? You just look at us and press your finger to your lips, and then you go out with him, leaving Sam to storm off to her bedroom and Henry alone with me, which is like leaving me with a Rottweiler with its leash taken off. But as long as you're happy, Mum, as long as you have your little bit of happiness.

These words bubbled inside me, struggling to find shape

and form and put themselves into sentences; I felt the truth, which I had clamped down for so long in the pit of my stomach, rising up, clawing at my heart, bursting to be let out. But then I thought of Mrs Robson's reaction to my story: *the old man doesn't make any sense*, and I thought angrily at how wrong she was, *Hamlet* didn't make any sense, did he, not one of us in class got him, and yet that was because he was real. I thought then that people in real life could never really be captured in books because they would be such a confusion of contradictions, such a chaos of senses and nonsenses, with so many cracks to explore the reader could never understand them and therefore could not believe in them. Then my anger was gone and a sadness swept over me. I couldn't tell anybody anything, not my mother, not Mrs Robson because words could not explain what was going on between Henry and I –

I woke up suddenly. Something hard was sticking into my forehead. I opened my eyes and saw Henry standing above me. I'd always imagined the tip of a rifle to feel cold but it was like a brand burning into my skin.

Oh God. I had told myself to **stay awake** but I had let myself slip into the noose of sleep. And now he had me.

'You're not my brother,' he said. His eyes were circled so heavily his bags looked like part of them, making his eyes look monstrously huge. 'I warned you if you slept that I was going to shoot you.'

I stared up at him with pleading eyes. A calm voice sliced through the black panic: he's not really going to shoot you. Henry would never go the whole way. He wouldn't risk it. Think about it.

'Say it!' his voice was high. 'Say you're not my brother!'

'I'm not your brother.'

'You're not my stepbrother.'

'I'm not your stepbrother.'

'When you were a baby, you turned up on your mother's doorstep in a carrier bag. You were a monster, but your mother took pity on you and let you in. Say all that.'

A pause.

'I said, say all that.'

'I'm not a monster.'

'Yes, you are.'

'No, I'm not –' and then Henry pulled the trigger.

I saw myself from high above, looking down. My body was lying sprawled on the floor. Henry dropped the gun and it hit the floor soundlessly. He knelt down and burst into weeping. He held my face, my hands. See, Henry, now look what you've done. I swooped and smiled through him and over him. I felt his pain and squeezed his heart to make him feel the pain even more acutely. I wrapped myself around his soul and he lay down and we curled up inside him like twins in a foetus.

I woke up suddenly, seeing the gamekeeper's face as the bullet hit his leg, and I let out a faint cry.

**M**y body was aching all over, as though I'd been beaten up, and I'd been lying with my left leg squashed up beneath my right one. It had gone dead. I sat up and tried rubbing and massaging it. I stretched it taut; when I released it, pins and needles prickled up my shin.

I lay still for a while, my mind still foggy; the nightmares had left a residue, like black ink flowing between my thoughts. I was aware of how dry my mouth was, my throat thick as though filled with dried moss.

I heard a noise from below: Henry was coughing.

Panic blew away the muzzy cobwebs in my mind. I pulled myself up. *Move, quickly, before he comes up.* I crawled down the corridor and into the bedroom I had been in last night. The faint light made a mockery of my fears. There was no body in bed: just ivory silk sheets, faded like the colour of an old person's skin. A tatty carpet and peeling wallpaper and a heavy wardrobe and a chest of drawers.

On the top of the chest of drawers was a mug. A dead fly floated in its dirty water. I wondered vaguely how long ago that water had been drunk. Perhaps the gamekeeper had lingered in this room, or had it been left by one of the owners?

I crawled to the window and pulled apart the velvet curtains. A shower of dust rained down softly. After the darkness of the night, the light was shocking. The grounds were filled with a vaporous mist, the trees poking their dark heads over the top. The dawn sky was covered with a fine layer of cloud, which the rising sun gave a translucent quality, and here and there broke through in bursts of aching brightness. I knelt down before the window and let the light bathe over me. I wanted to wrap it around myself and lie down and not wake up for ever.

I peered out of the window. Perhaps there might be a house close by; perhaps I could call for help. All I could see was the rolling green of the grounds and, above and beyond the forests, the haze of the horizon. It was white and contained a hint of a silhouette, which might have been the sea, or a cliff, or a city. I pictured the people out there, doing their daily things, shopping and eating and cooking and loving, and I wished so desperately that I could tie my voice to a bird and let it take my message to them, to come out and save me. But that was impossible. I felt like a prisoner stuck for his life in a cell looking at one patch of sky through a window and I heard Henry's voice saying *We're going to be here for ever* and I found myself turning into a girl. I felt tears seeping down my cheeks; I rolled up on the floor like a baby and sobbed. Anger flared in my stomach at the unfairness of it all. Why had God put me here in this house with Henry to deal with? Maybe Henry was the devil and I had to fight him. But I didn't have the strength to fight. I just wanted to be home in the softness of my bed looking at the stars through the gap in my curtains. My tears stopped and I felt them dry up in itchy lines on my face but I didn't brush them away. I felt snot pour from my nostril on to my lip but I let it. I decided to give up. I wouldn't move. I would just lie here and let Henry find me, or die on the floorboards.

I heard my father's voice in my head: *Be strong in yourself*. I remembered how, in the last months of his cancer, I had confided in him that PE lessons were becoming hell for me, how the coach knew I hated all sports. My father had said it was just a case of finding what I was good at. He said he had a hunch that I'd be a fine runner; he'd said he'd be my secret coach. He would sit in the front garden in a deckchair with his stop watch, making me run round the block, yelling exuberantly as I came panting up the hill, hug-hitting me every time I beat my record. And then came that glorious day at school when I had run in the race and everyone had thought old James the square, who kicks the ball into the wrong goal in footie, he's going to come last, and I felt myself soaring down the green strip, my body pure liquid, as though I was sweet music, floating past the other bodies, jumping over the finishing line, in first place, and I ran home and showed Dad my medal and he wept over it.

I sat up and my father's voice told me: stop crying and be strong. Everyone said you could never make the running team. Well, nobody would ever think you could survive this, and you can, and when you get out here, you're going to tell them all. You're hungry and thirsty, aren't you? Well, do something about it.

I was thirsty. So thirsty that I licked my palms, trying to scoop out one drop of sweat and moisture, but they were sandpaper, as though my body was turning to dust.

Right. You have to go back down into the hall and find water.

I can't go into the hall. I'm scared. What if he tries to shoot me?

Go into the hall. That's it. Creep down the corridor; silently. Can you see a bathroom? Yes; there; at the end of the corridor. Go in. That's right. See? You can do it. Be strong.

In the bathroom, there was a large bath with curling feet and a sink. I ran to it. The taps were very ornate, curved into elaborate swan's heads. Mildew crept like a green rash down the wall and over the top of the enamel. I grabbed a tap and twisted it. It was too stiff to turn.

There was a mirror above the sink; I caught a sudden glimpse of my reflection. My face looked like a stranger's, a foreign collection of dirt and smears and hollows. I ducked my head, refusing to catch my eye again.

I grabbed and tried again, harder. The sunlight streamed through the window; sweat burned on my forehead. It wouldn't turn. I heard myself cry out and kicked the sink. Be strong, be strong. Heat fissed beneath my armpits; I went to the window and yanked it open. Slumping down, I listened to the birdsong flowing in. In the distance, there was a sudden explosion, like a gunshot; the birdsong turned to shrieking as they rose from the trees in a fire of black wings.

I sat up. Henry was *outside*. Which meant, if I ran out and down the stairs and –

But no. It was no good. I would have to go out through the main entrance; and I'd have to walk across that wide, open no man's land of gravel driveway. I thought of the trapdoor again, though I feared it might lead only to a deep dark dead-end . . . then the kitchen . . . but the window I had seen was too small to climb out of . . .

I caught sight of my reflection again; the top half of my face, cut away at the nose. I saw the water filling my eyes and I quickly went back to the sink.

Right. Be strong. I can do this. I unbuttoned the dirty white cuff of my shirt and pulled it down over my hand. Then I grabbed the tap again and pulled until I felt the pain behind my eyes and in the roots of my teeth. It swivelled. I tried again, harder, and it twisted again.

Nothing came out.

Then there was a gurgling noise. A rumbling in the pipes. It belched out a spat of pale yellow water. I let out a noise that was somewhere between a laugh and a gasp.

I leaned into the sink and licked it. The enamel tasted like sea salt and dirt. I licked until all the water had gone and banged the taps but nothing more came out. My tongue felt cleansed, but the dry ache in my throat was even worse than it had been before I'd found the water. I wanted more.

Another gunshot. I ducked and cowered instinctively.

Something large and black whizzed in through the open window, hit the mirror and exploded into the sink.

I fell back to the floor. I wrapped my arms round my knees and buried my face into them. I heard the sounds of the mirror shards hitting the bath and floor with twinkly twangs, and then there was a strange sound: tiny little gasping cries. For several minutes I lay frozen, terrified by the sounds.

I got up, small shards of mirror tinkling from my trousers. There was something black in the sink. At first I thought it might be a rock; Henry had glimpsed me from down below and thought he'd fling up a nice little present.

Then I heard the cry again and I realised what it was. I felt dumb then, for being afraid; this little thing could hardly have hurt me. It swivelled a beady eye up at me and opened its yellow beak, showing a V of scarlet, letting out a plaintive caw. I wondered if Henry had hit it with a bullet; or perhaps a bullet had terrified it and it had flown in the window in a frenzy and hit the mirror. It seemed to have lost over half its feathers on impact; black clumps of them were strewn over the porcelain and they were wet and dark with blood. The bird was lying on its side and it kept lifting a wing in a stiff, mechanical motion, as though it was a broken toy. Perhaps I ought to pick it up and hold it by the window; then it might be able to fly off. I reached out and gently touched it, but it suddenly squawked and flapped, pecking at me violently. I stepped backwards in shock and fell on to the mirror shards.

I sat and let out a noise. It sounded strange; I hadn't laughed for a long time.

I laughed and felt better. I laughed some more, but each laugh became thinner and more fragile until they threatened to break. I got up then and went back to the bird.

'It's okay,' I said to him softly. 'You're going to be okay.'

For once in my life, I knew what to do. My father had taught me. Once or twice, he'd even suggested that we set up a proper animal sanctuary in our back garden, with a name and a logo and leaflets and cages and everything; Sam and I had gone mad over the idea, but Mum hadn't. She had rolled her eyes and said, 'I think we have enough to deal with in this household as it is', and that was that. Even so, we still cared for them. We healed a squirrel, two injured birds and a hedgehog, keeping them in our garage, feeding and caring for them. I remember how we had once let the sparrow free from its cage, how my father had gripped my hand tightly and my heart had thumped as it fluttered its healed wings cautiously and then soared into the clouds like a dream.

The bird needed a box, but I was scared to move it, so I figured the sink would be okay as long as it had some bedding to keep it warm. Birds go cold when they're in shock, my father had told me, and that's when they're in danger of dying.

Going out into the hallway, I felt a genuine surge of courage. I didn't even bother to crawl; I walked down the hallway and into the bedroom, and there were no gunshots.

In the bedroom, I opened up the stiff doors of the wardrobe. It was filled with clothes, with old-fashioned suits and beautiful ball gowns with floating skirts of chiffon. As I sifted through them, balls of grey dust flew out.

*What are you going to do about Henry?* a small voice said. *How are you going to get back down?*

*It doesn't matter. No need to worry about him right now. Just look after the bird and then worry. Take the pink dress with the frills on it.*

*What about the others? What about Matthew lying injured groaning for help?*

*I . . . I don't know . . . soon . . . soon I'll get out . . . I'll just protect the bird and then I'll face up to Henry, I will face up to him, I will . . .*

Back in the corridor, I heard a sound from below and I ran then, too quick for Henry to shoot or catch me. Back in the bathroom, I shut the door and found a lock with a rusty bolt; I pulled it tight.

My father had had a knack with animals. He had a certain voice that he used with them; it sounded a little like the jazz singers he liked listening to, a sort of husky, soothing croon. The animals loved it; it seemed to make them understand he was on their side. I tried to use the voice as I curled the dress around the bird's body. It still pecked me, but with less violence this time. Then it drooped its head back on to its pink pillow and closed its eyes. I stared down at it and one eye half-opened again, looking up at me.

'We're going to be all right,' I whispered.

*It's an omen. If the bird lives, I'm going to live. I'm going to keep him alive, whatever happens, and when I get out of here, I'm going to take him home. I'll smuggle him back on the ferry if I have to, and then I'll tame him and train him like a hawk; and he'll be my friend and attack the people I hate.*

'I know you're hungry. So am I. I'll go and find some food. I'll be back.'

**J**ames Frost is no ordinary teenager. Last year he narrowly escaped a tragic coach crash and then found himself facing death again when his stepbrother tried to murder him. We spoke to this extraordinary young man on how he managed to survive . . .

Q. So, James, you were in an impossible situation. You were trapped in a mansion; you had a psycho keeping you upstairs. How the hell did you manage to get out of your situation?

A. Well, that's a good question. At first I admit I panicked, but then I thought to myself: just sit down and be logical. I thought to myself: there must be a way out. Maybe a cranky old fire escape or a ladder. So I set about exploring – I had to be cautious and quiet because Henry was below. I walked down the corridor and I came to a curved door. This is just what I was looking for – a turret. I remembered seeing that there were two turrets at the front of the house, one in each corner. So I opened it – there was a winding spiral staircase and I walked up it. I found that I came out on the roof.

I broke off interviewing myself. It was a game I played a lot, especially when I was scared or sitting in lessons. I imagined that I was a famous writer; my book was number one in every country and made into a movie and everyone wanted to know the secret of my genius.

I stood on top of the roof. The view was beautiful. In all four directions, I could see hills undulating in glorious curves, patchwork fields, trees waving softly in the breeze, birds spiralling into the softly clouded sky. For a moment I felt all my cares drop away and I was like the wind: infinite and glorious and unbounded.

*Q. But what next, James? How do you escape?*

I couldn't find a fire escape, I composed the answer in my head. Or a staircase. But then . . . oh God . . . what, what?

Then I spotted the tree. My last hope.

But no. A false hope.

It was a beautiful tree, a mighty, magnificent oak that had stretched up tall and broad as though competing against the house for grandeur. But it was just that little bit too far away. No thick gnarled branch I could grab and swing from. Its leaves teasingly brushed the jagged stone edge, their twiggy wrists too slender.

I turned away, sick with fury. If only the tree had just been a metre closer. Why did it feel as though everything in this house was conspiring with fate to mock me?

Then I turned back and my eyes glided across the thick branch.

*Q. What did you see, James?*

A possibility. A crazy possibility – but what choice did I have?

I sat down on the edge of the roof. The drop was dizzying, blowing up spirals of hurricane sickness in my stomach. I reached out with one hand, hanging on tight to the stone with my other. I could just touch the branch with my fingertips.

I knew the only way was to jump. To jump and grab the branch and hang on tight. And if I did fall, pray the other branches would catch me . . .

I'd done this sort of thing as a kid, climbing trees. Though not from this height.

I stood up, balanced on the edge of the castellation. *I'm the King of the Castle.* The wind, unfettered at this height, raked furrows through my hair. I'd read stories about guys who did this sort of thing and they always triumphed by telling themselves *not to look down.* But I looked down. It was better to face it now, to get used to it. I looked down at the stretch of stone, at the curve of an open window, down past the mildewed base to the gravel, where a snake was slithering in circles of eight. I pictured my body hitting it, smashing it to black pulp, its venom spewing out over my puppet body.

I nearly climbed back down. But anger grabbed me by the scruff of the neck. This was the only way.

In my nerves, I became silly with superstition. I shook a twiggy arm of the tree, wishing it to be my friend, to guide me through its strengths and weaknesses.

I fixed my eyes on the branch. I focused. I drew in a breath. And then I saw Henry.

I nearly fell off the roof. I staggered, took a step back down on to the safe stone, arms windmilling, heart screaming.

Henry. He stood by the entrance of the house. The gun was slack by his side. He gazed up at me with curiosity, like a tourist watching a novelty act.

*I'll wait until he's gone*, I told myself.

But, of course, he didn't move. He waited. He lit up a cigarette, patient, intrigued. I heard him let out a sigh of faint boredom, as if to say: *I thought he'd never have the guts.*

*Okay*, I thought with a snarl of anger, *I don't care. He can watch. He can watch. I'll show him.*

I climbed back on to the roof edge. I tried to blot Henry out but he remained a figure in the shadow of my vision, like a Grim Reaper waiting in the wings.

And then –


The moment I jumped, I knew it was a mistake. I never really wanted to jump, never would have jumped, if Henry hadn't been there. *Idiot*, I screamed at myself, *what a stupid fucking way to die – all for Henry –*

I sailed in the sky, green leaves flying about me like clouds. I flailed out for the branch but in my panic I didn't even know where the branch was. Suddenly, it found me: I thwacked right on to it. My chest howled and I started to slip –

With a sob I curled my arms around it and held on tight.

I lay there for a while, clinging on, my cheek raw against the bark, feeling the branch creak like a ship in the wind. In the racing of my heart-thoughts, a spurt of triumph came: *I did it.* I opened my eyes and gazed through the criss-cross of tree to the ground so far below. And Henry.

He was pointing the gun right at me.

I felt a rush of glee before the fear. I'd shown him. I'd surprised him. He wouldn't be pointing that at me if he didn't feel put out, feel he had to score one back up on me.

Then I felt afraid. I saw myself spending the next hour picking my way down the tree to the bottom and then, just as my sole touched the gravel, then his finger would curl and –

*Just ignore him*, I told myself, *just move.*

I slowly sat up on the trunk, legs dangling, twigs caressing my ears. My chest still ached. The wind rolled through the tree like a woman and the tree groaned and arched back.

*Q. So James, how did you climb all the way down the tree?*

I looked down for the next foothold. I saw another, deeper branch below. I brought my legs up so that I was sitting on the edge of the branch. All I had to do was drop. It was simple.

I looked over at Henry. The barrel was still pointing; it seemed to sneer at me like a black pig's snout.

I dropped down on the thicker branch, hanging on to the one above while I found my balance. My chest hurt, but this time with happy pain. *I can do this*, I thought.

I realised that I was now opposite an open window. I could see the porcelain curve of a sink – it had to be the bathroom. I thought of the bird and promised silently I would be back soon.

Now for the next branch.

This one didn't look easy. In fact, it looked even harder than my first jump. I looked up at Henry again. *No, don't look at Henry.*

I sat on the edge of the branch. I paused again. My stomach curved like a bowling ball as the gravel shimmered below. Was this a good angle? Or should I move in towards the thicker end?

Suddenly I lost my nerve. The first jump had been spontaneous, crazy, innocent. Now I felt tangled in calculations of confusion. It hit me then, the cruelty of fate. Up until now, I had defied death but, if I missed this fall, I would still die. I'd climbed a ladder but I could easily slither down a snake. I wanted to believe that, having come this far, nature would reward me, but deep down I feared there was no logic, no fairness, no guarantee to any of this. I tried to psyche myself up, I battered my fear with loud words telling myself I had to think big, I had to think positive, I had to do this, and I just rolled up every drop of courage into one ball, when –

'All right there, James?' Henry called.

A click travelled through the air. The sound of cocking.

*He's going to shoot.*

No, he's not, no he's not –

*He's going to shoot. I can't go down, I can't go down.*

I'm going back, I'm retreating.

*You can't, you can't climb back up, you –*

I know how to get back in, there is a way.

I slithered down the branch towards the bathroom window. The bark rasped against my trousers, ripping eyes in the cloth. The branch grew thinner. A vague voice told me to be careful. But I couldn't concentrate. All I could think of was that bullet, sitting poised in that dark chamber, point quivering, hungry for release. I reached out for the window sill. *Hurry, hurry, he's going to –* My fingers curled around the wood but a sudden strong surge of wind whisked the branch away from the window. A few white flakes of paint fluttered down, twirly-swirling into the leaves. I turned back, searching desperately through the leaves for a sight of Henry. His whole body was taut with tension, shoulders hunched, barrel bobbing as though he was fine tuning his aim. *Oh God, please let me make it before he shoots, please God, you killed everyone else in the crash so please just let me live, please can there be some hope, some justice in this world.* I reached out again. As I leaned forward, my body weight cracked against the branch. I heard the sound of breaking wood. I screamed at the wind to keep still; I felt the branch slipping away from me. I reached out and grabbed the window and lunged into it. The wood bit into my stomach. My legs dangled, kicked out, hit twigs and leaves and air. A loud crack – *a bullet!* – and I cried out in terror. With one last thrust, I pushed myself into the bathroom. As I slithered on the floor, my head banged against the bath. I cried out again, dizzy, cursing, hopeless.

I staggered to my feet. My knees were shaking and I had to grab the sill for support. Henry was standing by the door, the gun now casual in his hands. The wind laughed in the tree. Down below, my branch lay in the gravel – that had been the crack. Henry hadn't fired a single shot.

I looked at him. He was smiling.

I turned away, fist curled and yelled out into the bathroom. The echo rolled off the walls; my bird cheeped in fear.

I sat on my haunches, my face in my hands. I heard the interviewer's voice, only this time it was infused with Henry's sneer.

*Q. Why are you such a loser, James?*
*Why are you such a loser?*

And then a voice came back at him, a voice that sounded strong and a little like Mrs Robson's, *You're not a loser, James. You're going to get through this.*

*You're going to beat him.*
*You're going to win.*

**E**nglish had always been my favourite subject and our lessons, with a guy called Mr Watt, were okay for the first few weeks. The first time I entered the classroom, I was aware of everyone breaking up their chatter and sizing me up, working out which box to put me into. At the very front of the class was a small Indian boy with a pudgy face and big, dark eyes that pleaded with me. Halfway up, was one other new boy sitting on his own. He had dark hair and flinty green eyes and was chewing gum. I went up to him and said, 'Can I sit here?' He shrugged. I sat down. He offered me some gum. I took it. He told me his name was Matthew. I told him my name. I tried to hide the jubilation in my chest. I had pulled it off. I was sitting with someone cool; therefore I was cool. I had recreated myself.

Henry watched us the whole time with thoughtful, narrowed eyes.

It turned out the small Indian boy at the front was called Colin. I was full of fear and loathing for him because he had the role I'd had to suffer at my last school. He was the class square, the Shakespearean fool that everyone mocked and spat at and blamed for farts.

*

It was a Thursday, 3 p.m. Our new teacher was late. Everyone was laughing, talking, graffiti-ing, chucking aeroplanes, texting, Gameboy-ing.

Then Henry walked to the front of the class and stood up on the teacher's desk and clapped.

'Okay, now that Mr Watt's moved on, I think that Mrs Robson is going to need a bit of entertainment, to liven things up, don't you?'

A ripple of excitement in the class. Henry sure knew how to liven school up. A bomb scare here, a stink bomb there. Not that Henry ever dirtied his own fingers. He was just the *inspiration*, as he put it. Henry never got caught; he was like a politician who never inhaled. Three of his cronies had got suspended, but Henry had never even been in detention.

'Okay – Matthew,' said Henry, putting on Mr Watt's limp voice and making us all laugh, 'you – have to sneeze every time Mrs R addresses you. Brian – you have to stand up and sit down every time Mrs R addresses you. If she freaks, say you have a disability. James . . .' Henry narrowed his eyes at me. 'Whenever Mrs R addresses you, you have to swear.'

'Hey, she's coming!' Colin, who was guarding the door, called.

In walked Mrs Robson and the whole class became very, very quiet.

'Hi, boys,' she said. 'Now, you at the front – I'm sorry, I don't know your name – be a dear and close the door for me, I have all these *books*.' Wham, she slammed them down on the desk. Last Sunday there had been nothing on TV and I had found myself watching an old movie where Marilyn Monroe sang 'Diamonds are a Girl's Best Friend'. That was how Mrs Robson sounded.

'Well, I'm Mrs Robson, and it's an *absolute* pleasure to be filling in for Mr Watt, who, I understand, is on sick leave.' A smile teased her lips. 'Now, you at the front, honey – what's your name – please pass round these new exercise books.'

Matthew sneezed, very feebly, and she cried 'Bless you' and the class laughed gently.

'Okay – so – let's dive in. *Hamlet*. Can anyone tell me what *Hamlet* is about? You, what's your name, I'm so sorry to be rude, I will learn all your lovely names, I promise.'

When Brian answered, he didn't get up or get down. My head throbbed with confusion. Was the dare off? Or was Brian going to get a beating from Henry later that day?

Maybe if I just sat tight, the whole lesson would go and she wouldn't notice me. A lot of teachers didn't. I looked at the clock, swallowing. Just twenty-four minutes to go.

'And you –' she pointed to me. Her eyes were liquid, like honey pouring over you. 'Can you tell me what you think of Hamlet?'

'I think he's out for' – breath – 'fucking revenge.'

Nobody laughed. Nobody muttered *cool*. The room went very quiet. I felt Mrs Robson's frowning stare coating me in shame. I stared down at my desk. At that moment, I had never hated Henry more. I just wanted to get good grades and go to Oxford and be a world famous writer and this was just the beginning. How many more dares would there be before Henry screwed it all up for me.

'I don't like people swearing in my classes, James,' she said. Her voice like the Arctic. 'Is that clear?'

I nodded.

'Now – I'd like to read out one of the key scenes in the play. You – Henry – you can take the part of Claudius. James, you can be Hamlet.'

I realised she was giving me a chance to say sorry. But what

Mrs Robson didn't know was that she had put me in hell. I hated reading out loud. Beside me, I was aware of Matthew giving me curious, pained glances as my voice shook and slid from soprano to baritone.

Henry wasn't afraid of reading. He sounded like a bloody Shakespearean actor.

'Thank you, James,' said Mrs Robson, giving me a strange smile. 'Now. When Shakespeare wrote *Hamlet*, there were a lot of revenge plays about. But *Hamlet* was different from the others. Anyone know why?' She looked around the class. 'Well, generally in these sort of plays, the person who needed to take revenge killed instantly. But Hamlet's different, isn't he . . . why is he different?'

'He's a pussy,' Henry said, grinning as everyone laughed. 'He thinks too much and he doesn't act.'

'But if you were about to kill someone, wouldn't you want to think about it? I mean, surely Hamlet's thinking is part of his conscience? Part of his moral fibre, part of his humanity? In the Bible it says we should take an eye for an eye, a tooth for a tooth, but if we all went around doing that, then what?'

Henry shrugged. 'Still a pussy. If someone hits you, you have to hit them back, or they'll hit you again. If someone bombs your country, you have to bomb them back.' He made an aeroplane noise, followed by a bombing noise (aided by the banging of his pens and ruler on the desk). Then everyone cheered, and the cacophony increased.

'Thank you for the sound effects, Henry,' said Mrs Robson, drily.

I stared at her intently, waiting for her to say more, but to my confusion, she asked us to read some more. This time she gave Matthew the part of Hamlet to read.

At the end of the class, a group of boys formed around her, offering to take her books, her bag. I followed at a safe distance until they had gone. I watched her packing her stuff into the boot of her car, stuffed my hands in my pockets and walked up to her.

'Mrs Robson,' I said, 'I'm sorry about . . .' I trailed off, my throat thick. Her shoes, I noticed as I stared at the ground, were the brightest neon pink.

'James, it's fine.' She looked at me and I felt as though she understood. She reached out and gently touched my cheek. I jumped as though she'd burnt me. 'Can I –'

'Mrs Robson,' I blurted out over the top of her, all in a rush. 'When Henry said all that stuff about war being a good thing, about it being a good idea to take revenge – do you really agree with that?'

'Everyone has a different point of view, James,' she said. For a moment she sounded like our pompous head. 'And we have to allow people to express those points of view.' She looked into my eyes. 'Does that make sense?'

'Um, yes. I mean – I . . .'

'Can I offer you a lift home?'

'I'm fine, I'm fine.'

I spent all the journey home hating myself, twisting myself in knots, wanting to tear apart the present and find the past, that moment again, and hear myself say *Yes, yes, Mrs Robson, oh yes, I'd like a lift home with you.* I felt as though it was a bad omen, as though the rest of my life would fall another way like a set of badly carved dominoes and everything would go wrong now because I hadn't grabbed this opportunity, walked through this door held wide open for me.

When I got home, I went into the kitchen to get a Mars

bar and Henry said, 'Hey, I saw you and Mrs Robson flirting in the car-park. Teacher's pet.'

He took a step closer and then my mum came in and Henry grinned.

'Hey, Mum,' he said.

When he called my mum 'Mum' I wanted to kill him.

'Hi, boys. Did you have a nice day at school?'

'It was great,' said Henry.

'Great,' I said, forcing a smile. I thought of a cheap shot. 'We got our essays back, the ones Mr Watt marked before he went, and I got an A.'

'Oh, well done, darling. And what did you get, Henry?'

Henry stared down into his can of Coke. 'I got a B.'

'Well, darling, I expect Mr Watt wasn't all that reliable, after all, they have got rid of him, haven't they?'

Henry looked up. 'You won't tell Dad about my B, will you?'

Mum put a finger to her lips. 'It's our secret. Between the three of us. Isn't that right, James?'

'Yes, Mum.'

When Mum had gone, Henry leaned over and whispered in my ear: 'You're not going to be a teacher's pet for long. I'm going to get you expelled.'

'Oh, I'm scared.'

Henry's face was taut and sullen. 'You should be,' he said. 'You should be.'

I was scared and I wasn't scared. His words jiggled about in my mind all day long. Sometimes at night I woke in the cold darkness, shaking with fear and at other times, I thought: how can he do it, how can he touch me? My grades are fine. He can't steal my homework; he can't do anything.

But Henry found a way.

**P**orridge. I could smell it, in my imagination. Thick gloopy milk and floating flakes of oat and gritty sprays of sugar.

It had been so long since I'd last eaten. The tree climb had used up every last drop of energy, and the energy beyond that, the nervous supply my body kept in reserve. Suddenly my hunger had become ravenous. Every cell in my body was crying out like a starving child. I couldn't think into the past or the future any more, just here and now and this violent obsession to eat.

I started to look for food. I crept into the bedroom. But there was nothing: just clothes, old books, journals written in French.

I had read books about people stranded on desert islands. They fought evil jungle tribes, or else they befriended them, saving themselves at the last minute from being added to a stew with some fast talking. They discovered rare and delicious fruits, or searched for berries in the bushes, or cooked some fish. But there were no fruits or fishes or berries here.

There was another book I'd read where people had been stuck on the top of a mountain with only snow to eat. But several of them had died and in the end they had eaten each other.

Then I remembered another book about a man who had lived off almost nothing for a week and an answer came to me.

I peeled up the frayed edge of the carpet and then I unlaced my shoe. A hot, phuttish smell filled the room. My socks were sweaty; my shoe was still caked with mud from the forest. I tried to calculate how many hours the gamekeeper had been lying downstairs and how many hours it might be before it was too late. I was normally good at maths but trying to work out the hours seemed as hard as a quadruple equation, and then I was distracted by the arrival of my first prey.

It scurried out from the floorboards, then froze. I held up my shoe and approached the spider. It sensed the vibrations of danger and paused. I inched forwards. It didn't move. I inched again. The shoe was tight in my hand but the sweat from my palm made the leather slippery. I raised the shoe – its elongated shadow fell over the spider –

and slowly brought it down

when the spider moved

scuttled into a corner and crouched there, in a black ball.

I let my arm fall slack and emitted a deep, shaky breath.

I swapped the shoe into my left hand, rubbed my sweating palm against my right trouser-leg, then took the shoe back and crept forwards again. The spider stretched out a few tentative legs. I tried to still the shivers convulsing over my body. The spider crept along the dusty skirting board a millimetre. I leaned in; it tensed. *Wham!* I smashed my shoe against it.

Silence. My hand was shaking. I crouched and I wanted to be sick but all that came into my throat was saliva. I closed my eyes and drew the shoe away. I made myself think of Mrs Robson, of the soft silk of her hair. I opened

148

my eyes and saw the spider had slid down the skirting board. It made me think of the children's book *Flat Stanley* which my mum had read to me and Sam when we were kids. The spider was now Flat Spider.

I did the deed swiftly. I picked up the spider and put it in my mouth and then chewed it quickly. I had expected it to taste of poison and pain, but it was pretty flavourless – a dull, black sort of taste. I swallowed. As I felt it going down my throat I thought of its legs again, pressed against the skirting board and began to retch. I made myself swallow fiercely, forcing it down.

I waited for some miraculous burst of energy, a straightening of my dizziness. But none came. I felt like crying. I felt cheated. In the book I'd read, the man had survived for five days by eating spiders and grubs. He only needed to eat one to feel better; but then, he had been in the jungle. I was probably going to need to eat at least ten spiders before I squeezed any sort of nutrition out of them. I told myself not to be a baby and keep going. If I was going to survive Henry I needed energy in any form; in my present state of hunger he could blow me over like a stalk of grass. So I spent the next hour or so sweeping along the skirting board. I ate two woodlice, another spider, even half a caterpillar I found curled around the window latch. Each time they got easier to swallow.

I went back into the bathroom and tried to feed the other half of the caterpillar to the bird, but it wouldn't eat; the green wriggle lay uselessly in its beak, then fell on to its chest. I stroked its black feathers and it cheeped softly. I realised then in horror that I wouldn't be able to drink any more water from the tap while it was in the sink.

Eventually, I found the answer; I dipped my face down so that my cheek was pressed lightly against its body and stuck out my tongue, collecting slithers and droplets from the tap.

Then I sat in the bathroom, the sun lying across me in hot bars. Minutes seemed to last hours; I felt as though I had been in this house for days.

*Q. Now what? How do I get down? How do I get past Henry?*

A. I don't know.

*Q. So now what?*

**T**wenty-seven, I counted. Twenty-seven. Who was I missing out?

I kept seeing the faces of my class, floating in front of me. I went through their names as though I was calling a register, and as I saw each face I tried to focus on whether eyes were wide or open, mouths firm or slack, as if through some intuition I might guess they were still alive. But there was just one name I had forgotten and no matter how I banged at my memory, I could not remember him, and I felt wracked with guilt.

My mind drifted and, just as I had let the idea go, his name came: Colin Rabindarath.

Colin Rabindarath.

It was no surprise that I'd wanted to blot him out.

One morning, on the way to school, Henry caught up with me before I went into a phone box and said, 'Meet me by the back gates, four-thirty.'

All day I toyed over whether to show. I felt tired, for Henry was beginning to grind me down. I wasn't sleeping. My grades were sliding. My head felt cloudy, unfocused; it felt as though I was using every last drop of energy to keep up my guard, like an animal who can't sleep fully, who must keep one ear pricked for fear of an enemy attack.

I had decided not to go. Then, I was just coming out of Latin when Matthew stopped me.

Ever since that day in English when I first sat next to Matthew, we'd been friends. In truth, he was my only friend. For a while I was hardly able to believe he liked me, that he wanted to sit and chat about movies, that he wanted to go and hang out ironically on the local swings, that he wanted to go running after school. Then, as I'd feared, things had changed. We still sat next to each other in English, but Matthew barely spoke to me any more. He was always too busy twisting round in his chair, shouting to Henry, sharing private jokes, tossing planes at him. I knew what Henry was doing and I tried to hide my desperation. I found myself alone in my lunch-hours again, sneaking out to Burger King, chewing soggy chips and wondering: why is this happening to me again? Why is history repeating itself? Why can't I hold on to my friends? What is it about me that isn't cool?

But now Matthew was being all chummy, saying come on, let's go to the back gates.

'I've kind of arranged to do something else,' I said. Despite myself, I felt an ache inside, and realised just how lonely I was.

'Come on, I've got some smokes.'

I knew Henry had put Matthew up to it. That's what I hated about Henry. He knew how to look into a person's heart and see their deepest hopes and fears, those little secret dreams that thud softly inside you like a heart within your heart. He knew that however much I hated him, I wanted to be part of his group.

By the back gates, I lifted my Silk Cut to my lips and blew out a stream of nothingness. Matthew didn't seem to notice.

'Man, I should just give this shit up,' he said. 'But I'm like on ten a day, y'know?'

'Uh huh.' I blew out, rearranged a few more air molecules.

'I mean – look at this.' He showed me the tip of his cigarette, where a dark bruise had formed in the centre. 'That's only after two drags.'

My tip was white all the way through, but Matthew only seemed pleased that it highlighted the depths of his nicotine depravity.

One by one, Henry's gang joined us. Terry, Dave, Jason, Charlie, Evans, Ralph. They all bummed cigarettes off Matthew and he made such a stir about having to give his precious fags away that it was obvious he was secretly wetting himself with delight to be King of Cool, Dispenser of Sins, The Tar Demon. None of them looked surprised to see me. They all said 'Hi,' grinned. A kind of pleasure drifted through me, like a leaf swirling from a tree, and settled on the bottom of my stomach. Maybe the War was over. Maybe I was cool enough for Matthew. Maybe Henry was ready to be friends. Maybe I was going to get on with his father and everything at home would settle down and everything was going to be okay after all.

Then Henry appeared. You could feel the atmosphere change, as though we were all bound together by a slack chain and it had suddenly been pulled taut.

'Hey, guys.' Henry didn't have to ask for a cigarette; immediately one appeared. A flick of the lighter flame; two demon orbs in his dark eyes; he blew out tiredly, as though he was some Mafia boss wearily having to dispense yet another mission. His eyes flicked around the group, then rested on me.

'James, we've got a mission for you.' He checked his watch. 'We'd better get going, or Phil will be wondering where we are.'

Phil? He was one of Henry's fat bodyguards.

We walked through the woods. I stuffed my sweaty hands in my pockets. I'd heard the rumours that in order to join Henry's gang you had to pass some kind of initiation.

We came to a clearing, deep in the woods.

'Hi, Phil,' Henry greeted him.

Someone else was sitting on the log beside Phil. Colin. He was looking scared, his eyes wide, hair dishevelled, the front patch on his blazer torn. The leaf of pleasure in my stomach withered to ashes. A voice inside me told me that this wasn't good, that Henry had reached into the horror videos we watched and pulled out something shadowy to play out in real life, that I had to walk away right now, no matter what they said.

'Hi, Colin,' said Henry. 'Glad you could make it.'

A few titters.

'I didn't want to come, I've got homework to do,' said Colin, with his usual lack of irony.

'You don't say,' said Henry.

I winced. It was hard to feel sympathy for Colin when he sounded like a six-year-old. Even I thought: *Just get a grip, play it cool, for God's sake.*

Henry turned his back on Colin and faced me.

'I'm afraid that Colin has behaved in a rather underhand manner recently – I'm afraid I found him copying my English homework,' Henry informed me, ignoring Colin's background protests of 'I didn't do it' and 'He's making it up and telling tales!', cut short by a thump from Terry. 'So we'd like to teach Colin a lesson and we figured you, James, would be just the guy to do it.'

'Me?' I said, only the shocked word didn't quite leave my mouth, remained locked in the 'O' of my lips. Then it all happened so quickly. Terry dragged Colin up and thrust him forwards. They formed a circle around us. We faced each other like boxers in a ring.

I paused. I knew this wasn't about punishing Colin. It was about finding out what I had in me. If I'd really been one of them, I would have searched inside and found anger. I would have drawn the anger up so that it pumped around my bloodstream and beat a drum in my heart and forced my fists into balls. But when I looked at Colin's pudgy face, his trembling chin, I only felt something tender inside, an urge to shake him and tell him to run home, to change schools, to keep away from Henry and keep running from all the Henrys he'd meet in future. The thought of hurting him felt like taking a knife to my own body or punching my reflection. I looked in his eyes and wished I could find a signal to make a pact with him. Two was better than one; one, in fact, was never any good.

Nine pairs of eyes on me. My breath thumping in my ears. A cloud passing over the sun. Trees leaning in. My arms slack at my sides, fingers like putty.

'Jesus, we might as well have set two goldfish on each other,' Henry sneered.

Colin looked at Matthew. Something passed over his face. Something hopeful. The tide might change, he was thinking, and I might not be the class square after this, if I play my cards right. Colin was no different from anyone in this group. Everyone was just looking out for themselves. A tiny flare of anger ignited inside me, enough for me to curl my fist and strike him.

Colin let out a gasp of surprise and took a few stumbles backwards. The blow had been light; it had barely brushed his chin. No mark on his face, except the pain in his eyes.

'So, Colin,' said Henry, behind him. 'Are you going to let James get away with that?'

'My religion forbids violence,' said Colin.

'Oh dear,' said Henry.

Colin swallowed. He looked up at me, scared, face flickering with conflicting emotions.

'My religion forbids violence,' he repeated.

The blow to my stomach was sudden and harsh. Now it was my turn to be surprised: by the force, the hate behind it. I staggered, found myself on my knees. My lunch – chips, a burger, Coke – moved about. My head swam. Jeers blurred in my ears. I opened my eyes and saw the sneer on Henry's face. He thought I was a chicken. A wimp. A girl.

I got to my feet and went for Colin. Just before I struck him, he stammered, 'My religion forbids violence my religion forbids violence my religion forbids –'

*Wham!* This time, when my fist sank into him, I felt a kind of pleasure. As though I wasn't striking a human, but I was at home practising punches in my pillow. My next blow encountered a crunch of ribs; another flash of satisfaction, like stamping on dry branches in the woods. I felt him sink before me, whimpering, begging. I felt power surge through me, pumping into my muscles. I raised my fist to finish him off – and then made the mistake of looking up at Henry again. The same sneer on his face. I realised then that he'd tricked me, that it was another lose-lose, for me and Colin, for being reduced to this – not human, sheer animal.

I tried to back off but Colin grabbed his chance. He seemed to have been forming a strategy while I was pummelling him to the ground. It was this: to leap up, grab my ear and twist the lobe hard. I let out a scream. I tried to tell him I gave up, he won, the fight was over, but he kept hanging on, his mouth a slit of determination. Henry and co. were laughing as though they were punters watching a dog-fight. The pain was excruciating, as though someone was driving a nail into my ear. I had to respond; the opening was too easy.

A second later, Colin collapsed to the ground, clutching his balls, sobbing.

I turned to Henry and shoved past him, breaking the circle.

'Hey!' said Terry.

'It's all right,' I heard Henry said. 'Let him go. Well done, James!' he called after me. 'Well done.'

I heard Matthew and Evans yell that they'd won the bets on me in the Battle of the Squares, that Terry owed them money.

I spat out and a tooth came flying out, falling into the grass. I bent to pick it up, when a frightened earwig shot out from its grass cave and hovered on it, antennae quivering, terrified by this big bad world it lived in, then scuttled away.

Back home, I waited for Henry in the kitchen. I had never realised I was capable of such rage; it was worse than when my father had died, this urge to tear down the sky, break up the earth, kick the moon out of the night, destroy the universe. I paced around the kitchen in circles of eight; every so often my anger simmered a little and I stoked it back, yelling silently: you mustn't let him get away with it this time!

The moment he came in, I did it. My fist meeting his cheek. For a moment, it was lovely: the surprise on his face, the pain watering in his eyes. Then I suddenly became aware of someone in the doorway, watching us.

'Sam,' I said. 'We were just – fighting.' I grinned, knowing she'd be on my side, knowing she hated Henry's presence in this house as much as I did.

But Henry's face was alive with confidence.

'You're so vile, James,' she said, shaking her head. 'You hit Henry, and he didn't do anything!'

'I'm not, Sam, I'm not – please – don't tell Mum – I was just mad –'

But Sam had walked out.


The next day at school I walked into English and found Henry sitting with Matthew. They had shuffled the desks around so that the only place I could sit was next to Colin.

I thumped myself down next to him and we sat there, loathing each other for our likeness: two squares in one pod. For the rest of the lesson, we didn't look at each other.

**I** stood at the top of the stairs. I had spent the last half an hour persuading myself not to be afraid of Henry. Think about it, I told myself. Remember the expression on Henry's face when he warned you that you might go to jail. He doesn't want to end up in some stinking French cell, either. If he kills you, he goes to jail; therefore Henry will not kill you. He might hit you; you might have to fight it out; but he will not kill you. After all, he could have shot you just now, in the tree, but he didn't. He would stop the game before we reached THE END.

But for all my reasoning, my body was betraying me. I stood at the top of the stairs and I felt weak and exasperated with my inability to control my shaking and sweating. The fear felt like a spirit possessing me, usurping my reason.

I looked back up at the sweep of the gallery. I looked back down into the Grand Hall. I had taken off my shoes and I slowly lifted my right foot. I placed the tip on the step below. The cold marble was like a sea creature that sucked away all my warmth. Slowly, I lowered my foot centimetre by centimetre: arch, sole, ball, until finally it was flat. Then I lifted my left foot and lowered it in the same way.

I had not made a sound.

I took another step down.

And then another.

And another.

And another.

Halfway down, I paused. I was in full view now. I swivelled my head to the left. I swivelled my head to the right. I slid down another step. My chest winced like a crab, clawing air in and then grabbing as it left my lungs.

Another step; another; another; another; another.

Another.

And then: my foot hit the dry roughness of the wooden floor.

A feeling of unease in my stomach.

But Henry had to be outside. Or I would have felt a bullet screaming through my body. Or his cries singing in my ears.

I lost control. Beyond the display cabinets and the Grand Hall, I saw a long window, looking out on to a paradise: trees gushing in the breeze, sun-splashed fields, blue sky puffy with clouds. I slipped my shoes back on and moved towards it, crouching down and darting through the cabinets, head twisting this way, that way, ears pricked.

Then I stopped short.

I had known that something was wrong and finally my head understood my heart.

The blanket, which I'd pulled over the gamekeeper, lay in a pool on the floor. Light slid through the stained-glass windows and lay in coloured fragments on the stone floor, blurring a trail of blood that led from the blanket.

I edged forwards. The bloodstains trailed down the corridor and circled and disappeared at the front entrance.

My first impulse was that the gamekeeper must have crawled away, gone to find a phone, call the police. Then another more troubling possibility flickered through my mind.

I circled around. I noticed that under one of the museum display cabinets, Henry had a stash of stolen cigarettes and food. God knows where he had got it from – but it was a sight to make my stomach whimper. A tin of baked beans, a hunk of French bread, a packet of butter, with grooves smeared out, studded with crumbs and bits of crust. A bottle of wine, half drunk. My fingers twitched; I could already feel the rough dustiness of the bread between them. I paused, listening nervously, for I knew the moment I took a bite, I would be lost and would drop my guard around my ankles.

Then I heard the footsteps. I darted back between some cabinets. There was a swinging, creaking noise: the front door opening. In a matter of seconds, I saw my only escape. I didn't stop to think it through. I lay down and pulled the blanket over me. As Henry's footsteps came closer, I curled the blanket under my toes and pulled the top over my head and then lay still. It smelt of blood and sickness. The wool was thick and scratchy against my face.

I heard Henry's footsteps in the Grand Hall. They stopped, started, stopped again.

I closed my eyes, picturing the rapid rise and fall of my lungs. I pictured a long, slender white hand curling around my lungs, soothing them, slowing them down. Gradually, I managed to soften my breath. But it harshened again with panicky thoughts. Surely Henry knew the gamekeeper had already gone, surely he would have seen his absence this morning? Or what if Henry didn't notice me under the blanket at all and he hung about in the Grand Hall for hours and I was stuck lying here? Or what if he *didn't* know the gamekeeper had gone and suddenly decided that the gamekeeper's life was no longer worth preserving and put a few bullets into me? I couldn't survive under here for much longer. My breaths gathered warmly until they felt like a hot pad being pressed against my face.

I was about to wriggle out and edge down a corridor to find a room to hide in. But it was too late. Through the criss-cross thread of blanket, I saw a dark shape cutting away the light.

'So, Monsieur Gamekeeper. How are you today? Done any other shootings?'

I lay still. Was he teasing me? Or was he fooled?

'I thought not. Looks as if you're not going to last much longer. I figured you might be happier if I just gave you a grave for your *un petite mort*.' He laughed, a high, hysterical laugh, and then muttered something, only the words got tangled up in the laughter and I couldn't fully understand them: '. . . waiting . . . or you'll . . . retaliate . . .'

Then, loudly: 'So, Monsieur Gamekeeper, what shall I put on your headstone?'

Laughter again, and more blurred words: '. . . too late . . . I heard Matthew . . . forgiving . . . oh God . . .'

'Okay. Let's go.'

A hand curled around my left ankle and I let out a faint cry. The blanket must have muffled the sound, for he began to drag me down the corridor. My head bumped against the floor; my shirt rucked up and the boards scraped their nails down my back. I squeezed my eyes shut, trying to endure it, but it was useless; the blanket fell away from my face.

Henry stopped. He was still carrying the rifle, slack in his hands. He bent over me theatrically, like Sherlock Holmes examining a curious corpse.

'*I zee.*' His imitation of the gamekeeper's gravely voice was perfect and utterly horrible. 'What have we 'ere? A small boy who thinks he can play around with guns?'

I tried to struggle up but he placed the tip of his shoe against my shoulder with a gentle pressure.

'So *mon petit garçon*, you want to play with zee guns, do you –'

A sudden slam cut Henry off. He dropped his rifle in shock and I leapt to my feet.

'What was that –'

'It came from the front –'

'It's the gamekeeper!' Henry hissed. 'Hide! We have to hide!'

'So he's alive –'

'He must be coming back to get us, oh God –'

I turned to dive under a cabinet, but Henry grabbed my arm. We ran through the hall, out through the left door and down the corridor that I had explored yesterday, when I had discovered the trapdoor. It turned out that Henry had discovered my secret place too.

I heard a distant thrumming sound; for a moment I thought it might be the police, coming through the back. Then I realised it was the flies in the kitchen.

Henry and I spotted the trapdoor at the same time and reached for it, him tugging to the left, me to the right, fingers overlocking.

'Let me do it!' Henry hissed. My arms dropped uselessly by my sides. When he prodded me forwards, I didn't hesitate. I grabbed the ladder, rust biting in my palms and hauled myself down, feet dangling and scraping for a hold.

I had climbed down enough for Henry to follow, when I heard him cry 'He's coming!' and then I saw the trapdoor arching over me, eating up the light and I cried 'No!' but he slammed it down.

When I opened my eyes, I saw that the trapdoor had not shut properly. A two-inch slit of light slithered into the dark, highlighting my surroundings: the earthy walls, the rust-crawled ladder. I could just see the black of Henry's trousers, the barrel of the rifle slack by his leg. What was he doing? Why wasn't he hiding too? Was he paralysed with shock? Was he keeping his cool, was he about to shoot the gamekeeper? Or was there no gamekeeper; had he too discovered that the gamekeeper had gone; was this all another of Henry's games?

I remembered that day we had got into the lift, Henry and I and Henry's father. Five floors; they had felt like five hundred. *Are you okay?* Henry's father had asked when we got out and I'd shrugged nonchalantly because I knew the way Henry worked, the way he looked for weaknesses in his victims, cracks to slip his fingers into. But Henry had seen; there was a glint in his eye; and now I was trapped in a tunnel and Henry was guarding the entrance and what if he didn't let me out? I felt the first wave of claustrophobia beginning to lap against me. That was the way it always began: softly, fooling me, thinking I could handle it, and then rising, and swirling, and foaming and spitting and then engulfing me in wave after wave, drowning me in fear, sucking out my breath, filling my lungs and heart with the waters of terror and I had to stop it, I had to stop it now, I had to remember the doctor mum had taken me to and the things he had told me to do. Picture your fear as a colour, he'd said. My fear was the colour yellow. Picture your courage as a colour, he'd said. I dipped myself in blueness; I lost myself in swirls of sky; and the fear began to retreat a little, when suddenly I heard a noise.

It sounded like a plaster being torn from a wound. I looked up for Henry. Gone; nothing but a patch of ivory wall. Then I felt the air swaying dangerously around my body and I realised that the ladder was coming away from the wall. I cried out 'Henry' softly, fearing the gamekeeper might hear. I could see the ladder physically tearing itself away, rusted bolts wriggling out of slots and falling into the darkness.

Up or down, my mind ordered. You have to make a decision either way and you have to make it now. But my body was frozen. I stared down into the unfathomable blackness. Then something clicked in. I took one hand from the ladder and pushed the flat of my palm hard against the trapdoor, but it was too heavy, a thick slab of wood, I needed two hands but if I took the other hand away I would fall and the ladder was coming away and Henry was nowhere to be seen.

Down, then.

*I can't go down.*

Yes, you can. You have to. If you fall, you'll break every bone. Think of skies, think of peacocks, think of the sea –

*Oh God.*

The fear caught me then. I found myself lost, swirling in currents. My body shook. Sweat slippery all over me. A tiny dribble of warm pee passed down my leg.

With a loud chink, one side of the ladder wrenched itself away from the wall. I clung on. The ladder swung and I hit the side of the shaft. A spray of dirt showered down. I heard myself calling out. I clutched the metal with both hands, curling my feet around it, like a drowning man clutching at straws. I was going to fall, and this was my punishment for letting Matthew and the others die and shooting the gamekeeper, I was going to fall –

And then there was light all around me, bright and dazzling. I screwed up my eyes, whimpering like a child. I felt warm skin against my face. I clung on. Give me your hand, he said. I grabbed it, squeezing so tightly our hands fused into one and I felt pain ripple through my shoulder as he hauled me up. He let out a groan at the weight and stumbled backwards; I lay like a beached fish, halfway across the floor, legs still dangling in the shaft. How I cherished the floor: my cheek against the hard grain of the carpet, my nails tearing into its flesh.

'Come on,' said Henry, grabbing my shoulders and pulling me out.

And then I was out and I curled up into a foetal ball, my face pressed to my knees, not wanting him to see the fear on my face. It took longer than usual for it to recede; my shame only seemed to draw it out.

I rubbed my damp eyes and looked up. Henry was strolling down the corridor. I noticed that he had left the rifle lying on the floor, by the trapdoor.

'Henry –' My voice was cut up by the palpitations of my still-quivering heart. 'Henry. Where's the gamekeeper? Are we safe?'

'He came and went,' Henry called, without looking back.

I sat up.

'What d'you mean? Did he see us?'

'I shot him.' Henry shrugged, a half-moon smile on his profile.

Though I knew he was lying, I nodded. I did not look at

the gun as I stood up. I did not look at the gun while I licked and sucked my raw hands. I did not look at the gun as he began to walk backwards, and yet with his sixth sense, he knew what I was doing. Oh, Henry had a sixth sense all right; so often, he said just what I was thinking or feeling, I swore he could see into my mind. He began to run, but he was too late. I grabbed the gun and pointed it at him. He stopped, a mild look on his face.

'I just saved your life,' he said softly.

I gulped.

'I didn't think you'd dare do that,' he said. 'Well done. You're winning now.'

I held the gun tightly.

'There are loads of other guns, you know,' he said, as though I was a child with a toy he wanted to take away. 'There's this room, back there, obviously the gamekeeper's haven, and shit, it's just chock full of them, old and new. I mean, there's even this antique, a Napoleonic rifle, dating from 1802, with two barrels, it's totally awesome. I could go and get it for you, I could give you that if you like and then I could have that one back.'

He stepped closer.

'Back up,' I said. 'Put your hands up, too.' I felt stupid saying it, like a bad actor in a lousy cop film. I was convinced that Henry knew me too well; that he would think I wasn't capable of shooting.

But he put his hands up flat, widening his eyes. There was blood on his palms. It looked wet and fresh; where had that come from? Had he really shot the gamekeeper? But surely there hadn't been time for him to move his body? I pointed the gun at him, frowning and slowly we progressed down the corridor, step by step, until we came to a choice. On one side: the Grand Hall. On the other, five red-carpeted steps that led down to the oak door that led to freedom.

That was when I made my mistake, the mistake the spies in the movies never make. Instead of focusing on my target and watching every twitch, every flicker, every heartbeat, I glanced at the door. It was slightly ajar and fresh air was slithering in. It smelt of freshly cut grass and new leaves, of sky and freedom. A dragonfly suddenly darted in, a shimmering, iridescent blur. It was followed by its mate. They darted around Henry's head, playing a blue courtship, teasing and flirting and winging each other. I felt as though I had been holding my heart tense, like a muscle, and as I breathed in the air it slackened.

Then the doorway was blocked. Henry was standing on the third step down. He spread out his arms, a cat's smile on his face.

Suddenly I felt very tired, the gun heavy as lead in my hands.

'Henry, get out of the way.'

'I said, get out of the way.'

Henry bobbed from side to side; my rifle barrel wobbled after him. I looked through the little hole, lining up his face. It was strange; like seeing someone through the comfort of a window. When I looked at him through the hole, I didn't feel afraid to stare into his eyes. Exhaustion had painted them different colours: yellow gunk in the corners, red lacing on the veins, blue puffs under his eyes. I stared into the black pinprick of light in the centre.

A dragonfly darted across my sights and broke the spell; I shook my head, finding my anger and focusing it again.

'I will shoot you,' I murmured. I held the rifle taut; it cut into my cheek, appling my words. 'I mean it.'

Henry stood up straight and crossed his arms. The blue of his eyes flashed.

*Henry's got eyes like an angel, aren't they the bluest of blue?* my mum had once said. I remembered that, then, how she had laughed, and Henry had flushed and a smile had hooked itself on to the corner of his father's lips. I had gone up to the bathroom and examined my eyes. Whatever light I stood in, the blue in them was faint, the grey predominating, the grey of slate and concrete.

'So shoot me,' Henry said.

The dragonflies swirled up on high, giddy, drunk on love, on life. The air wafted in gently, curling around my legs.

'You wouldn't dare,' said Henry.

I felt for and found the trigger, curled my finger around it.

'It isn't even cocked.'

'What?'

'Want me to show you how to do it?'

'I can do it,' I shouted. I lowered the gun and took several steps back, running my eyes over the gun and rapidly swinging them back to Henry, ready for an attack.

But Henry shoved his hands in his pockets and started to whistle.

In the seconds it took for me to cock the gun, Henry took a few steps forwards and I found myself backing up, edging between the museum display cases.

'Stop!' I yelled. 'I've cocked it now, okay!'

Henry stopped.

'What happened to the gamekeeper? Where is he?'

'Fuck knows. I just woke up this morning and he was gone.' He shrugged. 'Really. That's it.'

'But before you said . . . you're lying. Tell me the truth.'

'Maybe I do know something you don't know.'

'Where is he? What did you do with him?'

'I'm not talking about the gamekeeper, ne-cess-sar-ri-ly,' Henry drawled the last word in a Texan accent. He stood another step forward and I stamped my foot on the floor. The echo made him twitch. He stopped.

'You've been wanting to do this for a long time.'

'What?'

'Kill me.'

'No . . . I . . .' I wished he would stop talking. I was too tired to play our usual word-games, to bat back clever responses. The gun, muscular and warm, was beyond words; it was simple. I thought of Mrs Robson and our class discussions on *Hamlet* and on wars, and in that moment I had a vague understanding of why the news was always so dark, of how fighting became more obvious, of how guns only did one thing, whereas words, with their tricks and grammatical traps and double doors and labyrinths and masks and layers, did many things, so many things, were so complex. It would be so much easier just to stop talking and . . . 'You – you were the one who first said you wanted to kill me, it was you who . . .' *started it*, I nearly said, like some kid in year seven.

'Oh, but what about the Knife Incident? You were keen then.' He knew I would bristle at the mention of that; I saw his smile twitch. 'I heard Mum telling Dad she thought you might need medication. When we come back from France, she's sending you to a doctor. Hey, maybe they'll put you in a home, in a padded cell, eventually, and then you can just sit all day and dribble. But don't worry, I'll come and visit you, drop in, say "Hi", maybe once a year.'

I was so riled I was close to bringing up the subject of his mother. Did I dare? Then I thought: you can do whatever you like, you have the gun. A deeper wave of weariness pulled me down. Why couldn't I just put down the gun; why couldn't we just shake hands and walk out; why was life so complicated?

'Why do you hate me?' I burst out.

I flushed at the whine in my voice, but for once, Henry was silenced. Almost surprised.

Then he said softly: 'Shoot me, then. There's nobody here now – no parents, no teachers, no rules. We don't have my dad hanging about, saying "Have you done your home-work?" like we're sodding five-year-olds.' He seemed to forget that his father didn't yet have the nerve to impose his rules on me and Sam; we floated nervously on the edges of his discipline. 'Come on, shoot me.'

He lifted his chin, spread out his arms and arched his back: a living crucifix.

I clasped the gun again; it was beginning to feel familiar, like an extension of my hand. I relived the moment when I had shot the gamekeeper. Yes, there had been the terror, the horror, the fear, the guilt; and yet in the centre of the black hole was a delicious sensation of power. I felt it now.

I had the gun; whoever had the gun was God; therefore I was God.

Henry had shrunk to the size of a tiny chess piece; I could curl my palm around him and throw him from the board. *I really can do it*, I realised in a flash of amazed excitement, *I can do it. I know I can do it because I've done it once before.*

It was as though the boundary I had broken through when I shot the gamekeeper, that taut band of conscience holding me back, had become soft and tattered, easier to break through this time. Look at the way Henry's leering; I could show him. I didn't have to kill him. I could shoot him in the kneecaps. I'd read somewhere in a book that the most painful place to be shot is in the kneecaps; the pain is overwhelming.

I felt a fine ooze of sweat form at the tip of my forefinger and trickle down the curve of the trigger.

Just me and Henry, alone in the Hall.

But there was someone, something else. It was as though my shadow had come to life. He had curled up like smoke and was sitting on my shoulder. He was laughing at me and circling around me. He was mimicking Henry and he was calling me a chicken. He was poking his bony fingers into me and reminding me that before the crash, my whole life had been filled with fears, things that meant nothing to other people, but were monumental to a chicken like me. Speaking in class, wearing the wrong thing to school, a smile from a girl, a teacher frowning at me, a bad mark: my whole life was filled with butterflies. If you shoot Henry, the shadow whispered, maybe you'll just show yourself, for once, that you can be strong. Maybe those other fears will go away. Go on, do it. Be a man!

My finger slithered and found tension on the trigger, a millimetre of tension.

I am God.

I can shoot Henry.

The problem is, I whimpered to the shadow, I don't want to hear him scream. I can hear the gamekeeper's screams in my ears. D'you know what they sounded like? They make me feel as though I have a needle in my heart. When I shot him, it was as though a part of me, a part of the good in me, died. If I shoot Henry, will another part of that good in me die? Will I lose my soul and feel empty, will you enter me and replace it and fill me up with dark thoughts, so I'm like some zombie in my comics? I don't know if I'm explaining myself very well. It's hard to put these feelings into thoughts; they're so murky; and Henry's looking at me, and I have to decide and I can't decide. Tell me what to do.

Shoot him, the shadow mocked me.

But what if the police come and see I've shot Henry and the gamekeeper? Isn't that too much of a coincidence?

But you can shoot the policeman too, the shadow whispered. You can shoot Henry and drag his body and hide it. There'll be a lake, a pond, something at the back of the house and you can leave Henry in there. If the policeman comes in, you can shoot him. Watch the policeman fall to the floor; go to him and see if he is dead, watch the blood flow from his head and see how easy it is. He'll be like Matthew, the one you first killed. A head is just a melon; you can crush it, break it, shoot it –

I withdrew my finger from the trigger, startled awake from the vision like a dream. Why did I have to kill the policeman? What thoughts were these?

'Stay there.' My voice sounded weak, like a girl's.

I backed up. Henry remained still. I backed up until I was between the cases, then up the stairs, one foot behind the other.

At the top, I said: 'I'm going to stay here. And if you come up, I'll shoot. And then – and then – in about an hour, I'm going to come down again. And I'll shoot you if you don't let me out.'

Henry didn't say anything.

The dragonflies took a dip between some cabinets and then soared up after me, swirling around my head.

I backed up until I was on the gallery. Then I lay flat on my stomach, pointing the rifle barrel through the marble banisters, training my sight back on him.

Henry saw, but didn't seem to care. He rummaged about in his food store and then, cool as the Buddha, sat cross-legged and set about devouring a hunk of bread.

How long had it been since I had eaten? Two days nearly? There had been the blackberries and the spiders, but they had hardly counted. Since this morning, I had become so hungry I didn't feel hungry any more. I had become accustomed to the grinding of my stomach; its perpetual cry was background noise. Now, at the sight of food, my stomach mewed piteously.

'I need some food,' I called out. 'Or . . .'

Henry ignored me and carried on eating.

'I need some food – I need it for my bird.'

To my surprise, Henry stood up. I thought he was about to launch another attack, but he broke off a hunk of bread and flung it up. It bounced on the gallery, six feet away from me. I left my gun dangling and ran to it, tearing it with my teeth, swallowing great lumps. Halfway, I slowed down, savouring the sharpness of the crust against its spongy white centre. I kept telling myself I should ration it out, save a bite for this evening, a bite for the night, but I couldn't stop myself ramming every last crumb into my mouth. After I had finished, I felt worse. My mouth swam with unsatisfied saliva and my stomach, conscious of a small gap plugging its emptiness, only howled for more.

'What bird?' Henry suddenly called up.

'What?' I lay down and picked up the gun again, but Henry was unperturbed.

'I said, what bird?'

174

I panicked, then. If Henry touched the bird, I would kill him. The bird was mine; he couldn't touch it, he mustn't touch it.

'If you come up, I will shoot,' I yelled. 'I mean it. This is my territory. From there.' With a shaking hand, I pointed to the middle stair. 'I don't come into yours and you don't come into mine.'

'Fair enough,' said Henry, but there was a smile on his face.

I lay there for some time, the gun on him. The bread lay in my stomach like rocks.

Kill him. Go on. You chickened out last time but this time you know better. The shadow was back, leering over my shoulder, squinting through the sights at Henry. If you don't kill him, he'll come up and kill your bird. Are you going to let him keep on destroying everything you love? The shadow slipped inside my body, drummed a rhythm of anger in my heart. Don't-let-him-get-away-with-this-any-longer. Do something!

I half-closed my lids and everything seemed to sway and swing and turn upside down. My finger was on the trigger. I heard a dragonfly buzzing overhead. It sounded like the thrum of a lawnmower. I thought of a man plodding up and down a lawn, creating freshly cut stripes; I was locked in a room, staring out of a window, trying not to breathe in the hot, ripe air, coloured with the scent of decay. I turned and I saw him, and I –

No.

I dropped the gun with a clatter. It nearly fell through to the Grand Hall, but I yanked it back and then tossed it down on the floor. I rolled into a tight ball. I won't be bad, I won't be bad, I repeated. This is just what Henry wants, he wants to make me like him, he wants us to be one, my dad always said be good and Henry wants to destroy that, he's taken everything away from me, Matthew and Sam and my mum and Mrs Robson, but he can't take this, he can't unravel my soul and run his hands through it as though it's a piece of cloth to be bought and sold.

You were so close to shooting him then. Closer than ever. One split-second and you might have pulled that trigger; your reality now would be very different.

I rolled over on my right side. My forehead felt hot, my eyes burned and thoughts swam in feverish circles. I won't be bad, I'm not bad, I'm not bad. Think of Dad. Think of the bird. Think of Mr Bellow. Remember the story he told. Remember the second day of your trip, when the class went to visit the Somme and the coach going back was delayed and it was raining, so you all had to shelter in the church. Mr Bellow tried to 'entertain' you for an hour – or at least distract you from desecrating the hymn books – and he told you the story of his grandfather, who had fought in France in the war, and how one night, after so many nights of darkness and tiredness and shooting and mutilation and red bodies, one night the Germans began to sing across no man's land *'Stille Nacht'* and in return the English soldiers sang back 'Silent Night' and there was peace that night, the stars hung in the sky without bullets to dodge and the moon looked on in relief. All the boys sniggered when they heard the story, except for Colin, who cried, and they made violin noises around him, but you liked the story, didn't you? Didn't you? Because it reminded you of being a kid and going to church on Xmas Day with your dad and singing and watching the candlelight flicker on the stained-glass windows he'd made . . .

*

I lay there in the hallway, looking up at the ceiling and I sang and sang it over and over again in my heart, like a verbal medicine to keep me pure:

*Silent Night*
*Holy Night*
*All is Calm*
*All is Bright* . . .

Above me, the dragonflies darted around each other, as though they could hear my silent voice and were dancing to it.

For some time, Henry had been threatening to kill me. He hissed it fiercely, when we were swimming and held my head under water; he whispered it casually, under his breath, when he was asking me to pass the butter at the breakfast table; he sung it jestingly, when we were in the kitchen and I borrowed his pen by mistake to add something to the shopping list and his 'I'm going to kill you, James!' made my mum chuckle.

I was sure he wasn't joking. I had sensed a shift in his bullying recently: from the subtle to the deadly. When he'd first moved in, he'd played with me almost for fun, seeing how far he could go, like a scientist watching a new rat scuttling through a maze. But now he meant business. He wanted to be the only son in the family; he'd started doing his homework with feverish pleasure, showing off his good grades to Mum; he'd even bought Sam a pack of hairbands as a present. Now he wanted to shove me out of the nest as though I was the cuckoo. And I'd heard the rumours at school, floating whispers of awe, about how Henry had been involved in the death of his mother. And got away with it . . .

It was just a question of time.

I wished that he would be specific about his plans. The abstract idea was like a virus in my mind, spawning permutations and possibilities. I began to lose weight. At dinner, Henry only had to eye up my plate and I would push it away, declaring I wasn't hungry. Mum got angry, accusing me of snacking on my way home from school on crisps and sweets. In football, I always made sure I was the goalie, so Henry couldn't kick me in a tackle. At night, I piled a stack of books by my door that would topple with a warning crash if he crept in to push a pillow over my face. Then I told myself: he'll be clever about it. He'll make it look like an accident, he'll conjure up alibis. Every night, I checked the screws in the bookcase by my bed; in cars I kept my eyes fixed on the locks. I reached a point where I was so worried I couldn't be worried any more. Just when I had convinced myself that it was an empty threat, Henry gave me a warning.

I bought the knife in ASDA. I tried looking for one on the internet, but I needed a credit card, and my mum's purse sat on the kitchen table all evening but an opportunity never arose. My mum dragged me out to ASDA, saying she needed help with the shopping, which was all a cover for having A Talk. On buying peas, she said to me, 'Perhaps you don't much like Henry and his father'; burgers 'Maybe you should make more effort'; spring onions 'We could always go back,' she pleaded, in a voice that said if we went back to the way things were, she'd commit suicide. I just smiled and said 'Yeah, Mum I'm fine, I'm fine', and then she went to buy a rolling-pin and I saw the knife. My heart stood still.

When she was getting baked beans, I took out the toilet rolls and put them back on the shelf. At the checkout, she suddenly cried, 'James – I forgot the toilet rolls, can you run and get them?' I ran, picked them up, ran to the kitchen section, found it was clear, took the knife off its silver rack, slipped it into my blazer, ran back to the checkout and stood watching things beep through the till until my eyes stung with green flashes. It was the longest five minutes of my life. But we left without trouble and I felt for once God was protecting me.

As we got out to the car, I watched her putting the shopping into the boot. Her hair kept blowing in her mouth and she kept having to brush it back. I saw she looked tired. Suddenly I did have an urge to blurt everything out. But I knew she wouldn't believe me.

I sometimes wonder if that knife is hanging framed in the head's office, with a little plaque underneath saying: *ASDA weapon, used and removed from psycho boy who tried to stab his stepbrother.*

That night, I couldn't sleep. Lines from *Hamlet* sliced into my dreams like flashlights suddenly piercing through darkness, making me squint and duck.

*I'm Claudius, you're Hamlet.*

*I'm going to kill you.*

*Now I might do it, now he is a-praying . . . but do you dare, dear Hamlet, do you dare, or will you let the old king go like the scaredy-cat you are?*

*I'm going to do it tomorrow,* Henry had said, *we'll act it out for real. Be prepared. Pistols at dawn ha ha ha.*

The whole thing might not have been as bad if it hadn't been the day a visiting author came to talk to us. His name was Kevin Ross and he'd written thirteen Young Adult novels. We all had to read one in preparation. I'd hated mine. It was full of all these *cools* and *yeahs* and *I was hangin' out with Barry* and long sentences without punctuation, as though teenagers talk in some sort of breathless way all the time and can't think in full-stops. Listening to him was like watching your parents trying to dance at a high school disco.

Kevin Ross gave a long speech about his latest novel, about a juvenile delinquent who shoplifted for kicks. I didn't hear a word he said. Everything was a blur except for the cold feel of the knife, tucked inside my blazer, plastering a strip of shirt to my chest.

Then the talk came to an end.

Everyone clapped.

Butterflies exploded in my stomach.

I walked up to the front.

Henry walked behind me.

I was vaguely aware of Kevin Ross, sitting next to Mrs Robson with a faint sneer on his face, as though warning us that we were never going to make it to the RSC.

I tried to put the teacher's table between us, but Henry came around to the other side so that we were only a foot apart: face to face. His eyes held mine, telling me his threat was not a hollow one.

Then he turned away, with his back to the class. He hunched his shoulders and bowed his head, feigning deep prayer. Occasionally, he shot me a narrow, sidelong glance.

'"O my offence is rank, it smells to heaven;
*It hath the primal eldest curse upon't –*
*A brother's murder. Pray can I not,*
*Though inclination be as sharp as will,*
*My stronger guilt defeats my strong intent,*
*And, like a man to double business bound,*
*I stand in pause where I shall first begin,*

*And both neglect. What if this cursed hand*
*Were thicker than itself with brother's blood,*
*Is there not rain enough in the sweet heavens*
*To wash it white as snow?"'*

It was then that I saw it. A glint in his blazer. He brushed
the right lapel of his coat open, so that the silvery shimmer
was hidden from the rest of the class. Then the cloth fell
back. So. His weapon of choice was the same as mine.

I felt as though I was underwater. The rest of the class
seemed far away, bobbing on a distant shore. The clock said
3:43. Every tick sounded like a bomb going off. I felt the lines
spill from my lips and, ironically, I found I could suddenly
voice my soliloquy with clarity and calm; I was so afraid of
Henry, I forgot to be afraid of speaking aloud. I was even
aware of the warmth of Mrs Robson's pride emanating across
the room. 3:48. The school bell would shrill at four, pouring
pupils into corridors. If I could just survive until then, I might
have a chance. I could tell Mrs Robson; I could finally confide
in her, tell her everything; she could call the police.

Henry drew his hand into his blazer.

I thought in shock: he's going to do it now.

Not in the park after school.

*Now.*

In front of everyone.

He's lost it. He hates me so much that he's going to take
the risk.

'"*And am I then revenged,*
*To take him in the purging of his soul . . ."'*

My speech trailed off. I was aware of the class rippling
with laughter. But the words were stuck, like a pebble in my
throat. A voice wailed: *I don't want to die, I'm too young,*
*I don't want to die.*

Henry's hand stayed inside his blazer, knuckles protruding through the cloth, rippling the gold school crest.

I heard Mrs Robson in the background, asking me to carry on. Henry didn't take his eyes off me. He stepped forward. And then it all happened at once. I screamed. Drew the knife out. I was too scared to hold it against his throat, against that delicate bubble of Adam's apple that rose and fell as I held the knife to his cheek, against the warm, soft skin, dotted with black for the beard he was not yet old enough to grow.

Later, when the white-faced class had been sent home, when my mum had been called and embarrassed me in the head's office by bursting into tears, I was able to tell my story. Finally, I was able to tell it all. All about how Henry hated me, how he had threatened to kill me, how I had acted in self-defence because Henry had a knife too.

But who could believe me?

Who could believe me when Henry told them his threats were just jokes, playing, like Cowboys and Indians, and when they checked his blazer, there was nothing but a long, silvery strip of chewing gum wrappers.

'Maybe I've been selfish,' my mum sobbed, 'maybe it was too soon after your father died to try this.'

The head declared that I was suspended. I, who had never even been in detention before – suspended. But I was more afraid when I found out I was grounded; I would have to stay in every day; there would be no more trips to the park, to the library, to the burger bar, which meant Henry had an even greater chance to kill me.

Now Henry's dream had come true. We were in a house alone together. I knew that he was just treating me like a hunter with a fox, enjoying the thrill of the chase, letting me hide down holes and then scramble up again. He would kill me: tonight, tomorrow, the next day, next week. He'd do it, I had no doubt of that.

It didn't matter that I had the gun now. He would get another gun from the room he had told me about. And when it came down to it, it wasn't even about weapons, who had the bigger bullets or the fastest bullets or the best aim. It was about my mind versus his mind. And I wished that my mind could be as sharp as his, as ruthless as his, as cold as his.

I lay down on my side. Despair stung my eyes but when I shed a few tears the wracking of my stomach was too painful and I made myself stop. I felt the tears slowly slide down my cheeks in dry lines and spool over the tips of my eyes, wetting my hair. Out of the corner of my eye, I looked through a vase-shaped gap in the banisters, at the sharp edge of a museum cabinet. It would only take a minute. To run at the marble, to vault over, to feel the air gushing up around me, carrying me, caressing me, embracing me to death. I would break my back, my neck; blackness would instantly seep through my mind like ink, blotting out all my fears and worries. I pictured my body as a ragdoll, bones and joints bent out of place and winced. But, compared with what Henry might enact, surely it was a nicer way to die?

I slowly hauled myself up and the frayed edge of the carpet shifted. My foot hit something hard. I crawled over and peeled up the edge. There was an oblong slab of wood and a handle, identical to the one I had discovered downstairs: a trapdoor.

It took a long time to open the trapdoor, for I had to heave it up and lower it very slowly, so as not to make the slightest noise that might alert Henry to my find. I was weak from lack of food and my arm muscles strained in protest.

I stared down into the black depths and I could not make them blue. After hours of turmoil, of dipping a leg into the darkness and then hastily drawing it out, I slowly closed the trapdoor and sat for a while, waiting for my shaking to subside. It was ironic; I needed Henry to be here, next to me, goading me on; alone, I was unable to force myself. Inwardly, I raged at myself for my cowardice, for not being able to climb my mountain of fear, but I could not forget how I'd felt earlier in the tunnel: the choking smell, the darkness putting its hands all over me. I told myself that if I was going to be such a girl there was nothing left to do but fly over the banisters and I deserved the punishment of death, and yet I could not stand and do it. I began to play games: if I hear a noise from below in the next minute, I'll do it, or: if I hear three bird calls in the next minute, I'll do it. I realised that a sense of hurt was keeping me alive. I wanted the universe to respond to my tragedy and show me that it cared, to feel my existence meant something to someone, that I was not going to end up just another schoolboy in the news who had died in these last few days, a statistic that rounded the total up to twenty-nine.

Twilight came on quickly and I promised myself that I would not spend another night in this house, that by the time darkness had set in I would choose either the hole or death.

Down below, Henry had discovered a torch. He sat and spun it about, creating patterns of light on the ceiling. As the torch swerved, it left echoes of light that looped and danced with the stronger shimmer of the beam. I thought of a story my father had told me about oceans and phosphorescence, the glimmers of coloured light that danced in exotic waves. My mind was becoming too weak for thought or fight; I lay on my side and watched Henry's show with wide eyes, hypnotised by its strange beauty.

**S**omeone was coming.

I had been dozing, drifting between sleeping and dreaming. Now I pulled myself up and into waking, shaking my head as though I might dislodge the remaining flecks of sleep. I heard the noise again: light footsteps, heavy breathing. Someone on the stairs. *Where am I?* I panicked. I spread out my palms, flat on the carpet. In the bedroom, in the doorway . . . yes, I had fallen asleep here, too nervous to decide on the bedroom or the corridor. My hand banged something: the water bottle I had filled before sleep. I scrabbled about again, found the rifle. I grabbed it. My fingers were shaking like butterflies' wings. I smoothed them over the length of it: the cool, long nose of the barrel, the marbleish feel of the butt. I found the loop of trigger and slotted my finger into it. Now I was prepared.

Oh God, I thought, this is it. Finally. Henry versus James. One of us going to die; one of us cannot get out of this alive. Why, why hadn't I plucked up the courage to try the hole under the trapdoor? I should have forced myself. Oh God, should I fire now, into the dark? A pre-emptive strike? Should I take the risk? Because something isn't right. He doesn't sound like Henry.

Something was wrong with the sound of his breathing, the rhythm of his footsteps. A *thump* and then a *scratch*, as though one foot was dragging behind the other. A beat between steps, and an intake of breath like a sucked hiss.

Unless it was another one of Henry's games.

His breathing was lacerated with sobs. To my amazement, he murmured that he wanted his mummy. I thought: my mother or his mother?

It couldn't be Henry. It had to be the gamekeeper. Or one of the burglars – what if one of the boys who had burgled the house had come back for more and Henry had shot one of them and now they were staggering about looking for jewellery in a dazed state, leaving trails of blood in the darkness?

Or the gamekeeper. Maybe he had woken up and had killed Henry, shot him dead and now he was coming up to get me, only that didn't make sense, for he was speaking English, well, trying to speak it, his frail voice clawing air.

Maybe I should get up, run into the bedroom. I told my body to retreat but it didn't respond.

And all the time he was getting closer, and I was still sitting in the hallway.

He seemed to reach the top of the stairs. Then he came down the corridor, heading straight towards me. If he was a *he*. Or a *she*. Or an *it*. Now that he was closer, he seemed more of an *it*. His breath an entity in itself, hanging in the darkness.

I thought: what if he's . . .

Ghosts don't exist, I told myself. It's a scientific fact. But if you are functioning under the illusion that this is a ghost, then remember that he can't harm you. He might just need comforting, someone to help take away his sorrow for a night before tomorrow he wakes up and forgets and walks through the mansion alone, knowing he'll walk through these rooms for all eternity.

The dragging breath was coming closer. Now I could smell it. A smell of rotting. Of blood and dirt. A smell of pain.

It didn't seem to sense me. I drew in my breath, my nostrils tingling with the agony of its smell, and held it in.

It was coming closer, and if I didn't move my leg, it would trip over it, or walk through it. I pictured its coldness seeping through my muscles, my bones. It might leave behind a lingering of itself, an icy curse that would slowly seep into my soul.

I was sitting so still it felt as though every muscle in my body was stretched to breaking-point. My lungs were running out of breath but I dare not take another gulp.

He came closer.

I let out my breath in a gasp and he whimpered hoarsely, 'Is there anyone there?'

Relief softened my muscles. His voice was English. He sounded like a boy, three or four years old.

I opened my mouth but my tongue lay in my mouth like a piece of leather.

He collapsed against me. I went rigid. His hands pawed me. I let out a breath and quickly drew another in. He was sobbing and whispering, 'Oh, Ganesh, please help me, please help me, oh, Ganesh keep me safe keep me safe please help me Ganesh keep me safe . . .'

In my terror, I pulled the trigger. I did not hear the sound of the bullet firing; it seemed to shoot from barrel to skin with no gap of air. And then: silence.

I reached out to feel his body, to feel something warm

and wet, but my fingers trembled in the air, the thought of touching him too awful, and I curled them back, around the gun. I sat there, fingers rigid, breathing hard, silently singing, the words tumbling and jumbling over each other *silent night all is calm bright all is silent bright calm silent.*

I was woken suddenly the next morning by the sound of a distant gunshot. I saw that I was lying on a floor, on my side, facing a dirty, streaked skirting board. A bewildered thought rose through the muzziness: *Where am I?* My fingers were curled into my palms as though I had been clutching something in my sleep, and there was blood on them. I knew then that terrible things had happened but I pushed them to another part of my mind and closed my eyes, wanting to sink back into sleep, into the purity of ignorance. The terrible things began to fly into the front of my thoughts again and I pushed them to another part of my mind, and then another. I told myself that it was a Saturday and I was having a lie-in. Yet the things beat harder and faster, their black wings pounding against my temples in flapping strokes, screaming to be heard, and I couldn't push them aside any more, I could only lie flat and let them peck me. And I remembered it all in a trembling fit: the crash, the gamekeeper, the chase, Henry, the boy in the dark –

Where was the boy in the dark?

I sat up and saw him. He was lying by the window, in a ball. He shocked me, for he wasn't a three- or four-year-old boy at all. I went over and examined him, wide-eyed. His hair was sticky with blood. He lay with his thumb in his mouth. I bent down and looked into his face, to be sure, and that was the biggest shock of all.

I pulled back the velvet curtain, letting the sun pour over his brown face, slack and pudgy with sleep. It was streaked with dirt and razored with cuts. He was wearing a school shirt, so filthy it now looked as though it was brown with patches of white, a pair of blue, soiled Y-fronts and one sock. It was a school sock with a grey stripe and his name-tag had been sewn on the outside, loose loops of black cotton spooling out like a string caterpillar. Though I had no doubt who he was, I checked the name-tag, to reassure myself this wasn't a hallucination.

'Urgh.' I had tickled his feet and woken him up.

He squinted up at me.

'James!' he cried. His voice was hoarse and scratchy. 'James.' I continued to stare down at him, dazed. 'James, it's me – Colin!'

'I know it's you,' I said. I searched his body for signs of a bullet, but there were none. I missed him; oh thank God, I had missed him. I closed my eyes and in that moment of sweet relief I swore to God that I would never kill or harm anyone again, not even a scratch, not even a splinter.

I smiled down at him, a big, goofy, desperate grin that made my mouth ache.

'God, Colin, it's good to see you. How did you get –' I broke off, seeing a glint in the ripped pocket of his shirt. 'What's that?'

'I –'

'What is it?' I felt my skin quiver like rising fur. I grabbed out at his pocket, drew out half a bar of chocolate. It was French chocolate, the gleaming dark slabs covered in gold foil and a crumpled, dirty black and red wrapper that said *Valrhona*.

'I'm hungry,' I said, my smile becoming deranged. 'I'm very hungry.'

'You can have it.' There was a pleading in his voice and his eyes: *Don't eat it all.*

'I mean – how the hell have you got chocolate –'

'I bought it in Paris, I forgot it was there, I had to crawl –' he broke off in a fit of dry coughing.

'We'll share it. Are you thirsty? Have some water. It's precious, you see, it took me an hour to fill it, there's only a little dribble coming out of the tap. It's a fair deal.'

I passed him the water bottle and watched him knock it back, droplets slithering over his chin. The chocolate caressed my palms; I felt as though there was an animal in the back of my throat, mewing and purring with pleasure.

Then I couldn't hold back any longer. I broke off three slabs and crammed them into my mouth. They were warm from his body and the sun. The chocolate slid down my throat like ebony honey. When it hit my stomach, I felt a shudder of bliss convulse my body, and a feeling of relief so intense it was almost like I'd been running and running and running and then stopped; like an impulse to lie down and sleep. I took another slab and another and another and before I knew it, there was only one piece left.

'Go on,' he said.

But I shook my head and pushed it back at him.

He pushed it back to me with resigned eyes.

I wrapped it up very obviously and carefully and pushed it firmly back to him. He pocketed it reluctantly.

'We'll have it later,' I said loudly.

The caffeine buzzed around my brain like flies. My stomach convulsed, wailing for more.

'How did you get to survive?' I asked, grabbing the water back from Colin and taking a swig. I let it slosh around my mouth, mingling deliciously with the chocolate sludge still on my gums.

'Well, the coach crashed.' His voice was clearer now he had drunk the water.

'You don't say.' The caffeine had sharpened my tongue, but in truth I felt delirious with the pleasure of human company. I wanted to hug him so tight till he couldn't breathe; I wanted to tease him and tackle him and laugh with him and shout at him and just talk, talk and talk and talk all these thoughts that had been locked up in my head for days.

'It did, though, James – it crashed, it crash –'

'Okay, okay, but keep your voice down,' I hissed, glancing back nervously at the door. 'Or he might hear.'

'Who?'

'Didn't you see him on the way up? Has he gone?'

'Who? I didn't see him, it was dark –'

'Why didn't you cry out! I thought you were a ghost, I thought, I mean, I nearly –'

'I was tired, I was too tired, I was so tired I couldn't speak any more, I tried to yell out but my voice got lost in my throat and all I could do was sink down and – James, James, the coach crashed – after you got off to go to the loo, the driver drove off. Mr Bellow went up to the front and started yelling at him, it was really freaky because you wouldn't think Mr Bellow could yell, but he did, and he went all red, and then Ms Cave went up and tried to drag Mr Bellow off and he told her to go and sit down and then the driver *socked* him! – he punched him! – and Mr Bellow fell back against the seat and blood was running from his nose – and then the next thing we knew, the sky had come in through the windows and we were flying.'

'Matthew – is he still alive?' I clutched the bottle tightly.

'I don't know. I think he might be. Kevin is. He told me to go and get help and I ran, I ran, and then I saw the shirt –'

'The what?'

'It was an omen. I didn't know where to go. I was scared and they'd all cheered at me but I felt I was going to let them down and I prayed to Lord Ganesh and then I saw the shirt. It was a sign – I thought, so I came into the forest and then I saw the house and I came to get help.'

'But Henry – didn't you – he must have heard you –'

'Henry? Is he in the house?'

'He's – yes – but – but how did you get out from the crash – were you hurt?'

'No, because I'm protected,' said Colin.

'Protected? What –'

'Lord Ganesh, we do a *puja* to him every day in the temple and he protects me,' said Colin. 'It's a miracle. I woke up and I was lying in the grass. I could feel a weight on top of me and I suddenly realised it was Raf, and I screamed and I pushed him aside and he flopped into the grass and he was . . .' Colin swallowed, his eyes shiny. 'He saved my life. I closed his eyes and whispered a blessing in his ear. Then I prayed to Ganesh to say thank you for saving me because I wasn't even hurt, Raf's body had taken every blow that I should have taken, all the glass was embedded in –'

'Did you see Matthew's body, did you –'

'There was Steve. His body was in two pieces.' Colin shuddered. 'I mean – really, like someone had taken a knife and cut clean through him, cos one half was on a tree stump and the other half was lying on the grass. I was sick. But I could hear one or two people groaning. I could hear Mr Bellow, but he was trapped. I couldn't see Mr Bellow's face, it was hidden under the metal but I could see his hand. I knew it was him because he had his tweed coat on, and he said –' Colin was trying hard to keep his chin from quivering '– he said I had to try and move away the stuff on top of him. And I tried and I tried –' Colin uncurled his palms, which were cut open with red whorls '– but I couldn't. Then he said – well, he could hardly talk, he was talking but he kept hissing, breathing in and out like this – he said I had to go and look for help. He said I had to be brave. He said I had to climb the ravine and then I had to run and find help. And then I said, "I'll find help", I shouted, "I'll find help, there might be more people trapped alive", and in my head I heard them all crying at me to find help. I went up to the ravine and started to climb, but all the rocks were loose from the crash – I couldn't keep my grip – I fell.'

'You fell?'

'Yes, I hit my head, I think. I remember just before it went black that I'd failed everyone, that they were all going to die because of me, but then I woke up again and it was dark and my head hurt, it was really throbbing hard. I started to climb again and this time I made it, I did it, and when I got to the top I could hear them all cheering me – in my head, I mean.'

I saw the light in his face and I smiled.

'You've been very brave.' I sounded like a parent, for God's sake. 'Well done,' I tried again, hopelessly. Looking at his bright, earnest eyes, I felt another surge of relief and a wild appetite to hold him again, to touch human skin with my lonely hands, but that would have been gay or girlish, so I gave him a light punch and he was so weak he fell over and I laughed and he laughed and then we caught our breath.

'So what happened, what happened when you got to the top?' I asked. 'You have to tell me everything, you have to –'

'I climbed up the ravine and I ran down the road. My trousers got ripped and I took them off because they kept falling down and I felt I should run, only then I got lost. I got lost and I kept shouting out but all I could see were fields and nothing but the sky and the moon. I tried to go and look for that café where you went to the toilet but I couldn't find it, I thought I was going the right way to find it but I must have gone the wrong way, I just found myself in fields and then I couldn't remember how to get back and I was lost and I was frightened and then I saw the shirt on the railings and it was another sign only when I got here it was all dark and I knew I should find help but I was so tired, so tired, and I'm so glad I found you James, I . . .'

As Colin repeated his story, my mind began to whirr. Had Henry seen Colin? Did this mean that Henry was still down there? Perhaps he had left. And what about the bodies? Matthew might still be alive. Mr Bellow was alive. I wasn't a real murderer; if we went and saved them, I might be forgiven for causing the crash; I might be a hero. Relief oozed through me. Then my stomach clenched as I thought of Steve and his body in two halves. Maybe Colin and I could go and find a phone and then I could run. Colin would be too slow to catch me, stop me. I still had the last piece of chocolate; I could save it. Yes; I could save it and eat it, just after the call, give myself one last drop of energy to run. I could lie low in forests, find work on a farm, like an undercover spy. People would forget me and I would never have to go to jail.

I looked into Colin's eyes again and in a flash of deep and selfish longing, I wished we could just stay up here, eating chocolate and play-punching. But –

'We have to go back down,' Colin panted.

'But what about Henry?'

'No, we have to get help. We have to help Matthew.'

'But Henry's down there. I mean, he might have gone, but I think he still –'

'So? He's your brother, he's not going to hurt you.'

'Colin – he's got a gun. He's the reason I'm trapped up here. I mean, d'you really think I'd want to hang around this house all by myself –' I broke off in exasperation; it was like trying to persuade someone to be afraid of the dark. 'Colin, we just can't go down there, okay?'

'But – but –' Colin stared down at the rifle, lying by my feet. 'You have a gun.'

'I know, but he has more guns. And he . . . he'll use his, because he is a psycho.'

'We don't have to use it, we'll just take it,' said Colin stubbornly. 'We have to get help. Henry might have a gun but he won't really use it, come on, James, I know Henry's mean but he's not that bad. We'll tell him about Matthew. He likes Matthew, Matthew's his friend, he'll want to help.'

I stared at Colin and a revelation slowly came over me. Colin had every reason to be afraid of Henry too and yet he believed that we would be safe. Suddenly the shadows fell away from my mind, the chains snaking around my thoughts fell unlocked. I realised then that I was free: my fear was my own construction, that the real house of terror was the one that I had built in my mind.

'Before we go down,' Colin whispered, 'we'll sing "Silent Night".'

'What?'

We had crept out of the bedroom and we were crouched low in the hallway now, preparing our battle plan. I was carrying the gun. Colin hadn't wanted to take it.

'Don't you remember?' Colin whispered. 'That story Mr Bellow told us on the coach about the soldiers who sang. It was the most amazing story I've ever heard in my life –'

'I remember,' I whispered. 'But it's crazy.'

'It's symbolic. Henry heard Mr Bellow say that story too, he'll know what we mean by it, it's like asking for a truce. I mean, I'm sure Henry wants to help us, but just so he knows we're his friends.'

At the top of the marble staircase, however, Colin paused. He swallowed.

'He's down there?' he whispered, gazing through the marble balustrade, running his eyes over the glinting jumble of museum cabinets.

I nodded.

'HENRY?' Colin called out.

I shook my head frantically, but Colin shrugged.

'Henry, it's Colin! Colin Rabindarath. Me and James are coming down! I managed to get out of the crash alive – it was a miracle – and – and – and we have to find some help. Mr Bellow's hurt. We need help.'

Silence, and then a rustling, whispery sound: an intake of breath?

We went down the stairs. We began to sing. Colin's voice was hoarse but full of gusto; mine was weedy. I wanted to run. I knew that to delay was madness; I knew the only way to go was to sprint and take cover behind the cabinets. But Colin was holding back, climbing down a couple of steps and then stopping, glancing round, dropping down another step, glancing round again, singing, all the while. I signalled to him to *hurry*, but Colin looked at me blankly, warbling, *'Sleep in heavenly peace . . .'*

Then I caught sight of Henry. He was hunched up behind the case, his silhouette merging with the shadows and those scorpion instruments. The rifle barrel rose until it was pointing in our direction. I turned, but my voice was too dry. I cried, 'Colin!' but it was too quiet, too late, and then the shot came.

Colin slumped back on to the stairs, screaming.

'Colin – Colin –' I pulled at his clothes, looking for blood, my heart exploding with fury. I wanted to run down those steps, to curl my hands around Henry's throat and *squeeze*. I wanted to rip the gun out of his hands and kick him to the ground and hold the gun above him. Not strike him or shoot him, just hold it above him and see the fear in his eyes.

'I'm okay,' said Colin incredulously. 'Hey, I'm okay, he didn't get me.'

'Right.' I swung the gun in Henry's direction. My shadow

rose and clapped his hands in glee; I yelled at him to go away. I lifted the gun so that the viewfinder no longer showed the brown of his hair but a distant door, a foot above his head. Behind me, Colin began to sing 'Silent Night' again. I closed my eyes and fired.

Nothing. No sound, no bullet. I curled my finger tighter and pulled the trigger again and in that instant, my heart exploded, for I realised I had fired without aiming, that he was right in my sights, that the bullet would strike him and –

But nothing. Silence. *Silent Day.*

'What is it?' Colin broke off.

'There's no bullets in it,' I said blankly, everything falling into place. Henry wouldn't really have given me, the Enemy, a loaded gun, would he? It was another one of his tricks.

I thought of yesterday's agony, the way I had torn and tied my soul into knots.

I was ready to kill him then. But my sense of survival was stronger than my fury.

'Back up!' I grabbed Colin's sleeve. 'Up the stairs.'

'But we're meant to be singing "Silent –"'

'Up!'

Another bullet came and a shower of blood sprayed across Colin's shirt. In my numb shock, it struck me that the pattern looked like paw prints, as though a baby kangaroo with bloody feet had bounced across the cotton. Colin lost it. He started screaming and bawling like a baby and I had to slap him.

'I'm the one who's been shot, you wanker – get up, get up –' I broke off, mouth clawing at the pain of it, the throbbing pain, as though my finger was swelling up to the size of a house, a big red house.

'I'm not a wanker!' Colin yelled. 'Oh God, look at your –'

'Don't look at it, just move –'

'Yes, yes –'

'D'you want to get shot too?' I'm sorry I called you a wanker, but I'm the one who's been shot, okay? So we have to get up those stairs and –'

'Yes, yes!'

Colin started to mutter prayers in Hindi. We clutched each other, clambering up the stairs, crawling and stumbling into the bedroom.

We slammed the door and sat with our backs to it. Colin looked at my hand and cried out, 'I'm going to be sick, I'm going to be sick!'

He crawled to the corner and hunched over, but the only thing that came out of his mouth was a spool of drool.

When I looked down at my right hand, I felt as though I was looking at an image on a TV screen, as though this scarlet mess of bone and skin belonged to a stranger, some soldier, some victim of a distant war. I slowly spread open my palm. It was wet with blood, all the lines – life and love and that other one, did palmists name it fate or work or kids or maybe all of those – were highlighted as though sketched in with crimson biro, the type Mrs Robson used to mark our work. The top of my little finger was cut clean away. I noticed then, in a way I had seen but not seen a thousand times before, that each finger is divided into three parts. My little finger was cut neatly halfway up the second segment. The top was slightly jagged; it reminded me of the way I used to cut the wrapping paper for the presents we took to my father in hospital and my mum would tell me off for clumsiness. I'd seen the rest of my little finger lying on the stairs, a red raw lump that I'd wanted to kick away.

Now I longed to have it back. I wanted to stick it on, even if I had to use tape, string, whatever; anything to make my finger whole again.

Colin kept on faking throwing up in the corner. He turned and saw my finger and cried, 'Put it away.'

'I can't help it, it's not my fault, I told you, I told you we couldn't go down!' I shouted.

Colin stared at me with big, hurt eyes, then turned back to face his wall and carry on spitting at it as though he was delivering oblations to some God of Wallpaper.

I staggered to my feet and walked out, down the corridor, into the bathroom. Blood dripped on the floor, like a Hansel and Gretel trail of red breadcrumbs.

In the bathroom, I went to see my bird. He looked asleep. For one terrified moment I feared he was dead. I reached out, and a splurge of blood dropped on his body, seeping into the black. Then I saw his breath, quick ins and outs pumping away beneath his wing, and relief swam over me. For some time I stood there, mesmerised by the stream of his breath, by the magnificence of the life flow that kept him alive despite the broken fragility of his body. The rhythm soothed me; the waves of pain lapped into the distance.

A wave of dizziness forced me to sit down, to slump by the sink. I closed my eyes, the tide of pain rapidly coming inshore. I could feel sleep tempting me like a snake, twisting around me, gently hissing that I should just let go, just relax, just let it bite me and put me out, but I feared the poison would be so delicious I'd never want to wake up. I remembered a story I'd heard, maybe from Henry, about some guy who'd lost a toe – or was it an ear lobe? – and even though a small flow of blood was pouring out of him, he ended up dying. I tried to pull my shirt off over my bloody right hand, but the cuff was too tight. I pulled harder and then stopped – what if my left finger was pulled clean off, or worse, my hand fell off? I shook my head – *That's stupid, your hand can't fall off.* Even so, I pulled the sleeve back and tried to undo the button fastening the cuff, but I was right-handed and the fingers of my left hand were fumbling jellies of uselessness. Time and time again, I nearly got the button out of its cotton eye, only to have it slip back. I kept thinking that I should call Colin and ask him to do it but it had suddenly become a matter of pride, that I had to prove I was also a survivor; the way Colin had surprised me with his bravery in climbing the ravine. Finally, I got the button under a nail rim and tugged it out with a wince. The cuff flapped loose and I pulled the shirt off.

I held it in my lap for a minute. It reminded me of the blanket Sam used to carry around with her when she was a kid, maybe three or four years old, that she got so attached to she had to eat, sleep and bathe with it. The shirt was too big to wrap around my finger so I just muffled the whole thing around my right hand. A flower of blood immediately appeared. The thought of retying it was exhausting. I lay down on the floor, the tiles cool against my temple. I kept thinking: *Gotta retie it, gotta retie it if you don't all your blood might flow out while you're asleep flow across the floor seep out into the corridor and when Colin finds you you'll be drained dead like some vampire victim.* But I heard the bird cawing softly in the sink and then I was asleep.

'**C**ome here.'

Mrs Robson patted a patch of sofa beside her.

It was my first day back from school after the Knife Incident. Every classroom I walked into, someone made a wise remark; every teacher I dealt with refused to meet my eyes. I felt like running out and never coming back again, but I'd been warned that if I left the building at any time I would be expelled.

Mrs Robson had taken pity on me. She'd offered me a lift home and this time I'd said yes. Only she hadn't taken me home. She'd asked if she could just pick something up at her flat first and I'd stammered yes. Then she had pulled up, switched off the engine and stared into the whirred blur of her windscreen wipers.

'In about three hours' time my husband's going to come home,' she said. 'This is what happens to me every day. I drive up and I sit here and I wonder if I can stand it for one more day, if I can make myself go up and wait in that flat for him, or . . .'

This was not the Mrs Robson who stood at the front of our classes like a queen bee, maintaining order with the sting of her honey smiles. This was another Mrs Robson with cracks and colours and riddles and I didn't know who she was or how to handle her. I flicked her a startled glance, but she seemed slumped in vagueness now, as though barely aware of my presence.

' . . . or if I should just go upstairs and pack up everything I own and just walk out. I can just imagine the look, the *look* on his face . . .' She turned to face me and suddenly her face flickered, morphed into its teacher mask. 'You know, I have a special study guide on *Hamlet*. I have a spare copy. Would you like it?'

'Um, yes, yes, Mrs Robson.'

'Well then. You'd better come up and get it.'

I was bewildered by her change of mood. Her voice was brisk now, sharp as a pencil. As though in saying 'No' I'd be a bad pupil.

'Um, yes,' I squeaked in relief. 'Thank you, Mrs Robson.'

Entering her flat, I gaped at the pale walls, the bookcases crammed deliciously with books. Then, as she made tea, she started to talk more about her husband. About what he did to her. Night after night after night. I didn't know how to react. I desperately wanted to respond like an adult, show her I was on her level, but I found myself flushing and murmuring 'I'm sorry . . . I'm sorry . . .' until she came and sat beside me and said in a trembling voice, 'I'm sorry, James, I probably shouldn't have told you any of that.'

My heart was beating so loudly that the beat echoed in my mind, like a hammer pulping my brain to senseless mush. I could feel her staring at me; I was convinced she was about to tell me off. I stared at my knees, so hard I could see every individual thread of black cloth, the crisscross of knit, up to the thickened overlap where they were joined at the hem. She called my name, softly. I couldn't look up. She reached out and ran the tips of her polished nails up my temple, fluffing back my fringe, like my mum sometimes did. I recoiled in shock, pulling away from her.

We stared at each other with dilated pupils. I saw embarrassment rise over her face and mercurial drops forming in the corners of her eyes. I wanted to tell her that I loved her, but my throat was too thick, so I grabbed her hand and squeezed it tightly. I thought: What would Henry think if he could see me now? and then hated myself for such a thought.

I closed my eyes and thought of last night: how I entered their dark bedroom and saw them: Henry's father with his dirty paws on my mum's body. My body shuddered with a flicker of revulsion; Mrs Robson drew back, frowning. I blinked in confusion and leaned in, but she shook her head. I swallowed and stared at my feet.

Then she reached out and took my hand and raised it to her breast. My hand went stiff with shock. Then I let my fingers tremble against it and she smiled, gave me a slight, encouraging nod. A tear slid down her cheek. Her crying confused me. I wondered if I should stop, but I couldn't; the feel of it was so enticing, the sweet softness of it. I rubbed my hand over it and stroked it and trailed my fingers along the divide where the coarse cloth of her top contrasted with the warm bareness of skin. My fingers teased the edge of something lacy underneath and I felt desire. The strength of it shocked me. It was like a ravenous hunger, a kind of violence. I thought of her husband and the impact of her story suddenly seeped in: I wanted to find him, beat him to pulp.

I heard her sigh and then I stopped feeling embarrassed by the shaking of my breath. I leaned in to kiss her, but she pulled away again.

*

Even though she sent me home and gently told me to be good and keep our meeting secret and do my homework, I left feeling something I hadn't felt before. *I love her*, I shouted silently to the shoppers, *I love her*, I shouted to the bored line waiting for a bus, *I love her*, I shouted to the cars, and the sky, and the kerbs.

It was more than just wild happiness. It was a kind of peace. *Shantih shantih shantih*. All those nights I'd lain awake, fearing that no girl would ever love me, I'd die never knowing what a kiss was, never touching soft female skin. Even though people said you're too young to get married and marriage is just a piece of paper and one day marriage will die out because nobody believes in it any more and it's just about giving away half your house, I wanted to marry when I got old. I pictured myself walking home, and Mrs Robson opening up the door and planting a happy kiss on my lips, the way my mum used to when my father was well and worked in a factory and just did his stained-glass windows as a hobby.

When I got home, I saw that Mum and Henry's father were out, and Sam was at a sleepover. It was just me and Henry.

Instead of backing out and going to sit in the library and pretending to work, or the church and pretending to pray until I got too hungry to stay out and Mum swore at me for coming in late, I went inside. Henry was waiting for me. He started to bait me. He tore a page out of my French text-book. He did all the things he always did, but he could see something had changed: a part of me, deep in the core of me, the part he could normally reach, was untouchable. It belonged to her now. He pushed me to the floor and punched me. I pretended to groan. He walked to the door and said, 'That will teach you', and I said, 'Yes', and pretended to gasp. But he knew he had lost that day, because the moment he left, I lay down and there was a smile on my face.

I **felt something** touching my face and woke up with a start.

'It's okay, it's only me,' said Colin.

I knew something was wrong but I didn't want to face reality. I closed my eyes with a soft groan. I let myself slip back into the room, my lips meeting Mrs Robson's. Her lips so soft, like two apple slices.

'James – James?' He kept tugging my shoulder. 'Are you alive? You're not dead are you?'

'Yes,' I moaned.

I gave Mrs Robson a regretful kiss goodbye and opened my eyes. Then I checked my hand. Oh God. The shirt was soaked red.

'Can you help me? I need to tie it tightly, properly, to stop the blood.'

Colin, as though apologising for his earlier fit of wimpiness, undid the shirt and tore it into strips, winding them tight around my finger-stub.

'There's a bird in the sink.'

'I know. He's mine,' I said. 'When this is all over I'm taking him with me.'

Colin frowned and I felt embarrassed, as though I had shown him my journal or we were in the changing-rooms naked.

'Henry was shouting up asking if you were okay, you know,' Colin said, tying the knot.

I surveyed him through half-closed lids. I was fairly certain he was lying, but I didn't have the energy to tell him I didn't need patronising.

'So, did you go down?' I asked him.

'No.' Colin flushed. 'I mean, he's mad, right, he's totally lost it, he's mad.'

'I know. That's what I've been saying from the start, only no one would listen.' I swallowed, feeling my lids droop, Mrs Robson's smile hovering, Cheshire Cat-like, in the darkness. 'I want to kill him.'

'I've thought of a way out,' Colin said in a pleading voice. 'I've thought of a way. I can do it and then I can go and run for help.'

'What?'

I was almost disappointed when Colin told me his plan, though it was a good one. I was disappointed because it was an escape route, and I wanted war. The moment the bullet had hit me, something irrevocable had changed inside me. I wanted to kill Henry. A voice kept squeaking that I mustn't kill him, there would be consequences. But what consequences? Every time I tried to think of them, all I could see was a rage of red mist, too dense to see beyond. The shadow has won the battle for your soul, I realised, and I waited for a feeling of shock or panic, but there was none. I felt curiously numb, the only sensations in my body the throb of pain in my finger, chanting a battle cry: *Kill Henry, kill Henry, kill Henry.*

But Colin's plan did not include Henry. Finally, just as I was ready to go into battle, I was being forced to surrender.

**I**t took us a long time to make the rope. When we began – tearing dresses from the wardrobe, sheets from the bed, our arms stuffed with silk and net and cotton – the light outside had been bright. By the time we had finished ripping and shredding and tying the knots, the walls were tinted gold with sunset. The knots took ages because Colin insisted on using special ones that he had learned in the Boy Scouts. I teased him about going to Scouts, but I had to admit the knots looked impressively strong.

In between knots, I found myself fiddling with my wound. It became like a nervous tic, this perpetual urge to peel back the bandage and examine the damage.

We tied our rope around the gold pole of the four-poster and tried to pull the bed to the window. But the poles had wobbled dangerously and one of the chiffon curtains collapsed on Colin's head so that he looked like a dusty bride of death. The sight of him made me laugh and Colin got cross; then he started to laugh too and for about ten minutes we couldn't stop.

'Come on, we have to get it together,' I gasped, sobering up.

We lengthened the rope and then pulled it taut from the

bedpost to the window, where it slithered down the stone wall like a patchwork snake. It stopped short five feet above the ground.

'We need to make it longer.'

'No, when I get to the bottom, I can jump,' Colin insisted.

We had discovered a statue of Napoleon on the dresser. He stared down on us with a creased forehead and hooded eyes, as though hardly able to believe the stupidity of our plan. I pulled at my bandage; the end was starting to fray.

'Okay, ready?' I said.

Colin reached into his pocket and drew out the last piece of chocolate, lovingly wrapped in gold foil. He placed it down on the floor and we stared at it as though it was a priceless jewel.

'We should pray,' he said.

'What?'

'We should pray, before we do this. I need the chocolate.'

'What? Why?'

'I need it as an offering for Lord Ganesh.'

'Colin, we are not wasting this last bit of chocolate, okay? It's all we have left.'

'Don't worry. Once it's been used as an offering, we can eat it. It's even better then, because it's blessed food.'

Colin smoothed out the last of the gold wrapper to form a plate and placed the chocolate in the centre. Then he closed his eyes and bowed down, his nose tipping the floor. I felt embarrassed watching him. I closed my eyes too, for Colin had insisted that if we prayed together it would be more powerful, but my heart was a door shut against God. Nor did I have any idea who or what Lord Ganesh was.

I mouthed and muttered a few pleas. To my surprise, I felt a shudder of faith in my heart, as though it had seeped from Colin by osmosis. Then I felt afraid, for to feel faith was to be indulgent, to sink into weakness and hope that someone else might solve this for us. I knew I must keep whipping myself into facing the reality: that we, and only we alone, could get ourselves out of here.

'Okay?' I said to Colin in a fierce voice.

'Okay,' he said and suddenly we grinned at each other, sharing a ripple of frightened excitement.

Colin pulled himself up on to the window ledge, legs dangling inward. He made a confused noise and grabbed the sill, looking as though he was in danger of plunging head-first.

'Um, the other way,' I said quickly.

Colin waggled his legs.

'I mean – turn and let yourself down backwards, using the rope.'

'Oh yeah. I see.'

Colin, with much awkward arm-twisting and banging of his head against the frame, turned himself round so that his legs were now dangling outwards. He wrapped a length of rope around his hand. It looked like a bandage.

'Hang on to the sill. Then let yourself down slowly.'

'I know, I know.' He looked down past his shoulder and said, 'What if the rope doesn't hold?'

'It will – we did those strong knots, remember? Look, lower yourself down quick as you can, okay?'

'Okay.'

Colin drew in his legs. I saw eight pudgy fingers on the sill and the lopped-off, frightened top of his head.

'I've got the rope here,' I called. 'It's secure, you're okay.'

Colin's fingers uncurled, one by one. And then he was going . . . going . . . gone. I let out a silent whoop and did a giddy little dance around Napoleon. This was it. We were going to be saved. I went to the bedpost and checked that the knot was tight. Napoleon seemed to have a smirk on his face. I tried to work out whether I was superimposing it on his features or it was really a result of the sculptor's knife, until my vision blurred and his face became an abstract, a Picasso of brown shapes.

I heard a faint cry and ran to the window. I had expected to find Colin halfway down the rope. He was three inches from the window sill. His dangling body was twisted so that every inch of it was wound tightly around the rope: feet crossed, knees knocking, knuckles protruding like sticks of chalk.

'Colin?'

He opened his mouth to reply but only a gasp came out.

'Colin? Colin? Are you okay?' Was Henry below? Had Colin been shot? I had not heard a bullet. Oh God, we ought to have checked first; what idiots we were. But when I scanned the horizon, it was clear. 'What? What is it?'

He managed to squeak but his voice was too high for words, like those supersonic sounds only birds can hear.

'Colin, you have to hurry, or the rope will . . .'

'I'm afraid of heights,' Colin burst out.

A breeze laughed over my face. A smile and a grimace fought over my lips. There was a ripping sound and Colin bobbed down a few inches.

'It's breaking, it's breaking –'

'It can't be –'

'It's breaking, Oh God –'

'We did those special knots –' I broke off, and turned to the bedpost. The rope was stretching, multiplying, elongating itself. It was the lace and net that were the problem, weak links in the chain even though we'd folded them thrice. 'Okay – so you have to go down, really quick, hurry –'

'I –' Colin looked down and when he looked up again, his face was green.

'I can't move,' he whimpered. 'I'm going to fall, I'm going to fall, I'm going to fall.'

'Think of the colour blue –'

'What –'

'It might help – if you think of a soothing colour, it can cure you –'

'I don't like the colour blue, it makes me feel – I'm falling –'

'Okay, come up. Come on, give me your hand, give me your hand.' I reached out, the sill cutting into my stomach. Colin only managed to uncurl two fingers before gripping the rope again.

'Colin, take it, for God's sake, take my hand.' I brushed my tips over his hunched shoulder.

He took the plunge. He reached up suddenly and grabbed my left hand, squeezing my sawn-off fingertip. I gasped; my face went blue, my vein turned white; pain blazed into every corner of my body. I whispered at him to let go, but now he was too terrified. I forced myself to reach across the pain, to push it back and yank him up. As I did so, his whole body weight seemed to lean on my half-finger and I nearly blacked out. We toppled back into the room in a chaos of arms and legs and banging heads.

Tears exploded in the corners of my eyes. I looked down at the bandage on my hand and saw a fresh flower of blood. I held it between my knees and whimpered. The pain seemed to tremble from the very tip of my finger, shot up my spine and ripple in the roots of my teeth, making me bite and gag and gnaw my lip until blood mingled with the salt.

'I'm sorry,' Colin wept too, 'I grabbed your finger – I was just so scared – I shouldn't have gone down –'

'It's okay.'

'I wanted to be brave – I'm sorry –'

'You were brave, Colin,' I said fiercely, giving him a light punch on the shoulder and blinking back my tears. 'You were brave and it wasn't your fault it didn't work.'

'What shall we do now?' Colin whimpered. 'What shall we do? Maybe we'll have to wait until morning.'

I watched the last bars of sunset rise up the wall, bruised by the oncoming night. A third night in this house. My mind ran through a labyrinth of other possibilities, other escape routes, but it kept hitting dead ends, the centre seeming further and further away. Rage swelled in my chest. Why had fate done this to us? Why had Colin failed? Why were our prayers like dead letters? Why did Henry have food and we didn't? Why did God bless him and not us; where was the justice in that? The pain in my finger felt as though a hammer was continually being thumped against it, each stroke making it rawer and rawer, so acute I had to lash out at the world. I picked up the bust of Napoleon, ignoring the fresh shriek of agony in my finger, and took it to the window. I envisaged it hitting the ground with a satisfying smash; I wanted to see the shards fly and spin across the gravel. I heard Colin calling out and ignored him. He grabbed my arm and I elbowed him away with a howl. I lifted the bust up high; Colin reached out.

'Stop!' he cried, 'stop! Look – look what's in it?'

I frowned and drew the bust back. In its centre was a hollow, with a leather criss-cross of band holding in the treasure inside: a small, dusty bottle of red wine.

'It's going to be all right,' said Colin.

'Plan A failed, so we think up a plan B,' he said.

'I mean, we can't just give up,' he cried. 'We have to think of the others, waiting in the coach, waiting for us to save them.'

I didn't answer. The pain in my finger had lulled to a dry, persistent throb. I sat with my chin on my knees, staring out of the window. The sun had rolled across the sky and was beginning to sink tiredly between the trees. Despair passed through me like a sandstorm of grey dust; I didn't even have the energy to argue any more. I knew that there was hope, no way out, we were stuck here for ever. My eyes travelled to the bottle of wine, sitting on the boards. I didn't even have the energy to get drunk.

Napoleon sat next to the bottle, facing the wall.

'Are you hungry?' Colin asked.

I didn't reply, though my stomach did. It groaned at the thought of food, of hot dogs, of juicy meat, or dry crackers, slimy ice cream.

'The bird – the one in the sink – we should eat it.'

'Are you kidding?' I sat up; my head snapped backwards, my mouth an 'O' of outrage.

'But it's going to die anyway. You say you want to take it when you leave but it'll be dead by then – well, probably. And we can't drink the wine because then we'll get drunk and Henry will have the advantage, but if we ate the bird, then we could drink the wine and – and we need the strength,' Colin persisted. 'We need the energy. The chocolate's gone –'

'What?' My voice was like a whip. 'You ate the last bit of chocolate?'

'Well – well – I needed it to go down the rope, so I ate it just before, and you – you told me to eat it and you ate more than me anyway! And now I'm hungry!'

Silence.

'The last proper thing I ate,' Colin went on miserably, 'was two days ago. I had Marmite sandwiches for lunch. I can still taste them.'

I ignored his pleading look. But I couldn't help but picture the last thing I had eaten. Two days ago. I'd been too travel-sick on the coach to eat the day it had crashed. The day before I'd eaten some cheese sandwiches. I pictured the hard huskiness of the bread against the yellow squidginess of the cheese, the smooth cream of butter oozing between my teeth . . .

'We're not going to kill the bird, Colin.'

'Why not?'

'It's against my religion, okay?' I spat out.

I saw the look on his face and immediately regretted the words. But I wasn't in the mood for apologies. I turned away and carried on staring at the back of Napoleon's head.

Colin stayed silent for a while. Then I heard him rattling about with the chest of drawers. There was a crash as he up-ended one on the floor.

'Colin! Ssh! Are you trying to get Henry up here?'

'Sorry – but look!' Colin cried.

I looked. I looked at the spray of tissues, the books and hairpins and old cracked lipsticks and small diaries and keys and francs all tied up with yellowed string and a loop of green wool.

Something caught my eye and my interest: a collection of coloured silk scarves and a pack of playing cards. They were yellowed and old and had a strangely grotesque royal family on them: a sleazy jack, a queen wearing a mask, a king with a goatee beard and leering slits for eyes. I was puzzled by them. Some of the cards were thicker than others, and there were six aces, and only three fives, and some cards were stuck together, with glue, on either side of each other. A set for either a cheat or a magician.

'Look,' said Colin, who had been sifting carefully through the debris. He held up a small, turquoise lighter and flicked it. As the flame flared, my heart leapt. 'There's also a biro,' he said, frowning. 'I think it's just about the only other useful thing we can find.'

'Give me that,' I said quickly. I scrawled on the wall and the black ink began to flow.

'Maybe we shouldn't deface . . .' Colin trailed off as I gave him a look.

I turned away and swallowed, drawing some more and said, 'Well done. I should have thought of looking in the drawer myself, earlier. I could have done with the lighter last night.'

'You're just in shock,' Colin said gently. 'Otherwise you would have.'

'I have an idea,' I said abruptly. 'A Plan B.'

'Really?' Colin asked excitedly.

I took the biro, and on the cream wall of the bedroom I drew out a sketch of the top floor of the house and then the bottom floor:

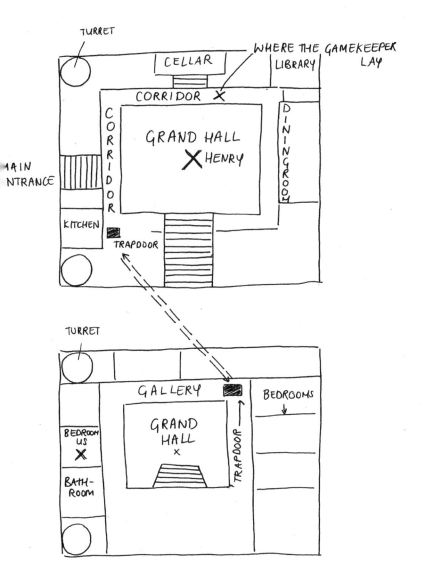

'There's a trapdoor down by the kitchen,' I said. I broke off with a yawn; Colin caught it and yawned too and then boomeranged it back to me and we laughed.

'Anyway.' I shook my head. 'There's a trapdoor down by the kitchen and another one just like it on the top floor. If we go down it, I swear they'll meet up. Then we'll come out in the corridor right next to the front entrance. We'll have to pass alongside the Grand Hall, that's the problem . . . but we can duck down low and make a run for it so Henry doesn't see us. But I think we can do it. He won't be expecting us to come out through there, he'll be looking up at the stairs, on guard there.'

'Why didn't you go down it earlier?' Colin asked, frowning. 'You could have escaped.'

'Well – I just . . . I just . . .' I broke off. 'I only discovered it . . . and then . . . I kind of forgot about it. I mean, I don't know for sure if they meet up, anyway. We just have to try, okay? Because there's no other way.'

Colin gave me a curious look, then shrugged.

'I think we should wait until 3 a.m. to go down. Maybe four. No – let's say three. The thing is, Henry has to sleep. If we go then, we'll catch him by surprise. He might even be outside. And it'll be dark, so he can't really see us. He does have a torch, though.'

'Well, we have a lighter,' said Colin defiantly, and the look on his face made me give him a jostling punch on the shoulder.

We carried on talking and plotting for a few more hours, testing the plan out, dipping into each corner, turning it inside out and back to front. Gradually we began to yawn more than we could talk and agreed that we should test a little of the wine. As we spoke and sipped, relief washed through me. We were going to be all right. Two were stronger than one; together, we would outwit Henry. Outside, the sunset melted and darkness seeped across the sky.

**W**aiting. In the bedroom. Waiting, waiting. Colin outside in the bathroom filling the water bottle. Nothing to do until 3 a.m., except run through the plan, looking for cracks and waiting. I yawned and sketched; then, nagging myself that I was wasting precious fuel, but indulging myself all the same, I flicked on the lighter, holding it up against the wall.

I looked down and saw that I was holding something black. It was *alive*. It trembled, then fought to be free; its leathery wings unfurled; yellow eyes blinked up at me. A baby bat.

I cried out and dropped it and it clattered to the floor. In the dark, I kicked out in blind fright; my foot connected with something. Then there was a rolling noise and the bang of something hitting the skirting-board.

I rubbed my eyes. Everything was fuzzy. How I loathed

this darkness that had gradually filled the house with thick ink, longed to tear it away like a curtain. I put my lighter between my teeth, tasting the plastic, and crawled across the floor cautiously. I flicked it on again, waving the flame in circles as a warning. The bat lay, as though dead, on the floor. My heart thudding. Was it playing a trick on me, luring me in? I drew closer, lowering my light. On the floor was a pen, glistening beneath the golden flicker. Not a bat, a pen. I picked it up and crawled back to the wall. Where was Colin? He was only meant to be in the corridor. How long had he been gone? What if he was in cahoots with Henry? What if this was a trap – no, no, that was crazy, I was getting paranoid. Tired and paranoid.

Every so often, a bubble rose up from the depths of my mind and popped on the surface. A vision of lifting the trapdoor and slipping down, down into the tunnel. *I can't do it*, a small voice whispered in my ear, *when the time comes I won't be able to do it, I won't be able to do it.*

Butterflies stirred in my stomach and I shouted at them to go away.

I reached for the wall, pressed my palms flat against it. I clicked on the biro and under the blind net of darkness, let its tip flow across the bumpy paintwork, the words and pictures soothing me, tranquillising the butterflies. After a while, however, my arm began to ache, and then to shake. My stomach moaned with hunger, though the moans were long and sighing, like a child who knows no matter how much he nags his parent his request will not be granted. My mind was grey with a liquid tiredness that sloshed from side to side. In places, it was beginning to solidify into exhaustion: odd throbs of pain that flickered from the back of my eyes to my temples, or suddenly pin-pricked my eyes with dots of black, taking the room and turning it upside down or stretching things sideways like those grotesque mirrors you find in funfairs.

3 a.m. Three hours to go.

Every so often, I flicked on the lighter to see what I had drawn, to inspect my blind collage of pictures:

Was that how to spell *Henri? Henri?* I asked Napoleon and his stone lips murmured a dry yes, but I was convinced he was tricking me. I held my lighter close to the H. I frowned. That didn't look right. Henri's name didn't begin with H. It began with a *huh* sound. An *uh* sound. Or was that . . . was that . . . I stared at it until the words blurred into black spiders. *Henri Henri Henri.* I repeated it over and over, tugging at the door of my memory that remained obstinately shut, until his name was no longer a word, but an essence beyond a word, and then beyond an essence, a transcendent nothingness.

**W**hat is he doing? I pondered. What is he doing right now? Sleeping, maybe? I closed my eyes and tried to picture him: below, in the Grand Hall, leaning back in a chair, legs swung up, gun slack between them, like some guy in a Mid-West movie, a smile drooping on his lips, waiting. At least I had Colin. Two against one.

'It's cold up here on the roof,' said Colin, shivering.

What is he thinking? There couldn't be much to do down there; he must have exhausted the museum cabinets by now. All that empty space to sit and think. He must think about Matthew and the others. Didn't he feel any guilt?

'I guess it's keeping us awake, though?'

A sudden, paranoid fear gripped me. What if, what if Henry wasn't down there at all?

What if he had left? Gone to find a phone. Wouldn't that be the cleanest victory? To simply leave and find a phone and tell them that his stepbrother had dragged him away, shot someone, hidden the body, gone crazy?

'My God!' I said out loud.

'What?' Colin cried.

It was just gone 2 a.m. now and we were keeping our-selves awake by sitting up on the roof of the house, looking up at the cold stars and talking, endlessly talking, keeping each other's spirits up.

'When did you last see Henry? Only, you never saw him, did you? When did we last hear him?'

'I heard a gunshot.'

'You did? When?'

'When you were down in the bedroom, drawing. Didn't you hear it?'

'No – but I . . .' I let out a deep breath; it created a white dragon in the freezing air. 'Okay. He's down there still. Okay.'

We remained in silence for a few minutes. When I looked up at the stars, I felt soothed. It took my mind off my chattering teeth by recognising and naming the glories my father had taught me. I half closed my eyes and the stars blurred into a gold bar. Their infinity was strangely impersonal, as though they looked down night after night and watched humans work and make love and sleep and make war with indifferent eyes.

'I can't understand why Henry's doing this,' Colin burst out. He chewed his lip dolefully. 'He must really hate us.'

'It's not our fault!' I cried, stung. 'He's the fucked-up one.'

'Yeah. Yeah. He's crazy.'

'You should try living with him.' I frowned too, fearing Colin was about to suggest another attempt at 'Silent Night' and negotiations, but instead he mused whimsically: 'I wish I was a magician. In the Vedas there are magicians called *sidhas* with amazing powers. They could move the sun and moon or make the weather. I could harness the wind and drive it through the hall and blow Henry away.'

'Yes . . .'

'Can we have some more wine?' Colin had brought up the bottle of wine and had it sitting between his legs. He was playing with the label, tearing off little yellow strips and rolling them into pellets and then tossing them into the darkness.

'Not yet.'

'It'll warm us up.'

'If we drink it, we'll end up drunk, we'll lose control. We've got to be sharp if we're going to beat Henry. I mean, Colin, you don't know what he's capable of, and we have to be ready for that, we have to be ready to retaliate. It's like in the Bible – well, maybe you have something similar in your Bible. If he takes an eye, we take an eye back.' I felt my hands clench into fists, the knuckles protruding like sticks of chalk.

'My religion forbids violence,' Colin said in an echo. I tensed, guilty with the memory of our fight in the woods. Then Colin looked at me and I saw in his eyes that he was thinking about the woods too; and suddenly we both laughed.

The sound shivered in the cold air and fled into the night.

'I'm sorry about . . . that . . . woods thing . . .' I said.

'It's okay. I forgive you.' Colin sighed. 'I'm hungry.' He gave me another look, but I ignored him.

Silence, for a while. Every so often, the thought took wings and darted across my mind: *You're going to have to go down into that tunnel.*

'Tell me about your worst nightmare,' said Colin.

I thought hard. I had a lot to choose from.

'Why?'

'Because if we tell each other our worst nightmares then we'll know what's happening now isn't as bad as anything that's happened in dreams and our minds, and it will make us feel better.'

I wasn't entirely convinced by Colin's theory, but I played along. Talking was certainly preferable to thinking.

'Well, I have a dream, a recurring nightmare that I have again and again,' I said. I could feel acid in my stomach at the thought of it. 'I'm in my house at home. I can hear foot-steps in the room above me, and as the footsteps move in a circle, the ceiling starts to crack and little fountains of plas-ter crumble down on to my head and my bed. I run out into the hall to climb the ladder up to the loft to tell him not to keep pacing, because it's bringing the house down, but the ladder's gone. I go into my parents' bedroom, but there's nobody there. I turn and – this bit always gets me – I grab out for the door, but just when I've curled my hand around the handle and it feels safe, I realise the door has pulled away from its hinges. I jump on to the floor in the hallway and it tips up like I'm on a ship in a storm. I try to run down the stairs, but each stair is sliding down on the other like it's folding on itself, eating itself up. I run to the bathroom and the wallpaper is sliding down the walls and the plaster is pouring down into white piles and the glass is dissolving into air. I find myself running from room to room as the house falls apart beneath my feet. I can hear the sound of footsteps in the attic above and if he'd just stop pacing then it would be okay, and I cry up at him, I yell until my voice is hoarse and I can hear my throat tearing, but he doesn't stop. And then it ends . . . well, all the end-ings are different.'

'What's the usual one?' Colin's eyes were like moons.

'Sometimes I find myself falling, falling down and it all comes crashing down on top of me and I'm buried alive.

The worst part is just before I wake up because it's dark and I'm lying under the rubble and all the crashing has stopped, but there's just silence. I can hear my breathing and that's all I can hear, and it's as though I'm buried maybe twenty feet under, deep, deep below the earth and it's not like one of those nightmares where you're buried alive and you die, because I can breathe, but I can't move, I'm suspended in blackness like a kind of earth space. I can see little particles of earth about, maybe the shadow of a worm wriggling past me, but there's not even room for me to cry out for help.'

'Gosh, that's horrible,' Colin shuddered.

'Yeah,' I said. 'Sometimes I wake up, and I'm in a cold sweat, and my heart is mad. But sometimes, actually, when I stop struggling and I just lie there, I feel almost . . . peaceful. Like I'm suspended between sleeping and waking . . . What about your worst nightmare?'

'I don't have any,' he replied abruptly. 'I have my dad, he stops me getting nightmares, 'cos I've got nothing to hide in the day that has to come out at night. I tell him everything. Like that day in the woods – I went home and told him all about it and that made it okay. You should do the same, you tell your mum about Henry, about what's happening.'

I thought about the look on her face when I had tried. The way her forehead would knit into a frown as though I was just some moaning kid who didn't want to make an effort.

'Look, I've tried. But she's kind of busy now. She's got a new job, she's working, and Henry's dad is keeping her busy and – I don't know. I don't care anyway.' I laughed and shrugged. Then I saw Colin looking at me with pity and felt a flash of anger. 'Look, I don't care, okay? I'm going to leave home soon anyway, I'm sixteen in a few months, I'm just going to pack my bags and go somewhere.'

'You care,' Colin said. 'I know you care. You pretend you're like Henry, but it's all crap. You have a good soul. You can't even kill a bird, and that's why you care and why you should talk to her,' he burst out in an impassioned rush.

He blinked as I jumped to my feet.

'Where are you going?'

'To get the bird.'

'James, I didn't mean –'

'No. You're right. We've got less than two hours to face the biggest psycho on the planet. This is no time to be soft. I'll kill the bird and then we'll meet in the bedroom, okay?'

It took me a long time to tiptoe down the steps of the turret. Every so often, black pinpricks danced across my eyes and I had to stop and rest and muster up more strength before attempting more steps. The bite of the cold air had cleared my head; now, in the heavy warmth of the house, my mind slumped with exhaustion.

At the entrance to the gallery, I let the lighter flame die, fearing Henry might spot it. I waited for a few minutes, hoping my eyes might adjust to the dark, but the darkness inside the house was too treacly for much night-vision.

As I crept into the corridor, I heard a noise from below. Henry. He was singing softly to himself:

"'Silent Night . . . Holy night . . . All is calm, all is bright . . .'"

His voice sounded ragged and out of tune and he was muddling the lyrics. I felt an unexpected flash of tenderness in my heart and I nearly called out to him. Then I caught myself roughly: *Are you out of your brain? You're getting as bad as Colin. Just use your fucking brains.*

I crept into the bathroom. The penknife was tight in my hand, the plastic indenting my palm. I kept telling myself: *I'm doing this to survive, I'm doing this to beat*

*Henry*, over and over, like a mantra.

In the bathroom, I stopped. A tap dripped. I couldn't hear the bird. Gently, I closed the door behind me.

I managed to drag myself over to the sink.

I flared the lighter. I didn't look down at the bird. I stared at my face in the mirror. Shadows danced skeletal in the hollows. My face blurred, quadrupled. I swayed again, blackness dancing in front of my eyes. And then, suddenly, I saw him. My father. I saw him in the glint of my eyes, in the curve of my cheeks, in the thin of my lips. His face in mine and his voice in my ear: *After the age of thirty, every man is responsible for his own face. That's a Japanese saying, James, did you know that?* And then, just as suddenly, my reflection was alone. I cursed and flicked the lighter again, looking desperately into every corner of the reflection as though he had hidden into a corner, but he had gone.

Down below, Henry was still singing in a ragged voice . . .

"'Sleep in heavenly peace . . . sleep in heavenly peace . . .'"

The moment I staggered back into the bedroom, I sensed at once that something was wrong. Colin flared the lighter, creating a blue halo around his body. He was sitting cross-legged, and the wine bottle was next to him, a red dribble running down the curve of its neck. I walked up close to Colin and he said, 'What?' I knew then. His breath was like a hot blast of rotting fruit.

'Colin, you've been drinking it, haven't you? You've been drinking the wine.'

'No. Did you get the bird? Where is it?'

'I can smell it on your breath.' I had his dirty collar clenched in my hand and as I shook it, it tore.

'I was thirsty,' he complained, the 's' slurring. 'I was thirsty. I only had a bit. You were gone for ages. You can have some.'

'I don't want some.'

'You can have some, go on.' He looked up at me with desperate eyes. 'There's loads left. Have some.'

'It's not the point. Colin, you're drunk, you're drunk, you stupid moron, you bastard, you idiot! We lost the bird, right! It flew away, I went in and it flew away because I left the fucking window open and now, now you've gone and drunk the wine, you idiot, I mean, how can we attack Henry if you're drunk –' I was taken aback by the anger inside me, as though my stomach had turned in on itself and was eating its own lining. But it was an anger born of despair. I had finally laid every piece of our plan in place, like a jigsaw, and he was like a clumsy kid who had pawed it into a mess.

Colin started to cry. Hearing his piteous sobbed apologies, I felt an odd sense of power, a strange and sudden flash of recognition, of what it might be like to be Henry, and why he did what he did. I knew it was cruel, to perpetuate his shame, but I did it: I yanked the lighter from his hands, went to the bottle and pulled out the shard of cork, just to see how much he had drunk. It was worse than I had thought: it was only a quarter full.

'I jus – just wanted to see what it tasted like –' he broke off, interrupted by a belch. It hung in the air like a bad smell. He giggled. Then he began to cry again.

I felt a flush of shame on my cheeks. After all, I had failed too. I had been unable to fulfil my task and kill the bird; I had hidden it in a small wicker basket in the bathroom, where it had sat bleating puzzled, making affectionate cheeps. I'd whispered a promise that I would come back for it later.

If there was a later.

'Look Colin,' I said, forcing a smile and flaring up the lighter.

He looked. I took a great big glug of wine and then wiped my mouth on my hand. I belched too. He smiled uneasily.

'Oh sod it,' I said. 'We'll just get drunk. It's all hopeless anyway.'

But now it was Colin's turn to admonish; he pulled the bottle from my fingers and set it away.

We sat in the dark for a few minutes, in silence.

'When we get back home, can we sit next to each other in class, I mean, properly?' Colin asked. 'You never wanted to sit with me in class, and I didn't know why.'

I bit back a smile and shook my head. At that moment I truly did love Colin for his naivety, for believing we were ever going to be home.

'I'll sit next to you. I already do.'

'No, but really, will you? I only want you to if you want to –'

'Colin, you're sounding like a girl.'

'Sorry.'

'But I will sit next to you, because I'd like to sit next to you,' I said, and I meant it, and we sat in more silence and this time it was warm with good feeling.

'Look,' he said, 'we still have an hour to go. You can sleep. I'll wake you. I promise. You'll feel better if you sleep, sleep's more important than the bird, than food.'

I knew it was foolish to agree, but I said yes. I lay down on the floor. My body felt strange: loose and light and strangely foreign, as though it was a collection of limbs borrowed from other bodies and sewn together. I felt my eyelids sink shut. Since I had entered the house, I had slowly felt a sense of reduction, as though the layers of my personality had been stripped off and there was nothing left but James, or perhaps not even James, just some essence of common humanity, some spark of universal soul that thumped weakly in my fading body.

Just before I drifted off, I heard Colin musing quietly, 'We have to sit next to each other, because when we get home nobody will ever understand this, will know what we've been through together . . .'

Henry had once caught me going into Sam's room but when he mentioned it to her, I had told her I was looking for a tissue and she had believed me rather than him. Since then, I'd been more careful. But now they were both enjoying their homework together downstairs.

Sam's new issue of *Teen Girl* was lying on her pillow, thick and glossy. I flicked through, eyeing up the fashion models: young girls standing in fields wearing outfits made of wool. Then I turned to a feature on 'How to Kiss'. I was so gripped by it that, too late, I suddenly became conscious of footsteps on the stairs. I quickly put the magazine back and slid under the bed. It wasn't as comfortable a hiding-place as I'd envisaged. Sam had used to collect teddy-bears and dolls, and when our father died, her passion had deepened into obsession. At one point her collection had reached a hundred and thirty, until every shelf and ledge in her bedroom was filled with something soft and grinning. Since Henry had arrived, however, she had got rid of the lot. I didn't realise she had shoved them beneath her bed. Thus, I ended up lying on a bed of toys, squashing furry faces, glassy eyes pressing into my back, claws snagging my blazer.

I was surprised when I heard his voice and Sam's giggle. Jealousy shot through me: how come Henry was allowed in her room and I wasn't?

Two sets of feet – one with thick black socks, the other palely stockinged – padded over to the bed. I saw the impression in the mattress as they sat down. I heard the rustle of the magazine as Henry picked it up and his voice, mocking: 'How to kiss the man of your dreams . . .' Sam giggled profusely.

'So have you kissed Tom yet?'

Had Henry been reading her diaries too?

'Noooo,' Sam said in her sing-song voice. Whenever I wanted to know something really important, Sam would always answer in a monosyllable, a stretched-out yeees or nooo. I waited for Henry to become irritated and I felt confused and disappointed when he merely said, 'Oh come on, I bet you have.'

'No, we haven't!' Sam squealed. 'Shush, they might hear.'

'They're not in. Come on.' Henry lowered his voice. 'How far have you gone? Have you . . .' I strained to hear but he spoke too quietly and Sam replied with a yelp.

'So, you're saying you haven't even kissed yet . . . ?'

'Kind of.'

'Well, what does "kind of" mean?'

'Well, we did and it kind of went wrong.'

'How?' The interest in Henry's voice echoed my own.

'Oh – well – this is so embarrassing . . .'

'Go on.'

*whispers.*

'Bastard,' said Henry.

'Yeah,' Sam echoed. 'Bastard.' She spoke the word uncertainly.

I heard a *thwack* and then intense giggling and 'Stop it, stop it!' and I realised that he was tickling her.

Their laughter faded and Henry said, 'Have you heard about Mum and Dad?'

'No, what?' Sam asked. 'What . . . *what?*' A giggle and a shriek. 'Hey, let me go. Just tell me. Tell me tell me tell me.'

'Okay, but only if you –' Henry's voice dropped to a whisper and Sam let out another shriek.

'No, no, I can't,' she protested.

'But it's a dare. It's only fair. You do that and then I'll tell you.'

Silence, and then Sam's small, excited voice: 'Okay.' A frown cut deep into my forehead. I pulled the stuffing out of a toy, bracing myself for the sound of their lips. But there was a rustling noise, followed by a puzzle of silence. I heard Henry sigh and Sam giggled softly and then Henry said, 'Okay, I'll tell you. I overheard Mum talking. She and Dad are getting married.'

'Oh wow. Wow.'

I closed my eyes. It's over, I thought. Henry's won. I pictured the years ahead, Henry's tortures peeling back the layers of me, until nothing was left but a raw pulp of me. I thought of the rucksack stuffed deep at the bottom of my wardrobe. On the honeymoon, I thought, as soon as they go, I'll go. I saw it all: the suit they would make me put on, the sickly smell of flowers in the church, Henry quietly taunting me all the way. Maybe I could flee on the morning of the wedding. But that would ruin it for Mum; I saw her mascara on clownish tears on her face, the bridal car roaming the streets for me. *Look after your mother*, my father had said. But surely he could never have seen this?

240

I opened my eyes and through the blur I suddenly became aware that something was wrong. Henry's feet were on the floor; the bed creaked.

'Please, Henry,' Sam was entreating him.

'You don't want them to marry. You're just like James. You're just as bad as him.'

'I'm not, I'm not, anyway, James does like you, he does.'

'Oh yeah, right. On the first day I came he showed me around like I was some piece of scum. I could tell he didn't want me here.'

'Henry, we do want you, Mum loves you, you know that, she said to me it feels as though you really are her son. She wants you to be one of the family.'

A creak. My fingers twisted against my wet, throbbing temples.

Sam's cajoling worked. Henry lay back down on the bed and began to talk, a high, whiney, girlish voice, about the death of his mother. I shifted and a teddy bear suddenly tumbled out from my left foot. I froze, but neither seemed to notice, they were too engrossed in Henry's confession . . . 'I was eating at the table, it was dinnertime, it was summer, I could smell the grass in the air, and this man just walked in. I thought he'd come to fix the meter so I just carried on eating my tea. The radio was playing in the background. The man said is your mum or dad in and I said my dad's out but my mum's upstairs on the loo, she'll be down in a minute. He went to the drawer and he was shuffling through the forks and knives and I just thought it was like the meter readings, only some sort of cutlery inspection . . .'

Sam giggled.

I was so tired, as though I was lying in a coffin made out of teddy bears and exhaustion was pouring in like embalming fluid, sealing me into their tufty ears and glassy eyes. Henry's voice began to blur away from me . . .

' . . . then Mum came downstairs and he waved the knife at her, grinning, and said –'

'Oh, Henry,' said Sam, 'he had a knife?'

'Yes, he had a knife and he said, "Give me your purse and Mum went white and I was so angry, I thought he'd come to check something, I'd trusted him and I picked up my bowl of cornflakes and threw them over him and if only I hadn't done that, if only I hadn't made him mad –'

'But it's not your fault,' said Sam.

'But it is my fault, by the time Dad came home I was hiding under the table and I could see it in his eyes when we went to the hospital that he thought it was my fault, I tried to climb on his lap and he kept pushing me away and just stared at the tiles.'

Sam said, 'He was in shock.'

'Yes, he was, but even now I can see he blames me still every second. He'd prefer it if it was just him and Mum and you two and not me, he never tells you or James off, never lays a finger on you, I'm the one nobody wants –'

'That's not true,' said Sam.

'But the worst thing is, when she died, she was carrying my sister, the sister that I should have had in her stomach, and I'm so glad I've got you, Sam, you're the sister I always wanted and –'

'Give me a hug,' said Sam, 'give me a kiss, don't you know, my mum lost a baby too, she was the same, she was meant to have a little boy after James and she lost him too, so now you're the brother we should have had . . .'

I was fully awake now. The wetness had dried on my face into an itchy prickling. Henry and Sam. Sam was *my* sister, she belonged to me. Was he playing with the line between them, or had he already dragged her over it? The thought of them together, locked in a naked embrace, jolted me with a hot, erotic flash. Then I felt sick with shame. Henry and his fucking stories. I didn't believe a word of it.

I was about to slide out, when Sam sighed and Mum called up, 'Dinner's ready!' and I heard a faint creaking and rustling and then silence and then another, 'Dinner's ready! James, James, are you up there or have you gone wandering off again!' And Henry said, 'James is hardly ever in the house now, I think he avoids me, I want him to like me but he won't', and my fingers itched to shoot out and grab his ankle and tumble him to the floor. But I let them go and then waited another ten minutes before following. 'Where were you?' Mum demanded crossly, 'I was calling you', and I yawned and rubbed my eyes and said in a shaky voice, 'Asleep', and I saw Henry and Sam roll eyes at each other.

All through dinner I waited and waited for the announcement, for the awkward clearing-of-throats and the bashful smiles and the aren't-you-happy-for-us but it never came.

**I didn't think** I'd be able to sleep, to put my trust in Colin. But as soon as I lay down, I quickly slid into a thick slumber. There were no dreams until the last few minutes before Colin woke me, and it was a strange one.

I dreamt that I was entering my house. It was empty, but for once I didn't feel afraid, for the house was full of blazing white light. I walked from the hallway into the living room. I stood and looked around the room, drinking in every detail as though I knew it would be the last time I would see it. I remembered the games of cards I'd played with Sam and my dad, the Xmas celebrations we'd shared, the love and the laughter. When I was leaving the room, the light went out. The same thing happened with all the rooms downstairs and as I walked upstairs, each step behind me dissolved into blackness. I visited every room upstairs, and as each light went out I felt a profound sense of peace. All that was left was the attic. I climbed the ladder and the board slid back and revealed a brilliant face, like the angels my father painted on his stained-glass windows, only the paintwork was gloopy and smeary on his glass wings. He smiled down at me. He reached out his hand, and said, in a voice like honey, 'You're safe now, there's no need to be –'

'James?' Colin was shaking my shoulder, holding the lighter flame above me.

'Uh hi . . .'

'Sorry to wake you . . .' He was still feeling guilty from the wine mistake. 'But . . . anyway. I don't feel drunk now, by the way.'

'It's okay. It's time, right?'

'Yes.'

I'd been so desperately tired that the sleep, though short, had refreshed me. The dream also seemed to have cleansed me in some way; a profound sense of calm filled me. I kept thinking of Henry, and waiting for that familiar feeling of fear, but it failed to penetrate the peace. It will be all right, I told myself. What will be will be.

'Ready?' I asked Colin.

'Yeah, I don't feel drunk any more.' The flagging lighter flame went out and he flicked it again. 'I –'

'Hang on. Wait. Sssh.' I paused.

'Wha –'

'Ssh. Listen,' I whispered.

'James?' a voice was calling. 'James?'

It came closer.

'James?'

*'Henry's coming.'*

He was *upstairs*. I grabbed the lighter, flicked it against my watch. 3:03 a.m. My heart felt like stone. If only Colin had just woken me ten minutes earlier, we would have made it . . .

'We should speak to him –' Colin began in a normal voice.

'Shut up!' I clamped my hand over his mouth. We struggled and I forced him down on the bed. Then there was the awful clatter of the lighter flying out of my hands and landing on the floor, somewhere in the sea of darkness. Colin cried out again and I sat on top of him, grabbed a pillow and stuffed it over his face. He went still. I peeled up a corner of the pillow. In the dark, his face was a black smudge that I hissed into: 'Shut up – unless you want Henry to shoot your finger off too, okay? Shut up, shut up!'

'Jaaaames . . . Jaaamees . . .' Henry must be out in the corridor now.

Colin and I lay still. His breaths evaporated in moist mists against my palm.

'Jaaames . . . Jaaaameees . . .' His voice was fading.

I sat up.

'If you don't keep quiet, I'll kill you, okay?' I hissed into Colin's face.

No answer.

'I said, okay?'

'Okay,' Colin whispered.

I clambered off the bed and padded out across the carpet, arms outstretched, fingers clawing darkness until they met with the panels of the door. I pressed my cheek against the grain of the wood. I heard heavy breathing; then I realised it belonged to Colin. The door was too thick for me to hear if Henry was right outside, or down the corridor, or creeping back downstairs. I hesitated and curled my hand around the twirled handle. A sweaty, shaky weakness gripped me, a loathing of having to make a decision, and a loathing of myself for not being able to make it. If I chose wrongly, would a bullet in the darkness end it all for both of us? I twisted the handle very slowly but at the last turn, it emitted an awful bat's squeak and the door opened with a heavy click. I froze. My heart pounded in my ears. I tried to hold in my breath. I couldn't hear anything; or was Henry outside, waiting, ready to . . . ?

I heard the faint creak of the floorboards as Colin came up behind me. I turned and felt his breath on my chin.

'We need to get the lighter and get out.' I spoke in a whisper more air than words. 'I think he's gone up the turret to the roof.'

'Okay.'

We knelt down on the floor, palms spreading, flat against the warmth of the carpet and the chill of the stone. I curled my fingers around something, then discovered it was a thimble. The drawer Colin had upended earlier had left a trail of false clues.

*Come on, come on, come on*, I shouted at myself. *Quick, before Henry comes back down.*

*Come on come on come on.*

I felt something again, then realised that it was Colin's foot. Our elbows bumped.

There was a whirring sound and then an orb of gold.

I could feel Colin's pleasure, so tangible in the darkness that I swallowed back my yell that he had ruined any hope at night vision. I patted him on the back and grimaced at the yellow spots in front of my eyes. I calculated, savagely, how long it would take for the darkness to thin again . . . ten minutes, perhaps? And now we had to slip down the corridor like blind men.

But we had no choice.

'Now we're going to go out into the corridor,' I whispered. 'We're going to go down through the trapdoor, and then down the tunnel to the trapdoor by the kitchen. We're sticking to the plan, okay?'

247

'Okay.'

'We'll crawl – it'll be quieter and then we can't fall. I'll go first and you hold on to my feet.'

'Okay.'

I set out across the carpet, Colin's breath circling my ankles. Reaching the door, I backed up; Colin's nose banged against my back. He let out a nervous, high-pitched giggle. Then, a second later, whispered a meek *Sorry*.

I felt like laughing myself. Lying on my back and screaming with laughter until I died of it.

Oh-so-slowly, I pulled open the door. Thank God, it did not make a noise.

It was time to enter no man's land. Better to go as fast as possible, I thought. Don't linger, don't look out for him, just move.

*But what about the tunnel*, a small boy's voice whimpered, banging his fists against my heart, *what about having to go down the tunnel and the walls pressing in –*

Shut up. Just get on, just hurry up. I crawled out quickly, padding down the carpet, a map of the gallery corridors clear in my mind. It wasn't too far to the trapdoor. Just crawl down the corridor, turn right, crawl down the corridor, and the trapdoor was in the corner. If Henry was still up on the roof, we would make it, easily.

'James,' Colin whispered.

'What?'

'Why don't we just go down the stairs?'

'No – it's too risky. He'll hear us, he'll come after us, we'll never make it – we don't have time to discuss this – this was the plan –'

And then I heard his voice in the distance.

'Jaaaameeess . . .'

I stopped. Colin stopped. We heaved in air.

I heard the sound of Henry's footsteps as he began to climb back down the turret. Within a minute, at the most, he would be on top of us.

'Quick!'

'Down the stairs – let's go back –'

'No – the trapdoor! Follow the plan!'

I crawled forwards in a tumble of arms and legs. The darkness pressed against my face like a black rag. Where was the end of the corridor, where was the turn? I swung sharply, banged my face against stone. My nasal passages stung and stung and streamed. I reached out, felt the marble bars of the gallery banisters.

Henry's footsteps on the stairs, coming closer.

I thought about standing up and running but the risk of falling in the darkness was too great. So I crawled on, touching the marble bars and feeling my way down the length, cursing silently at Colin to keep up.

'Jaaaammesss . . .'

Nearly there, nearly at the corner, just down this length and then the trapdoor.

Click . . . click . . . click . . . sang his footsteps, like exuberant gunshots.

The corner – here. I felt the stone turn.

'Colin?'

'Here,' he pant-whispered.

I kept on. My knees were raw against the carpet friction.

'Jaaammess . . . I know you're up here.' Impatient now. 'Where are you?' Almost . . . lonely. 'Where are you?'

Down the carpet – now – where was the trapdoor? I felt about but only found carpet and wall.

'Colin – I need your lighter – I can't find it –'

And then: a light. From the far end of the gallery. Henry's torch, spraying out a hose of yellow light.

It passed down the latter side of the gallery, finding nothing but bare carpet.

I crouched down, pulling Colin with me and that was when I found the edge of the trapdoor. I flung it up with a bang. I shoved Colin forwards into the tunnel, ignoring his cry.

'James? James?'

The torchlight was spiralling all over the place, slicing paths of yellow through the black.

I dropped down, felt my feet kicking against Colin. I swayed, reached out, found something wooden to hold on to.

I was about to pull the trapdoor down when I made a terrible mistake.

I looked up. I looked up and I did not see Henry, just the full, blinding glare of the torch in my face for several seconds before I swung the trapdoor down with a bang and we were in.

**A**t first there wasn't time for the fear to hit me. Colin and I were too busy blundering into each other.

'Did he see?' Colin whispered. 'Did he see us?'

'No,' I lied. 'We're okay. Just get the lighter!'

'I have!' Colin banged against my arm. 'It doesn't work. I think the fuel's running out, I can't get it to work, James –'

'Give it to me.'

I rubbed the ball of my thumb against the semi-circle of metal teeth. Nothing. Again: nothing. Again: nothing. Again nothing again nothing again nothing . . . was Henry above us? again nothing was he creeping down the corridor with his torch ready to pull up the trapdoor point his gun down and shoot blindly and again nothing again nothing again nothing –

A flame,

dancing in the dark.

I held it up, highlighting Colin's face, the rolling marbles of his eyes. I lifted it up to his hand. It was curled around a piece of beam. I lowered it to my feet. I was standing on a joist of wood – a thick beam about ten inches thick. I flickered it to the left. I saw the joists ran in two layers, above and below: thick wooden tightropes for us to stagger along.

The comforting infinity of the darkness was shattered; a sickness flared up in my stomach.

'I thought there was meant to be a ladder!' Colin cried. 'I thought we'd have to go down to get to the trapdoor downstairs . . .'

I crouched down in confusion, trying to see if there was a floor we could climb down on to. But all I could see was a knife edge of flame and darkness. I stood up.

'It will – it will,' I promised him roughly. 'There'll be a ladder, we just have to walk along the joists, follow it down.'

'Okay,' said Colin in a small voice. 'I'll go first then.'

'Well, you're in front. *Come on.*'

My thumb rolled against the lighter and the flame died out and we were in darkness again. We felt our way down the joists, our elbows knocking against the stone walls. The further we went, the more the space seemed to narrow and the ceiling began to stoop until it was brushing against the top of my head. I felt my breath begin to shorten and shake. I kept trying to still it, fearing that Colin would hear and it would multiply his terror a thousandfold. But then the panic, which had been perched in my chest, took flight. It flapped its wings and screamed up into my throat and batted against my ribcage: *Get out, get out, get out of here.* I swayed dizzily on the joist and the lighter slipped from my sweaty hands and tumbled into darkness.

'What was that? Is it Henry?'

I opened my mouth to say *nothing* but it was too dry.

'I think he might be coming down after us.'

The darkness swirled; the walls closed in. *I'm going to faint*, I panicked, gripping the joist so tightly splinters bit into my palms. *Oh, God, please don't let me faint.* I closed my eyes.

When I opened them and tried to move again, I found myself paralysed. I kept yelling at my body to move but it obstinately clung to the joists. The more I yelled at it, the more it froze.

Look at you, I yelled, look at you, you idiot. Henry isn't down here, he hasn't followed you because he knows you too well, he knows you've set your own trap and walked into it. You should have listened to Colin, you should have risked the stairs, you should have known you couldn't do this. But no. You had to try to prove that you're as brave as Colin who climbed the ravine. Well, now look at you. You're a pussy, you're a girl, now get a grip and MOVE –

'I can see light!' Colin called from ahead. 'There's some light – something – it must lead down!'

Dizziness put its hands on my shoulders and shook me. The creature in my heart sat on his haunches and screamed like a banshee. I grabbed it and held it tight: stop panicking, stop panicking, stop it. You're down here now. You can't go back. Think of Mrs Robson. Go on, think of her. See her face. You're kissing. Taste her in your mouth, taste her raw and wet. You're not in the dark, you're in an open space, on a hill. Feel her hair.

I stepped forwards.

And stopped again.

I saw her face on that day. Seven days after she had let me touch her. I was in the library, researching my project, when I saw her, in a corner, browsing. I walked up to her. She flushed. *Hi, James, what a surprise.* Silence. Then a few more stiff, stilted questions and answers. And then: her hand on my arm. Her voice soft: *James, I'm sorry. There's a line between teachers and students that should not be crossed and I'm sorry, I should never have . . . I didn't mean*

I didn't know what to do with the love inside me. I couldn't cut it away; it was rooted too deep. I tried to slash it back but it just grew back, overnight, in dreams and memories. And so the fruits of my love just fell and lay in the bottom of my stomach and slowly rotted.

And then, one afternoon after school, she had found me alone and suddenly held me. Not as a lover. Like a mother. Held me so tight, her cheek against mine, and made me feel safe, turned my love into seeds.

I heard a sob in my throat. I swayed again, ready to lie down in a ball and give up, let the darkness take me.

'James?' Colin called. 'I don't think it's what we thought.'

I staggered forwards. My body spun apart and I vomited into the darkness, coughing and retching.

'James – are you okay?'

'Yes,' I managed weakly. I sank on to the beam, crawling forwards, aware of damp sick seeping against my knees, an awful, sharp stench – I could smell the wine from earlier – forcing myself forwards like an animal being whipped, anything to get out, to get to the light, to find the light.

I came out into an open space, heaving in air, barely aware of Colin staring at me in terror, of the sick on my shirt, just aware that this wasn't right, this was all wrong, in fact.

We were in a small rectangular room, about five feet by three feet. A faint moonlight shone down in thin slices through some sort of grate in the ceiling. We stood on a wooden rim that ran along the edges of the room. In front of us was a large white oval, like the humped back of some prehistoric monster, which seemed to be made of plaster.

'What is it?' Colin cried, as though terrified the thing

might come to life and reach out with a plaster claw. 'It wasn't on the map!'

'I don't know, I don't know.' Shame stung too deep for me to admit my plan had failed. 'There must be a door somewhere, there must be. We're just not looking!'

I turned and banged my fists against the walls. They bit back against my knuckles: cruel, unrelenting.

'There has to be a door. Come on, Colin.' I fought back another wave of bile and another rush of terror, banging hard with my fists.

Colin began knocking too, and then –

A noise.

A noise that tore up through the oval –

– and then all of a sudden hard, jagged white birds were flying towards us and Colin clung to me, petrified.

I lifted my head slowly. Colin kept his buried tight in my chest; there was white dust in his greasy hair.

I realised that we had not been attacked by white birds but plaster. The oval now had a hole in it, and it had been made by a gunshot. Henry had calculated the path of the tunnel and now he was below us . . . in . . . the kitchen? I tried to redraw the map in my mind but my head swam and the lines and names blurred in my anger that I had messed up, muddled the routes, led us straight into a no man's land.

Henry called something up, but I couldn't decipher his words. Another gunshot; and this one made a huge dent in the oval's fragile loveliness, spraying plaster all over us.

'We have to go back up the tunnel,' Colin whimpered.

'We can't!' The thought of that darkness closing in on me scared me more than getting shot.

'He's going to get us, he's going to –'

Another gunshot, aimed at the rim of the oval. Colin panicked and dived away, straight on to the oval, one hand curled around the edges of its bleeding holes. I heard a cracking sound and my heart jumped. Tiny spider's-web cracks were running all over the plaster egg. Then a large chunk snapped clean away and Colin half fell and hung from a jagged edge. I looked down and saw Henry below. I realised then that the oval formed the curve of a ceiling. The torchlight blinded me. I screamed at him to turn it off. The light fell and I saw his dark shape jump on to something – a desk? – and realised we were above the library. He took hold of Colin's leg, crying 'I've got you, just jump!' and Colin started yelling at me, 'Help me, he's got me, he's got me!' and before I could reach for him, he had gone and the light spun away and two bodies half fell on the desk and on to the carpet.

'Here!' Henry stood below me, the torch wedged in his mouth, arms spread out like a crucifix. 'Come on, jump! I'll catch you!'

I looked down at Colin's eyes, moons in the flare of the torch; I looked back down the tunnel that led into random darkness.

I jumped.

And hit

hardness.

Darkness. Voices, like ribbons of light, spangles in the black. A light prised beneath my lids but when I tried to open them up I couldn't; the energy I needed seemed as great as lifting heavy weights.

I swam in the darkness, swam through the waves.

Then my head bobbed up gasping. I was in a room. It was hot, the air exhausted with heat. I knew this room; it was familiar. The sunlight beating down through the windows, lying on me like brown glass. The air rotten with freshly cut grass. I turned and saw him. My father. Sitting up in bed, smiling, smiling; my mother and Sam had gone out to the shops. Left me to look after him, left me to watch him heave his last breath and then exhale as though too tired to be alive any more, his head flopping like a broken puppet's on the pillow. No pulse, no breath. My breath desperate in his empty mouth. Running through the house, screaming for somebody to help me. I could hear my screams now, as the house collapsed in on me and then I was lying deep, deep beneath the rubble, and thousands of years had passed. I kept fighting against it, feeling things spray and hit me and thump, I kept searching through the layers of debris for a light, but there was no light: I had been buried alive.

'Leave me alone!'

'Come on, he's all right, he's awake, see?'

Arrows pierced my eyes; I saw a bird flying across the sheen of white light, laughing and squawking. *Come on, Dad, look, look at him, fly, James, look at him fly!*

'Don't do that –'

'He's all right. I broke his fall, see?' Henry. Henry's voice.

'You were meant to catch him!' Colin cried.

'I did catch him. I can't help it if his aim was terrible, if he deliberately tried to miss me.'

'I think he's got concussion.'

'He's all right, he's all right.'

I became aware of pain, singing through me with abstract notes, moving from arm to leg to torso and then settling in my arm, raising its voice to a higher octave.

'Get up, sleepy boy,' said Henry. I peeled open my eyes and he stared down at me. I noticed he had a new gun; this one a revolver or a pistol. He poked it into my shoulder. 'I've got something to show you. You're going to love this.'

As I staggered to my feet, I felt as though my body was a collection of glass fragments that might spin apart at the slightest knock. In the corner of my vision, a black bird seemed to fly round and round in dizzy circles before soaring into the dark edges of the library and disappearing. And there was just Colin, looking scared, and Henry, looking smug; and a torch; and the never-ending darkness, a night that seemed to be lasting for ever.

'Come on.' Henry banged the barrel of the gun against Colin's back and he yelped and stumbled forwards. I followed him into the Grand Hall. From over my shoulder, Henry waved the torch over the museum cabinets and the hanging cage. 'You Colin – get into the cage. And you – James – get over there.' The torch-beam rested on the gleaming blade of the guillotine.

'There's this story in the Vedas, Henry,' Colin calls out in a shaky voice. 'It's about – about Y-Yama. Yama means death and he goes to look for a man's karma but he can't find it anywhere. He goes looking all through the heavens, and earth, and hell, but he can't find it, and so he can't kill the man. And then finally he finds the man and he's at the top of the mountain surrounded by white light and Yama tries to reach out to take him but he can't penetrate the white light. The man has no karma, because he's transcended time and burnt his karma away and he's free for ever and even death can't hurt him . . . B-but you can't escape Yama, Henry, what you do to us will come back and be done to you.' He begins to cough and breaks off, retching up saliva.

'Uh huh. Sure, Colin. That makes a lot of sense.'

Henry lays the torch down so that it shines like a line of rope between us. There is just enough light to see Colin looking out through the cage with big, scared eyes. In my heart I feel a deep regret that Colin ever got involved, got dragged into our private war, like an innocent civilian damaged by a misguided bomb. I look up and see Henry's face, a harlequin of black and pale yellow. His eyes look like hollows, his face skeletal. I cannot win this fight, and

259

he knows it too. My eyes linger over his face, searching, searching for a crack. What is Henry's fatal flaw? What is the key that unlocks him? His mother . . . she is part of it. But I can only see how she might shape the colour of the key, not how its jagged edges might be made to fit and turn. Maybe he doesn't want to be here either, maybe he longs to be back at home, safe in bed, clean in a bath, maybe he feels compelled now to drive this through to the end?

'If you want to let Colin out – without me shooting him – there'll be a forfeit,' Henry says.

'Whatever you say.'

'You have to put your head on the guillotine, and then close your eyes. Then I'll let him go.'

'All right.'

I see surprise on his face.

'No, James,' Colin calls from the cage. 'No!'

'It's all right, Colin,' I say. I turn back to Henry. 'You promise me if I do this, you won't harm Colin.'

'I promise,' says Henry. He looks a bit confused.

'Okay.'

'Go on then.'

I go over to the guillotine. I am surprised at my calm. A part of me feels as though it has separated from the panic and pain of my body and is watching from above, aloof and pure.

As I gaze at the blade, I hear the clink of keys as Henry unlocks Colin's cage, and Henry warning Colin that he is holding the gun and if Colin interferes, he will be forced to retaliate.

I lay down my head and feel the wooden curve scoop around my neck like a glove. Henry stands by my side. He runs his fingers over the back of my neck and I shiver. I can hear a sobbing noise from behind me. I want to tell Colin that it's all right. I want to say: It's all right, don't worry, Henry won't go that far. I don't think he'll go that far.

'Ready, James?' Henry says, softly.

Henry's finger is on the button. I realise that perhaps Henry is not playing a game. Possibilities flitter through my mind with wild wings: I can stop. I can scream, I can turn and grab him, I can dart away at the last minute, I can I can I can. But then the thoughts droop like dying insects at the end of summer, fall exhausted to the floor of my mind. I am no longer watching myself from above; I am flesh and blood, here and now, and I feel so heavy, as though my skin is straining to hold my parts intact. My head hurts, my leg hurts, my finger hurts. I feel old. I feel like my father must have felt when cancer turned him inside out and ate him and spat out the roughness and ate him again. I don't want to go home, I don't want to be found, I just want to be in a green place with laughter and my father's hand in mine. I am ready.

I can sense Henry is pausing, confused, waiting for my cries, my pleas. My blankness is interrupted by a brief flicker of victory. Henry is a parasite that feeds on fear and in my lack of struggle, my pure surrender, my white flag, I have in my own small way, won. I think of how pleased my father will be when he sees me, of how I will tell him all of this, of how I will talk and talk until my voice grows hoarse, and then there is the sound of the blade falling and Colin's screams and a gush of air pouring over the back of my neck and a fury slams against my chest that Henry has won, it's not fair, Henry has won he's won –

'**D**'you have a girlfriend?'

We were standing in the garage when he asked the question.

My father liked teaching me stuff – the names of wild flowers, how to tame a fox, how to fix a bike. What I loved about my father was that he never treated me like a kid and made me sit on the side, having to Watch and Learn. Even when I was six or seven years old and we made a go-kart, he let me saw the wood myself, standing close behind me but never touching, let me sketch up the designs and paint the sides red and green.

That morning, we were standing side by side, painting stained-glass windows. My father hadn't given me any tips; he just let me get on with it. Our subject matter was the same, only my father's was an elegant, willowy angel whilst mine looked like a white UFO blob. And then he said it. *D'you have a girlfriend?*

My ears burned. I wondered if he was about to say 'Once upon a time, James, there were Birds and there were Bees . . .' I wondered if for the first time in my life he might disappoint me. If we were going to follow the same pattern as my friends and their fathers, slowly drift from friends to strangers to enemies.

'No, I don't,' I said at last.

Silence. We carried on painting. I pretended to be unaware of the glance he shot me.

Then he let out a sigh and said, 'Ah well. Love isn't easy, anyway, James. In fact, love can sometimes be a fucking pain in the backside.'

My father hardly ever swore; I let out a gasp of delighted, shocked laughter.

'I'm serious,' he said, looking at me with stern eyes. 'Love can sometimes bring you more pain than happiness. You don't realise that when you're . . . I mean, you watch the movies and you think love is going to be this great thing. Maybe I shouldn't be telling you this; maybe I shouldn't spoil your innocence.'

I nodded, looking down, though I didn't have a clue what he was talking about. His bewilderment frightened me a little.

'So don't worry if you don't have a girlfriend. I mean, when I was thirteen, it was such a big deal to me to get one. I laugh when I look back and think about how I agonised over that. Love isn't a big deal, not romantic love.'

'Love isn't important,' I echoed him, muttering.

'James,' he said, in a cross, gentle voice, 'I'm not saying love isn't important. Love is very important. But you can find love in all kinds of places – with your friends, with your family, for your teacher, or just a simple, everyday love of life.'

'Uh huh.' I drew a thin, shaky halo around my angel. It looked like a helmet. As we painted, I thought vaguely on his words, but they drifted away. I thought of all the things we were going to do that summer now that school was up. We had plans, we had Big Plans. We were going to go camping together and catch fish; we were going to climb trees and search for eggs; we were going to keep sketchbooks and draw nature; we were going to make our own computer game and it would be the best game in the world and then we'd become millionaires: it was all stretching out ahead of us like a beach, and a raw feeling suddenly burned in my heart for him, an urge to fling my arms around him, and I thought that if there was a love that existed that had value, it was my love for my father. But I didn't, I just carried on painting and then my father examined my effort and said it was excellent and then we went out to cook lunch for Mum and Sam.

'**I**t's a miracle!' Colin gasps.

'It's magic,' Henry snorts.

'It's a miracle, it's a miracle.'

There are tears in Colin's voice. Henry swings the torch to his face and Colin ducks from the light.

The blade has fallen and I am still lying with my neck on the block. I wriggle slightly, feeling the pull of the veins and muscles that link my shoulders to my head. I rub my thumb against the knobble at the top of my spine. I hardly dare rise, afraid that the moment I move, my head will sever and thump into the basket.

The click of footsteps. The torch slices on my neck like a second cut, then slides up to the guillotine.

'The owner', Henry says crisply, 'was a magician. There's a most interesting little pamphlet about him in one of the museum cases, how he used to entertain his kids with amateur shows, and this guillotine always went down a treat, until the day he put his daughter on the block and forgot that the safety catch wasn't on. It was the safety catch that saved you, James. See – there's this little black button at the top, and this slides like so, so . . .'

I let Henry rant on with his rubbish story in his smug

voice. I smile as I rise and stand up shakily. I nod as I step
backwards. I say 'Really?' and even manage some *mmms* as
though he is a fascinating tour guide. I reach for Colin,
clutch his elbow and whisper, 'Go!'

'What?'

'Go! Run!'

'I can't leave you behind, James –'

'*Go!*'

Henry senses a conspiracy. The torch swings over. Colin
freezes. I feel the whoosh of air echo over my neck again, as
though the blade had a breath.

And then Colin moves. He runs out of the torchlight,
beyond its fuzzy white halo, and into the darkness. There is
a thump as he hits a cabinet, and my heart contracts. Then
the slam of his footsteps again as he leaves the hall. There is
a sudden blazing ribbon-flash of blue-white, like a small,
intense burst of lightning. But Henry's shot has missed; the
footsteps clamber down the stairs; Colin is inches from the
front door. Henry puts down the gun and makes to run. I
lunge at him. The torch flies from his grasp, hits the floor
and rolls over and over, spinning undulations of light. The
light stops and highlights his body, breathing sharply, the
arch of his knees as he rises again. I feel close to collapse
but I cannot let him get Colin, my last hope. I spot the
museum cabinet and as Henry reaches out to grab it and
pull himself up, I hurl myself forwards. I feel the sharp
wooden edge punching my stomach and then the cabinet
topples and I hear glass shattering and the darkness is sliced
open by flying shards. Torture instruments fly and fall.
Henry returns to the floor. Silence. In the line of torchlight,
I can see the scorpion instrument lying with a bent-up tail,
spine broken. I hear heavy breathing.

'Henry?'

In the distance, a slam of the door. Colin has made it. My heart swells with pride for him and sweet victory sings inside me: Oh thank God, Oh thank God. I calculate how long it will take for him to hurry down the drive, through the forest, find help. And then they have to believe him, translate his bad French, find us. An hour? Too long; they will come too late. But they are coming. Oh thank God, they are coming; and Colin is safe; and Colin, more than anyone, deserves to be safe.

I grab the torch, stopping its spin of light and turn its hose on Henry. He is on his haunches. Blood zig-zagging on his face, his eyes white-blue with the intensity of his fury. I feel the echo of the air-whoosh on my neck and I picture the blade, slicing and thumping as my head falls into the basket. He lets out a groan, 'I'm going to get you for that', but he is too exhausted to rise. He ducks his head, as though trying to wave away the blinding beam of light. I keep telling myself to run, but I am transfixed by his face, caught in that light. The thought of the outside, of the world beyond what we have created here, suddenly seems more terrifying.

Henry is trying to crawl under a museum cabinet. At first I am fooled into thinking he is giving up, forced by exhaustion into surrender. Then I realise.

He nearly makes it but I run and kick it and we listen to the noise of the gun slithering across the floor and hitting a stone wall with a bang.

'See?' I hiss. 'We're staying here until Colin comes back.'

Dribble spools from Henry's lips and he blinks his eyes, shaking his head blearily.

Then he begins to laugh. The laughter echoes around the

hall, mocking me, until I want to put my hands over my ears. I feel anger rise in my chest, and I try to push it back, I keep telling myself not to lose control, not when the police are so close, just to stay calm and see this out; but every chuckle is like a fist punching my heart and it cannot help but clench and snarl back in rage.

'Shut up.'

His laughter increases. He rolls on the floor.

'I said, SHUT UP, OKAY?' And then I break. I go running through the darkness, the torch slicing a path. I stumble, I find the gun. I go back to Henry. I grab the back of his collar. He lets out a squeal of surprise and laughs. My arm, still sore from the fall, sings with pain as I hoist him over to the guillotine. I let him go and Henry collapses, his head falling into the curved groove, only he's the wrong way up: facing me.

But he's stopped laughing.

I reach up for the safety catch and then draw back, gulping in air. Henry widens his eyes. For the first time, I see fear in them.

'Let me go.'

'I've got the gun now.' My arm aches as I hold it up; my knees buckle, aching to lie still.

'You said Colin's coming back.'

'So?'

'I'll make a pact with you.'

'What pact? What? I'm not playing your stupid games any more. What?'

'I've got something to tell you. Something you don't know.'

I reach for the safety catch and flick it off. I stare at the black button, the smudge of Henry's fingerprint when he pressed it for me.

'Like what, you're going to tell me how you killed your mother? Don't move, I've got the gun, I said I've got the gun, okay?!'

'I didn't kill her –'

'You did. After the Knife Incident, my mum took me for a talk and she told me all about that mugger –'

'D'you want to know what your mum really wanted to tell you that afternoon?'

'What?' I rub my face. My legs tremble and I force them to still. Suddenly my exhausted mind is zinging and alert; my thoughts stretch out like quivering antennae. I sense for once Henry isn't playing games. His voice isn't sing-song any more. It has a reasoning quality to it; he sounds like a grown-up.

'She was going to tell you something else. I mean, it was an accident and I didn't kill my mother, because she isn't my mother.'

'Oh, who is she then? The Hunchback of Notre Dame? Sure, Henry, she's not your mother.'

'You think you know everything, James, but you know fuck all. Your mum thinks you're too young to know the truth, because you're Baby James, little James-y-boy who –'

'DO YOU WANT ME TO PRESS THIS BUTTON?'

'Our mum and my dad have been screwing each other for the last sixteen years.'

I shine the torch on the gleaming blade. Then I lower it to his face.

'No they haven't.' I keep my voice steady now. 'My dad only died six months ago, they can't have, my mum and him have been married for twenty years, you idiot, you don't know anything . . .' Words trail off into weariness. The house is closing in on me, the darkness pressing down on my face like a thick cloth. I want to curl up on my own and sleep, to be out of these spinning loops of taunts.

'Are you some kind of idiot?' His voice is savage, fragile. 'What kind of naive idiot are you? I mean, you think that people get married and then, oh, they can't be in love with anyone else because, oh, they're married. D'you think it's that simple?'

I lean over him, and he keeps talking, jabbering, his breath sour on my face, and though I can see his eyes twitching and cheek muscles flexing and mouth moving, he seems distanced, at the end of a tunnel. I watch his tongue flick and curl in his mouth, hypnotised, my mind whirring. It's like those movies where suddenly everything goes in reverse: toppled buildings stand upright, day-clouds surf back into the pitch-black of night, lava pours back into a volcano, a row of crashed dominoes rising back up. Rising back, all painted with different scenes of my life, of mum and dad's life.

' . . . your mum is my mum. You might have a different dad, but your mum is my mum, okay?'

'No,' I said. 'No.'

'Your dad wasn't any good at fucking so mum had to look somewhere else and that's why she fell in love with my dad, and your dad –'

'No, no –'

'– and your dad –' he is screaming in my face now '– your dad knew all about it only he never said anything 'cos he was too much of a wimp to tell her where to go, he just put up with it and that's why he got cancer, it drove him mad, it screwed him up and –'

'*NO!*' I reach for the button, my finger nearly a pressure against it. Henry – my brother – screams. His eyes are white with terror. I stare into those blue eyes and I see my mother looking back at me and then with a whimper I drop the torch and I run.

**A**t the main entrance, I stop.

I stand in the open doorway, teeter on the threshold. The night air whiplashes me; the starlit darkness is startlingly light after the intensity of the house. Everything is big and swooping: the trees stand like sentinels, ready to trap me; the gravel path seems an ocean. It terrifies me; I want to be back in the cramped safety of the house. I find myself turning back.

I realise then that I am still carrying the gun. I look down at it. How heavy it feels in my palm. A teardrop splashes on to it, then trickles down its black spine.

*Your mum is my mum. You might have a different dad, but your mum is my mum, okay?*

I have to go somewhere, do something. I want to be someone else, I want to flee the cage of my mind. *Your dad wasn't any good at fucking so mum had to look somewhere else and that's why she fell in love with my dad and your dad –*

I run down the hallway. I hear Henry call after me but I don't care. I find the trapdoor and shove it up. I toss the gun down into the darkness and it goes off with a bang. I jump violently and Henry cries out again.

The dark space still terrifies me, but now it also tempts me. I want to curl up in it like a womb; I want it to choke me into a ball; I want to be so scared my fear drives out his words, for terror to fill my mind so that there is no space for this tidal wave of pain I am holding back with both hands.

I forget the ladder has broken until it is too late. It comes away from the wall and I find myself slipping, banging, crying out; the last thing I see before I fall is Henry's face peering down at me.

The fall is not far but I hit the floor with a jolt. Pain screams through me, shooting up my spine and in lightning flashes across my ribcage. I relish it; I feel it roll around my body and tears stream down my cheeks. *Oh Dad, oh Dad, it can't be true, this can't be true, can it, it can't be true.*

I lie there in the tunnel. Musty smells fill my nostrils. Shivers of pain and fear wrack my body. *Oh Dad.* I feel as though I will die here in this dark place, as though I will never find light again.

'I'm coming down,' Henry calls. 'James, I'm coming down.'

'Leave me alone,' I call weakly. 'Oh God, just leave me alone.'

I roll up and scrabble about for the gun, curling, hiding it behind me. Henry lowers himself into the tunnel, then there is a bang and the faint sound of him groaning. I back up against a wall that feels damp and smeary with mud.

Silence. Henry's shaky breaths slow. I curl up tight, the gun poking into my leg.

'You were lying, weren't you?' My voice catches and I straighten it out. 'You were lying about my dad. Just another story.'

'No.'

'Liar liar liar.' I swallow. All those Sundays, all those nights Mum told us she was seeing friends and my father locked himself away in the garage, painting those stupid stained-glass windows; did he know? Of course he knew. 'How d'you know anyway?' Then something clicks into place, something that never seemed right. 'My mum – she lost a baby. She lost one and –'

'No, she never lost a baby. That was just a story.' Henry sounds weary now, his voice losing texture. 'Just after you were born, she got pregnant with me. And she had me – I was that baby. My dad took me home and she felt she should just tell you she'd lost the baby, she felt she couldn't handle the truth, you were too young –'

'You're lying, you're lying. God, you're fucked up, you know that?'

'Mum –'

'*Mum* – God, you wish – you're lying.'

'She used to come and see me. Every Sunday, she used to come and see me. She'd see my father.'

'My dad would never have stood for it, you're lying. He wouldn't have let her go –'

'He told her to go.'

'Liar. All lies, all lies . . .' And yet. The feel of all those Sundays haunts me: the street quiet, the house empty, church bells poignant in the distance. The way Mum could come home and there would be something sharp and strange in the atmosphere. And then I remember that one Sunday, when I was about five or six when she came home my father kissed her hello and she burst into tears. She sat down on the sofa and cried and cried and cried. I remember the bewildered fear; I had never seen an adult cry before. I

kept on tugging Dad's sleeve and asking what was wrong –
I felt too afraid to ask her myself; she suddenly seemed a
stranger to me and I was anxious for my real, sunny, invin-
cible mother to return. My mother suddenly sniffed, looked
me straight in the eye, and then she told me. About the
'miscarriage', though I was too young to understand the
word; six years ago you lost a brother, she explained, but
you were too little to know at the time. Every Sunday I go
to visit his grave. Dad cut in and told me to go to the
kitchen and get her some water, or fetch her a biscuit. They
lay uneaten on the table by her. I asked Dad if we could go
and visit the baby's grave and he wept too, then. Later, he
went into his garage and didn't come out for dinner and
Mum cooked me fish fingers, my favourite, and she kept
sniffing and ruffling my hair and telling me everything was
okay.

Now I realise she was crying because she had lost a baby,
in a way. Given him up to his father –

'Your dad didn't want to leave her,' Henry interrupts my
swirl of thought. 'He kept begging her to stay, even if it
meant she didn't love him, even if she just lived with him
for your sake. She kept telling him she was going to leave
him, but he couldn't bear it, he said it wasn't fair on you.
That's the only reason she had Sam – to try to paper over
the cracks.'

'What? That doesn't make any sense. Nobody has a baby
for that reason.'

'You know so little about the real world, James. In the
end, he only got her to stay by threatening to take her to
court and get you. He said he'd win because she was having
an affair. That's the only reason she stayed – not because
she loved him but –'

'Oh shut up, okay, shut up!' I yell and he is silent.

I sit there for a few minutes, shaking violently. And I know that Henry has won. Nothing that he has done to me so far has hurt me like this; the pain keeps ballooning and ballooning, filling up until the edges of my heart feel they will split open. I sink down into the tunnel, mud harsh against my cheek. I hear Henry call, faintly, 'Are you all right?' His voice is distant. I can feel the gun sweaty in my palms. I raise it to my temple, feel it cool against the skin. Oh Dad, why didn't you tell me? Even when you died, when I was trapped in that hot room, in those last minutes, you were smiling, forcing that smile across your lips and teeth, trying to pretend everything was okay. I taste tears, snot in my mouth. You could have left Mum, you could have taken me away. We could have lived in the country, I could have been taught lessons at home by you. You'd be happy, you'd still be alive, oh Dad, why didn't you tell me?

*I want to be with you.*

'James!' Henry leans over me, eyes straining in the darkness. And then he sees. 'Fuck. Give me the gun.'

'You've won,' I whisper. 'You've won. I hope you're happy now.'

'Give me the gun.'

Henry's hand closes tight and hot around mine.

'I want it to be over,' he says desperately. 'I don't want you to die, give me the gun, James, give me the gun, I don't want you to do this, don't do this. Your dad wouldn't want you to do this.'

His words jolt me. I look up into his eyes and a wave of relief rolls through me. Dad wouldn't want me to do this. I understand now. It's not my fault. Not my fault for not being – a good enough – son? – for not being a good

276

enough, good enough. All those prayers weren't wasted, Dad. You didn't die because of me, and you'll never die, I'll always keep you alive in my mind, always.

My hand slackens and Henry takes the gun away and lays it down in the tunnel.

'She's my mum too, you know,' he says in a trembling voice. 'She's my mum too.'

For a moment, there, when he took the gun away, I almost loved him. In an instant, the coin tosses again and lands on its other side. All these weeks, these months, these years that nobody has told me anything. I've just been stupid James, not worth telling the truth to. All those times Henry has taunted me and known everything while I knew nothing.

My rage erupts.

'But she doesn't love you,' I yell. 'She only saw you on weekends, she never loved you that much!'

And then I hurl myself at him. The gun goes skidding down the tunnel, but I don't care about it any more. I want to kill him with my bare hands.

I throw punches into him, then stop to gasp breath. He is crying too now, I can feel his body shaking, tears falling on my cheeks. Can I love him, Dad, can I love him for you? But I put my fingers around his throat and I see her in his eyes again and I want to blot those eyes out until they are empty, I want to kill whatever parts of her are in him.

And now it's too late and I can't say sorry, I can't wave a white flag because I can't – *breathe* – have to fight back have to Dad have to fight back have to.

**W**e both hold on tightly, thumbs against throats. We hear each other hissing for breath. I think: *We're both going to die. This is crazy.* I want to say to him, *If you let go, I'll let go.* But I can't speak, and I do not remove my thumbs.

Somewhere in the distance, I can hear footsteps. Colin? In the periphery of my vision, I see a swerve of light sweep across the edges of the tunnel entrance. I want to raise my head, but I can't.

The light provokes a desperate panic in me. I want it, want to claw after it, drink it in, be safe. But the light is fading away as black spots flower in front of my eyes. I realise: *We're not going to die together. One of us will die first and let go, and the other will be able to breathe.* And I summon every last drop of anger and energy into my pale body and force it into my thumbs and squeeze so hard I feel as though my thumbs will burst through his skin and into his throat.

*Let go, James, just let go. Wait for next time.*
*I can't I can't can't let him beat me, take every last thing from me –*

278

The footsteps. They're getting closer. Oh, my throat! My body is screaming in every cell. My feet kick and curl in the dust. Come quicker, come quicker. It's as though my throat is a rope being tied into tighter and tighter knots. A sharp pain spreads across my brain. A high-pitched ringing in my ears, like the E string on my violin wound up too tight. My thoughts are weak and sticky and colours become white. The tunnel seems to narrow into a dark line with a tiny light-spark bobbing at the end.

It's as though each part of my mind is shutting down in turn, like the lights in a house being turned off, one by one.

*Don't let go. Hang on to him hang on him Henry Henry Hen-ree please don't let me die I'm sixteen I haven't kissed Mrs Robson yet haven't*
    *Just want this to be over just want to try can't you just let go let's try to be, for the sake of my father, let's try to be –*

Suddenly, I have a clear vision. A policeman has come, come to save us. Or has he? I can't feel Henry any more can't feel anything any more. Because he's torn us apart and I was lying in the mud and now I'm in the back of a car. The leather against the back of my neck. My mother beside me. She's holding my hand and her other hand is stroking my hair softly. She's telling me, softly, that sometimes adults can love more than one person at the same time and she will never stop loving my father. I lean my cheek against her shoulder and she doesn't mind the blood that oozes on to her sleeve and we're driving down the sleepy French road and the first sun is washing over me like a baptism.

But I'm not there, I'm not there, I'm lying in the tunnel, I open my wet eyes and I see his face, and I see me in his snarl his eyes his mouth and I scream *HENRY* and I can hear footsteps behind me and I see his eyes close as mine close and

I'm in the back of the car, and I can feel her hand this is real I can feel it I'm safe now I'm alive or am I

and someone is asking are you awake now James are you awake

someone is saying, *Garçons?*

**H**enry's fingers fall away.

Light pierces my eyes.

Air sucks into my lungs, pierces my bruised throat like a vampire's kiss.

Henry gasps, 'He's come back!'

A torch, a face glaring at the top of the tunnel.

My sickly eyes spool and focus as Henry grips my hand.

The gamekeeper.

'I thought you said you'd shot him!' I whimpered.

'No, no, I never did, I was just saying that to . . . oh God, he's come back, he's come back to get us, oh God . . .'

'**G**arçons! Ça va?'

Henry and I both try to crawl back down the tunnel at the same time; Henry ends up clambering on top of me and we both tussle in a desperate scramble of arms and legs.

'Where's the gun?' Henry hisses. 'We need the gun.' He starts to sob. 'Oh God, we need the gun –'

'No! No! We can't, no, Henry, I won't let you –'

'*Laissez-moi vous aider, c'est bon, je suis là pour vous aider . . .*'

The gamekeeper stretches out a hand. His muscles shine like ribbons beneath the torchlight, which lights up every dark spindly hair on his arm.

'Oh God, oh God, oh God,' Henry is muttering.

We both shrink back against the mud wall.

'*Allez, montez! Je sais que vous n'êtes pas les voleurs, c'est bon de monter.*'

Just the sound of his voice and I'm back in the cellar, the scent of apples like knives in my nostrils and I know if I ever get out of here alive I will never be able to eat apples again and I can feel the gun digging against my hip and I dare not move, terrified Henry might discover it.

'Leave us alone!' Henry whimpers, his voice hoarse. 'Leave us alone!'

The torch lingers on Henry's face, smeared with dirt and desperation. I stare into his eyes and picture in that moment how it might have been for him, as a boy, six or seven, waiting in the porch every Sunday for my mum to come and see him, knowing even as she scooped him up in her arms that in a few hours she would be gone, leaving behind her perfume and empty embraces.

I want to live. I want us both to live.

'Please,' I call up to the gamekeeper. 'We're not thieves. Do you understand, we're not –'

'Where's the gun, where's the gun?' Henry's fingers are scrabbling about in the dirt. 'James where's the gun –'

Then, another voice. The torchlight slithers back up the tunnel, like a cat up a tree and we're left in darkness. Our terrified breaths mingle into one. Then another torch, a fatter, brighter, square beam, and another face: an elfish, craggy face, with a black moustache.

'*Ils refusent de monter,*' the gamekeeper cries.

'These boys are Engleesh,' the man with the moustache says, 'you need to try Engleessh. You – you boys – you will come up? How long have you been down here?'

'It's a trap.' Henry digs his fingers in my arm. 'It's a trap.'

'You are safe, your class, there was a crash, yes?'

'Yes,' I cry up, but Henry slams his hand over my mouth. I tear it away. 'He's here to help us, don't you see, Colin got help –'

'No.' Henry is hysterical now. 'No.'

'Listen.' The man leans in a little more and I see the black collar of a policeman's uniform slicing into his neck. 'The gamekeeper here – he understands you boys are not here for trouble – there was a mistake – we understand – now we must help you up. You are safe now.'

I look up at the policeman and I see compassion in his dark eyes. After all the cruelties I have suffered, the simplicity of that emotion makes my heart bleed with relief.

I reach up and grab his hand. He groans with the weight of me. My nails tear into the earth walls as I scrabble to climb up.

'It's all right, Henry,' I keep crying, 'it's all right.'

As the policeman pulls me out, the gamekeeper tries to help but he stumbles on his injured leg. I scream at the feel of his hands on my body but then I am up, up and out and the gamekeeper staggers upright and nods at me gruffly and I look down into the tunnel where the policeman stretches out his hand once more.

Under the glare of the torchlight, Henry curls into a ball.

**W**e walk down the gravel driveway. I can see the ghostly shapes of police cars at the far end. Henry and I stagger like drunkards on either side of the policeman. The gamekeeper walks a little way ahead of us, dragging his hurt leg. My gaze slides down, expecting to see a trail of blood following him. I shake myself.

A breeze caresses my face upwards and the beauty of it hits me and my fear drops away. After the curse of the house, this is Eden. The air fresh as apples. The arc of sky above, blazing stars, hints of dawn bleeding into the horizon. The trees, evergreens, with splayed frayed leaves; I want to walk over to them and trail my fingers through their spiky greenness, to know all of this is real.

But what if, what if I am being taken to a place where the air is dead and there are no trees, only stone?

I turn to the policeman desperately.

'I didn't mean to shoot the gamekeeper,' I say shakily, lowering my voice, scared he will hear and turn on me. 'I didn't meant to shoot him.'

'It's all right,' says the policeman. 'It's all right.'

'Tell him, Henry,' I say, 'tell him how we –'

I try to sidestep around to face him but Henry swivels

nervously back on the other side of the policeman. Rage flares in my chest; the new Henry, the Henry who took away my gun in the tunnel has gone; now he is the old Henry again, cunning and cowardice flashing in his eyes.

'I didn't mean to shoot him!' I cry. 'Henry will say, Henry has to tell you, Henry, Henry –'

'I said, it's all right.' The policeman shakes my arm gently. 'Nobody is pressing any charges, okay?' He looks fiercely into my eyes. 'Do you understand me? You're not going to prison. Okay?'

'But, I didn't mean to do it.'

The policeman carries on walking, guiding us along.

'There are no charges. We understand there was a misunderstanding. The gamekeeper – he was looking after the house after the owners left in a hurry, there was a family, how do you say – ah, an emergency, and he let some boys, some thieves, take some things.' He lowers his voice and says to me in a confiding tone, 'He is not a very good gamekeeper really, is he, hmm?'

'No,' I stammer. 'No.'

'He crawled out of the house, you know, back to his – how do you – his hut, his gamekeeper's hut – and passed out again. Then when he ah, woke up, he phoned us, the police, and we informed him about the crash and he realised you were from the English schoolboys. You are very lucky to have . . .' he breaks off awkwardly.

We walk in silence for a few paces, the gravel crunching beneath our feet. Henry asks, 'Did Matthew . . . is he okay?'

'There was a boy who survived,' the policeman says brightly. 'Colin Rabind –' he pronounces shakily. 'Rabind –'

'Colin Rabindarath,' I say quickly. 'Yes, but what about Mr Bellow?'

'What about Matthew?' Henry persists, tugging his sleeve. 'What about Matthew? What about Raf?'

The policeman stops and swallows and turns to face Henry and even before I hear the words *I'm sorry* I see the shadow of despair falling across his profile and I know.

I step back while the policeman comforts Henry. I shove my hands in my pockets and I look up at the sky and I think I can see the last shadows of smoke from the crash, wreathing up through the fading stars and I feel heavy with the burden I will have to carry for the rest of my life, of all those souls I have to keep alive in my mind.

**I** find that the touch of human skin is the most soothing thing. The feel of my mother's hands in my hair, the wet of her tears on my forehead: my hate dissolving instantly into a love that is like an appetite, my hunger for her touch insatiable. Her voice, though hoarse is like a lullaby: *Look at you, I thought I'd lost you in the crash, oh, you're all dirty, all those cuts, what have you been doing, my naughty boy, look at you, I thought I'd lost you . . .* I keep reminding myself that I should never speak to her again, but I find myself sobbing and burying my head in her breasts.

A policewoman drapes a blanket around my shoulders and gives me a hot drink. I sip it, but it seems tasteless. A balding officer asks me three questions in a heavy French accent; Colin watches with wide eyes and a pale, hollow face from the back seat of a locked police car. He smiles at me and I manage a wobbly grin. The officer's questions become thin air; all I can do is shrug. The policeman with the moustache taps him on the shoulder, gestures for him to leave me alone. I watch my mother holding Henry, clutching him, shushing him like a baby. I look for invisible threads between them: similar eyes, the curve of their eyelashes, the shell shape of their ears, the length of their fingers. She looks up and she sees in my eyes that I know.

I turn to the policeman and I find myself asking him if we can go and see the crash site. The words sound wrong, but still I ask them. The policeman gently replies that Henry and I need to go to the hospital now to be looked after. I ask again if we can go and he says that it is best that I go and be with my mother.

In the back of the police car, my mother sits in the middle, between me and Henry. She holds me tight and murmurs that she loves me, she loves us both and she will always be there for us. I look up at Henry and I feel my fingers curl into my palm.

The police car is about to drive off, when suddenly I remember my bird in the sink.

The policeman looks confused when I try to explain. My mother tries for me, and I think he understands, but then he only looks more confused.

'James, it is just a bird,' she says gently, stroking my hair.

I recoil from her and I glare into her eyes and say, 'I want the bird, Dad would have wanted me to look after it.'

She flinches at his name. She turns back to the policeman.

'I'll get it,' says Henry. His voice is blank, a strange tone I haven't heard before. He turns to me and smiles a dangerous smile.

'No!' I cry. 'No!'

'Really. I'll get it.' Henry opens the door, jumps out of the car and runs down the gravel.

'No! He can't, he can't, he'll kill it –' I scream.

'James, he won't kill it, he's trying to make up,' my mother says, holding me back.

I struggle wildly against her but my body is too weak

with exhaustion; I feel more air than muscle, as though the slightest tap will break my bones.

In defeat, I sink back into the seat. I close my eyes and think: I have lost. I give up. I give up on everything.

The minutes go by and Henry does not come back. A faint twittering in the trees. The drone of the police car radio. Smoke fading in the sky.

And still he does not come back. And then in the dark I hear my mother's voice:

'See?' she says softly. 'See?'

I look up and see him walking very slowly down the gravel driveway, arms outstretched, holding the bird like some priest holding an offering up to the Gods, and I look away. I can't stand this any more, I think, I will die, I will die of this hatred.

Then he is pushing the bird into my dead hands and I shake my head, frowning, numb.

My mother strokes my hair, whispering 'Go on, James, go on, James.'

He pushes it into my hands again and I see my bird quiver and open a beady eye, smiling up at me. I look up at Henry and he looks down at me with exhausted eyes. There is still blood in his hair and a cut on his neck that will become a scar. As he passes the bird over to me, our fingers brush. He smiles. I blink. I cannot see if his smile holds the promise of a smirk, if his kindness is a truce or a trap, if the war will continue or we are at peace, the bird our treaty.

Then the police car revs up and my mother puts her arms around us and holds us both close. Henry puts his head in her lap and sucks his thumb. He looks at me and I want to laugh but I force it back and we stare at each other for some time, the car rocking over the bumpy roads, our mother's hands on our hair. I duck my head and stroke my bird gently, inwardly replying to his *cheeps* as we drive into the strange openness of fields and sky and land without boundaries, bars of sunlight filtering through the trees as the night slowly fades away.

## Acknowledgements

First of all, huge thanks to my muse Tristan Rogers, who read this book chunk by chunk, inspired me to keep going, and kept me on my toes.

Thanks to my family – Mum, Dad and my brothers

Thanks to Matt Whyman for becoming my literay agony uncle and giving me all the right advice just when I needed it.

Thanks to Scarlett Thomas & Tom Boncza-Tomaszewski for inspiration and publishing a short story that inspired this book. To DBC Pierre for tails, to Tansy Troy for Macbeth, Graham Joyce for advice, Daren King for giraffes and Dan Gordon for correcting my French.

Huge thanks to my super-agent Simon Trewin, and Claire Gill and Emily Sklar at PFD. To my excellent editor Julia Wells, whose enthusiasm has been so exhilarating and everyone else at Faber, especially Helena Zedig, Nick Lowndes, Roisin Heycock and my copy-editor Martin Bryant. To Tessa Balshaw-Jones at ILA for her hard work and for thinking up the title.

Not forgetting special thanks to K – with all my deepest love.